LOOKING FOR ALICE

A GUNVOR STRÖM NOVEL

LUNA MILLER

For information address Publish Authority, 300 Colonial Center Parkway, Suite 100, Roswell, GA 30076

Cover design lead: Raeghan Rebstock
Translator: Aidan Isherwood
Editor: Gordon Jackson

A previous version originally published in Swedish as *Den som ger sig in i leken* by Luna Miller. This edition is translated from the original Swedish, and revised by the author.

Publish Authority
Newport Beach, CA – Roswell (Atlanta), GA USA
www.PublishAuthority.com

The Library of Congress has established a Cataloging-in-Publication record for this title.
ISBN: 978-1-7325347-4-2

To my husband, my son and my daughter for being my beloved islands of happiness in the stormy sea that we call life.
And to my friend Aidan for being my committed partner on the journey into my world of fantasy.

CONTENTS

*

I hate you.
I've hated you as long as I can remember.
Your big breasts and your pouting lips disgust me.
The way you look from behind your painted
    eyelashes; you think you're so adorable.
You make me want to puke.
You think your charm can get you anything you
    want.
You think everybody eats out of your hand.
Well believe me, nobody does.
In fact, it's your hand they're eating, down to the
    bone.
And they won't stop there.
You're condemning yourself to death.
And when it comes, it'll be too late.
I won't stand by you.
I'll choose death first…

1

---

etting mad always made Gunvor Ström's head feel like it was going to explode. If she could, she'd kick the little shit 'till he cried for his mother, and then some more. She was well trained in Aikido and prided herself as being physically fit, but she's a 65-year-old woman and wiser for it. She quickly accessed the potentially volatile situation in front of her and determined there was a better way to deal with this punk than to play as he wanted. So instead, she laid a protective arm on the young girl and glared at the big-mouthed idiot. "Why do you keep doing this? Can't you see what you're doing to her?" Gunvor was so tired of hearing her own voice repeating the same things she'd been saying for days on end. And what was particularly annoying was that she knew he'd come out with the same crap as always. Which was exactly what he did.

"Listen, you old bag, how many times have I got to tell you? Mind your own business and piss off."

Gunvor looked at him, waiting for her to reply with the usual placating words, *Just leave the girl alone. Go and pick on someone your own size instead.'*

So, he got a real shock when she snarled, "Once more and I'll sort you out for real."

She caught the surprise in his face before he covered it with a false laugh.

"Oh, yeah, what are you gonna do? Clip me 'round the ear? You can always try."

Humiliating as it was, it gave them the chance to escape without any more trouble. The sound of swearing and mocking laughter followed them down the steps, and out of the tube station. Gunvor loosened her grip on the girl but kept her close to her side as they walked out across Fruängenstorget and turned left towards the walkway between Konsum and the gym. They walked in silence, with Gunvor feeling a mounting sense of injustice. *This has to stop,* she thought.

It started on Monday, although it had presumably been going on longer than that. But it was on Monday that Gunvor happened to be on the same tube as the girl who later introduced herself as Elin. Gunvor had been sitting towards the back of the train, so when she got off in Fruängen most of the other passengers had already left the station, apart from Elin and the young man who had blocked her route through the barriers. He hadn't said anything, he just stood in front of her and grinned. When she tried to go past him to one side, he blocked her way and when she tried the other side, he moved and blocked her again. Gunvor noticed that he had two friends sitting on the bench nearby who seemed to find it all highly amusing.

"What are you two laughing about? You're a bit old for this sort of nonsense, aren't you?" Gunvor snapped at the boys on the bench before going forward to help the girl get past her tormentor.

Elin had thanked her and said it wasn't the first time it had happened. She tried to brush it off. She told Gunvor that the boys weren't doing any real harm. When Gunvor suggested that she get off the train at Västertorp instead, Elin demurred. Not because it was too long a walk, but because she didn't want to let them think they'd won. She didn't want them to think this was getting to her any more than it actually was.

She had swallowed her pride reluctantly and agreed to text Gunvor every day to say which train she would be on when she came home. Since then, Gunvor had taken the same train as Elin and got herself mixed up in similar incidents on Tuesday, Wednesday and Thursday. Now it was Friday, with no change in sight.

"Why don't you let me speak to your mother? We really must sort this out and put an end to it."

"No, I don't want to worry her. I'm nineteen, for God's sake. I don't go running home to mummy whenever something happens."

Gunvor didn't agree but she didn't want to go against Elin's will.

"He's just a wimp pretending to be hard."

"Okay, it's your decision. And you're right, he is a wimp. He's a coward too, and it's not right that he takes it out on you. So listen, if you don't want to report him, you have to defend yourself. If you knee him really hard between the legs, you'll hurt him and show him up in front of his idiot friends."

Elin looked at Gunvor and rolled her eyes to the heavens. "Where did that come from?" she asked."

"Look, if you won't let somebody else help you, you've got to help yourself."

"Oh, please. I don't want to lower myself to his level. He's the thug, not me."

"Of course you don't, but a taste of his own medicine wouldn't be such a bad thing. And think, if you can't be bothered stopping him, next time he might pick on someone who isn't as tough as you, someone who can't cope."

"Yeah, well, that won't be my problem."

Gunvor bit her tongue and managed not to say anything more.

They'd nearly reached the end of Fruängsgatan, which was where they usually separated.

"Look after yourself now."

"Bye," said Elin, before turning left into Fredrik Bremersgata.

Instead of going home, Gunvor walked back to the little shopping center in Fruängen. Her knee started hurting again, so she sat down on a bench to rest for a while. As usual she had ignored her doctor's orders to take it easy, preferring to push herself to her limits at the gym instead. She had kept herself fit for most of her life and found it hard to believe that rest was the best cure for the pain in her joints. She was convinced that strengthening her muscles to lighten the load on her joints was what worked best, even at her age. She always pushed herself just that bit too far at the gym and then found herself cursing the pain when she walked. But it was worth it if she could keep that old man´s walking frame at bay for a little longer.

She turned the conversation with Elin around in her head. Elin must see she had a duty to make a stand and do something. *People have to stand up for themselves*, she thought. Gunvor had been cajoling Elin for a week now and had started to lose hope that anything different was going to happen. David wouldn't stop bullying Elin until he found some other poor sod to pick on.

Back in Fruängen, Gunvor slipped into the library to see if any new crime stories had come in. She picked up a couple that she hadn't read before going over to the children's section to find something for her neighbor's daughter, who was ill and stayed off school. Standing with her back to the door, she heard a familiar voice.

"Can't I go home first?"

The lad! she realized. Suddenly, the "tough" punk from the tube station didn't sound so tough. Gunvor pricked up her ears but didn't turn around to take a confirming peek.

"Come on David. Can't you even do one thing I ask you to do for me? Sit down by the computer for a bit. I won't be long."

Gunvor guessed that voice was his mother's.

David let out an exaggerated sigh and a groan, but Gunvor heard what sounded like a chair being pulled out in the computer corner and presumed he was at least obeying his mother. She turned slowly and saw him sitting with his back to her as his mother browsed the shelves. Gunvor couldn't resist the temptation. She snuck up behind a shelf that seemed to have been put there to create an air of privacy for whoever was sitting at the computer, but it was not private enough. She watched him log onto Facebook. She smiled as he typed in his username and password. She almost laughed out loud when she saw the password he'd chosen.

Gangsta.

Gangsta! Since when has it been 'gangsta' to bully girls? What'll be his next gangsta trick? Tie a 100 kronor note to a piece of string so he can pull it away when someone tries to grab it?

Gangsta, my ass! she thought.

Suddenly she had an idea. She hurried to get her books ready and then pretended to be looking on a shelf for another book until she saw David's mother had had her books stamped and was ready to leave. With her handbag over her shoulder and her left arm hanging by her side, Gunvor pretended to be totally engrossed in a book she was holding in her other hand. She walked right into David and his mother as they made their way out. She bumped into them so hard she nearly lost her balance.

"Oh God, sorry!"

She looked up at David's surprised mother.

"Sorry, I really didn't mean to…"

"Don't worry. No harm done."

David's mother quickly composed herself and smiled at Gunvor. "It must be a very exciting book." She nodded at the book in Gunvor's hand before turning away and leaving the library. David had swung his head to look away as soon as he'd realized who had bumped into them.

He must have a modicum of shame in him.

Now she had to hurry. David and his mother were walking towards the central square, so she turned in the other direction. She turned right at the church and took the footpath that went through the underpass. A bit further on, she dug into her bag for today's catch—David's phone. She had noticed that he kept it in the back pocket of his saggy jeans. So it wasn't that hard to fish it out when she bumped into him and his mother. All it took was a diversionary move with her other hand while she fumbled with her book.

The phone didn't have a password, and she let out a small sigh of relief. She put it into flight mode and carried on past the school and down the path that ran alongside the football pitch. She crossed the road and went up the short street that leads to the open area between the blocks of flats. It was a warm afternoon in early September and a few of the local children were pedaling around and around the communal laundry in the middle of the open area on their bikes. Some young girls were playing on the swings in one of the area's three tiny playgrounds. Gunvor smiled at them before entering her block.

There wasn't much time, but she ran across the hallway to her neighbor Ciwan's door anyway and knocked. Gunvor imagined she would have been lying around in front of the TV most of the day with her daughter and would be sick of it by now. When the door opened, Tara was standing behind Ciwan, looking sorry for herself and very bored. Gunvor handed Tara the books. She took them with a smile and sat down on the deep red oriental rug in the hallway. "Thanks Gunvor, that's sweet of you! Do you want to stay for a bit of dinner?" Ciwan asked.

"Thanks, but I haven't got time today."

"Hang on then," Ciwan disappeared into the kitchen and came back with a plate of baba ganoush.

"" Oh, my favorite!"

"Have you got pita bread at home?" Ciwan only needed to look at Gunvor to know she didn't. She went back into the kitchen, ignoring Gunvor's protests. Back in the hallway she forced two big pitas into her hand.

"You take care of me and I'll take care of you."

They turned to look at Tara. She was sniffing and coughing, but she was already engrossed in one of the books. She was reading the first few lines out loud in a slow and serious voice.

Gunvor sighed when she finally closed her own front door. She stepped out of her latest purchase, a pair of white, green-soled espadrille-style Ecco shoes that managed to combine comfort with a certain panache. She pulled out the insoles to let them breathe before she wore them again and slipped her feet into her well-worn Birkenstocks.

Her one-bedroom flat was sparsely furnished. After the divorce, when she moved out of the large detached home, all she took with her were her clothes. She wanted to start again, she wanted to abandon anything that would remind her of the years she'd spent with Rune. But furniture and interiors had never really been her thing. Her bedroom consisted of a bed and a chair she just used to put clothes on. She read a lot, but hardly ever in bed, so she didn't see the need for a bedside table or a lamp. The windows had blinds when she bought the flat, so she didn't see any real need for curtains. The sparsely-furnished room gave off an empty echo, so she had started to think about at least getting a rug, but she'd gotten no further than thinking about it.

The living room had pale purple curtains hanging in the window that opened onto a balcony. Apart from the curtains the room was equally bare, the only real furniture being a dark purple sofa and a small coffee table. There was an imposing wooden framed mirror on one wall and a large yucca taking up space in one corner.

The kitchen was the homeliest room in the one-bedroom flat. It was where she spent most of her time when she was at home, except on sunny days when she could sit on the balcony. Along one wall there was a bookshelf lined with her current favorites and various work-related documents. On the windowsill she was growing tomatoes, chilis, a few herbs and a small lemon tree. A large rustic wooden table filled up most of the kitchen's floorspace. It seated four and Gunvor's computer was on it, along with a large pile of paper and books. She seldom received more than one or two visitors at a time, so she was happy to let the home office dominate the room. She sat down and switched on the computer and logged onto Facebook as David. First, she changed his password, to keep him out for a while. Of course, he would reset it as soon as he got back in, but with a bit of luck she would have enough time to mess a few things up. She thought for a bit before doing a status update.

— *I feel a bit sensitive today,* she typed.

It took just a few seconds before friends started commenting with question marks or laughter emojis. Someone suggested he had been Faceraped.

Gunvor picked up her iPhone and called Elin. She told her something had happened that they needed to talk about, then invited her to come around. Elin sounded surprised but accepted the invitation. In order to limit any potential over-reactions from Elin, Gunvor tried to make the scene more homely. She broke the pita bread into medium chunks and set them out in a serving dish alongside a handful of Kalamata olives, Ciwan's baba ghanoush and a bottle of wine. *The girl is eighteen, isn't she? No, nineteen,* she reminded herself, playing over their earlier conversation in her head.

From her vantage point on the balcony, she spotted Elin walking into the central outdoor area. Despite the hot weather Gunvor got the kitchen table ready. Sometimes when it was hot the guys living in her block would get together to smoke a water pipe on the deck below her first-floor balcony. Before opening the door for Elin, Gunvor closed the balcony door to make sure that no one could possibly overhear what they were about to discuss.

Elin, who hadn't been that talkative all week, rattled on nonstop after Gunvor told her what she'd done.

"You nicked his phone? But you're just a sweet little old lady. Sorry that's a bit rude—but it's true!" Elin sounded outraged, but she had a huge smile on her face. "It's sweet of you, really sweet, and so brave to help me like this. I still can't believe you took his phone!"

"I got his Facebook password too," Gunvor smiled.

"You know what Facebook is?"

"Give me a break. I'm not that old."

"Sorry. Facebook's not that complicated, but how did you even come up with the rest of it? The password and User ID?"

It was clear that Elin was impressed by her performance, but Gunvor wasn't entirely happy about her reaction. Looking like a boring old woman may well be an advantage in her line of work, but it hurt to have it confirmed so emphatically. Especially when she so actively loathed the whole idea of growing old.

"I'm a private detective."

"You're a what?" Elin drew a shocked breath, then stifled a laugh. Gunvor smiled and filled Elin's glass with Rioja.

"You're nineteen, aren't you?"

"How'd you know?"

"You mentioned it. We were talking about your mother, remember?"

"You don't miss much, do you?"

Gunvor shrugged. "We don't miss a thing, us private eyes."

Elin picked up the glass and took a couple of large gulps.

"Careful. That's wine, not blackcurrant juice."

"I know. I'm probably not as innocent as I look," Elin took two or three olives and then another gulp of wine, "But this is the biggest surprise I've had. Ever."

Gunvor took a slow sip of wine, then pulled the computer nearer and turned the screen so Elin could see it.

"I've started, but I want you to decide whether I should write anything more. And if so, what?"

Elin pulled the computer towards her and read the comments that were now flooding in, mocking David's apparent sensitivity.

"I don't know. Something humiliating, I guess."

Then Gunvor had an idea.

"I know." She laughed as she looked for a picture she knew she'd saved somewhere on the computer. Then she went back to the Facebook page, uploaded the picture and wrote in the comment box:

— *I love the feel of nylon on my legs and the way my feet look in my little red stilettos.*

Elin's laughter echoed around the small flat. "Oh my God! You're nuts!" She laughed so much the tears ran down her face. She couldn't stop looking at the picture Gunvor took on an assignment a couple of months ago. It showed the back, mostly the legs, of a man in a red sequin dress with nylon tights and red shoes with ridiculously high stiletto heels. You couldn't see who the man was, but you could tell it was a man.

"What the hell is that?"

"It's from work. A woman suspected her husband was being unfaithful after finding this little outfit in his wardrobe."

"And?"

"It was his. She could have saved a lot of money by just asking him to his face, but he had been a bit withdrawn for a while, and she thought he was having an affair."

"But he wasn't?"

"No. He was getting himself dolled up and going to a posh café somewhere. All he did was drink latte and look through women's magazines."

The photo abruptly vanished. They realized David must have logged in. He posted in his status that he'd been Faceraped. Gunvor immediately deleted his comment and reposted the picture and the comments on how he loved nylon tights and red stilettos. She and Elin carried on for about an hour, enjoying the nibbles, finishing the wine and laughing at David's friends' comments.

When it was time for Elin to go home, they decided they'd done enough—at least as far as Facebook was concerned. Gunvor had been working on another idea but she decided to keep it to herself for the time being.

2

The weekend passed slowly. Gunvor Ström spent most of her time on the balcony reading her unsolved cases. On Saturday she gave herself a whole-body workout in the gym. She didn't like the tacky, over-frequented gym in Fruängen, so she had joined the Flex Sports Club in Västertorp instead. She walked there through the newly-built residential area between Lidl and the motorway. When they'd started digging up the overgrown and undeveloped site a few years ago she'd felt invaded. She didn't like the idea that the inner city was taking over—even in the furthest outposts of Hägersten. Why couldn't they just leave the few remaining wooded areas alone for the kids to play hide-and-seek in? Where were they supposed to go now to avoid prying eyes when they shared their first kiss or learn to smoke?

But now the estate was nearly finished, and it looked pretty nice. The new residents had filled their balconies with lively, colorful plants in attractive pots next to mostly tasteful garden furniture. The area was alive now in a way it had never been before, Gunvor had to admit. She turned right, went past Shurgard, and stepped onto the footbridge over the motorway towards the gym.

Gunvor's time in the gym was usually one of the best times of her day. Talk about stress relief. Some days, she felt bone-tired going into the gym, and refreshed when she came out. Today, even if her body did hurt, she practiced some aikido high falls. Although she didn't train that sport for close combat much anymore, as she had for many years before, she still wanted to train the technique—on her own terms. She spent the whole session contemplating last night's idea on how to handle David, and by the time she set off back to Fruängen she had developed a plan. She called her nephew, who was delighted to help. They agreed to meet on Monday.

Happy with her training session and her plan, she made it to Systembolaget just before it closed, but even before she'd left the little shopping center at Fruängsgången, her purchase had started to make her feel just a little bit uncomfortable. She was drinking too much and too often. After a few glasses she lost her ability to decide when to stop and hangovers were becoming a regular part of her life. She shouldn't keep too much alcohol at home. But Gunvor didn't always take the easiest path—or the even most sensible one.

To put things right, she decided to invite her neighbor for dinner. Gunvor had made friends with Aidan almost as soon as she moved in. He'd worked for many years as an English teacher, but like Gunvor he had recently changed careers. He wasn't that far off from fifty when he finally landed his dream job as a consultant football coach in Manchester. It was only part-time, but Gunvor knew that the globetrotter in him embraced the challenge of working in both Sweden and England. When he was back in Stockholm, he always appreciated the chance to socialize. Aidan had a lively imagination and loved listening to Gunvor's stories—even if they mainly involved her standing around, waiting and watching until she could confirm whether whoever she was following was being unfaithful or not. And Gunvor loved telling Aidan her stories. She was sure he thought her job was filled with so much more excitement and danger than its rather mundane reality. They regularly sat and talked about her adventures over dinner or a glass of wine.

Aidan responded to her text quickly. Suddenly in the mood for a bit of a party she invited Ciwan as well. All of a sudden, one box of wine didn't seem quite enough.

3

By the time Monday came, Gunvor was ready to leave the weekend behind. It'd been fun, enjoyable and relaxing. She headed into T-Centralen on the underground in time for the shops to open. She had already decided which shop she was going to, but she took her time wandering through the shoe shops before arriving at Buttericks, Stockholm's best fancy dress shop. As soon as she walked in, she realized she had made a good choice. This would have the required effect without breaking the bank.

After making her purchases, she went to TUI on Sveavägen to pay for the trip to Gran Canaria she had booked on a whim last night. She even managed to fit in a walk to Kungsträdgården and back before lunchtime. She was determined to move as much as she could every day, however much her leg hurt. She went to the gym at least three times a week and took long walks and did sit-ups and press-ups at home every other day. Today it was hurting less than yesterday, so she should really go to the gym, but she'd have to settle for another lap of Kungsträdgården instead. She had enough to do as it was, so this time she'd walk faster. Afterward, she went to Kulturhuset to meet her nephew.

She watched him sauntering across Sergels Torg with a big grin on his face. "Hi Johan, good to see you," she said.

"You too." Johan gave Gunvor a hug. He hadn't time to join her for lunch, but he agreed to run an errand for her later that afternoon.

"It's great that you can help me."

"I'll always try, especially with something a bit mad like this. You do know you're my absolute craziest aunt, don't you?"

"That's not so hard. I'm your only aunt."

"Even if I had loads of aunts, you'd be the maddest and the best of the lot."

"Like I said earlier, timing is everything. Can you do it between your deliveries?"

"I've told them at work I've got a dentist's appointment at three, so they know they can't send me any express orders then."

Gunvor was satisfied with that answer and handed him a 500 kronor note.

"That's way too much," Johan says.

"But you're my favorite nephew, so I can give you as much money as I want."

Johan didn't need any more persuading. He took the note and slipped it into the pocket of his jeans.

They hugged each other again and Johan hurried away over to Sergels Torg. Gunvor went for lunch in Teaterbaren. She had time to relax now that she'd done everything she planned. To make sure she caught the same tube as Elin she didn't need to leave here until half-past two. She stayed at her window seat, people watching over coffee.

She wondered if David would dare show his face in the center after the photo on his Facebook page. But she guessed he'd be too restless to stay at home all day. He'd definitely be keen to see his mates and explain that he had absolutely nothing to do with that stupid picture. When Gunvor got to Fruängen later that afternoon, she was not at all surprised to see him standing by the barriers. Today, however, he didn't seem to have time to hassle her or Elin. She just managed to hide her smile as she watched the scenes developing around David and the parcel that a courier had just given him. David was screaming and swearing in an incoherent rant as his friends tossed a pair of size 45 red stilettos to each other and laughed so much they could hardly stay on their feet. Gunvor was delighted and nodded her thanks to Johan.

She started going down the steps to the square and saw Elin waiting at the bottom. Her eyebrows were raised in a look of complete bewilderment. Gunvor gave her a nod and a wink. Elin began to laugh.

"That was amazing! I've never met anyone like you. Not ever." Elin hugged Gunvor when she reached her. "I'll never forget this. I really owe you one."

"The pleasure was all mine."

Elin headed home while Gunvor lingered near Pressbyrån until the crowds busied their way to the bus station or the shops had thinned out a little. David and his friends had calmed down now, though their shrieks of laughter and delirious shouting were still audible in the waiting area on the level above. When she was sure she was on her own and out of their line of sight, she quickly bent down and placed David's mobile on the escalator then walked out into Konsum. Less than a minute later, David came charging out onto the square holding his iPhone with a wild look in his eyes. Gunvor was well hidden between the shelves of breakfast cereals.

4

Gunvor was looking forward to her spur-of-the-moment trip to Gran Canaria. She planned to fly out early the next morning. In all truth, it wasn't actually that spontaneous, she'd been putting it off for a while. But she had made a snap decision to book it last night, so it was at least impulsive. She had a new lover living out there, and now that she had sorted out Elin's little problem with David and wasn't involved in any other cases, she could escape for a while.

She had planned to devote her evening to packing and cleaning, but just as she finished packing and was about to get the vacuum cleaner out, Aidan knocked on the door with a bottle of wine, hoping to hear about today's coup. On Saturday she had told him what she had done and what she was going to do with the red shoes. Housework or wine and Aidan? It's an easy decision. Within minutes they were sitting on the balcony nursing large glasses of wine. The vacuum cleaner was stored away in the cleaning cupboard. After another bottle and some Thai food, they realized it was midnight. Aidan agreed to water Gunvor's flowers and plants while she was away and headed home a little reluctantly.

The next morning, she was furious with herself at her inability to resist the second bottle, but after a cold shower and a double espresso she felt better. She'd given herself plenty of time to make herself look good before taking the taxi to Arlanda. In her job she often chose to match her grey hair with a lack of makeup; blending in was part and parcel of her routine. But for this trip she wanted to make herself stand out for a change. She used a blow-dryer and a bit of mousse to fluff up her normally lifeless hair, knowing that a combination of mascara and dark red lips would attract looks. Especially when she was wearing her new green linen dress. She had always had the looks. And she knew that she still did, especially with a little help of makeup. Her body was fit, petite, and nicely shaped. Her intense brown eyes unleashed both intelligence and beauty. But she hated the fact that she was getting old. Every little wrinkle that reminded her of that inevitable fact was like a mini-defeat to her.

The six-hour flight was fun. She found herself sitting next to a chatty guy who insisted on offering her drink after drink. So, even though she stuck strictly to her plan of having a glass of water between each drink, she wasn't quite as assertive as she'd like when it came to negotiating the cab fare to Arguineguin. But her bartering skills had not entirely deserted her, and soon enough she was sitting on the sun-warmed back seat of a taxi drinking a bottle of ice-cold water she had bought at the airport.

Gunvor smiled as she looked up at the sun-scorched mountains and out at the beautifully sparkling sea. Now that she was here, she couldn't wait to see the surprise and joy in the eyes of Kjell, who had no idea she was coming. She was looking forward to some wonderful lazy days, but after a week, when it was time to go back to Fruängen, she knew she would have had enough. Not enough of him, but enough of lounging around and days with no substance.

She hoped he'd be at home. It would be easier to surprise him. If he was out, she'd just have to go and see if she could find him in one of the little tapas bars in the square, where he took every chance to practice his Spanish in simple but intense conversations with the local fishermen.

As the taxi drove past Bahia Feliz her telephone rang.

"Manuel?"

"Gunvor, a job's come in."

"I'm fine thanks. How are you?" She couldn't hold back the sarcasm. Manuel's manner, as always, was totally devoid of social graces. She heard him laugh.

"Sorry, I'll start again. Hope you're well and you've had a good summer. I really appreciate all the work you did while the rest of us were off. I'm also really grateful for the good work you've done over the year you've been with us. You are a quick learner and you are more than able to work on your own."

"Thanks, Manuel. Which is why I'm on holiday in Gran Canaria just now."

"Shit. I need you."

"Tough."

"Please Gunvor," a note of pleading had entered Manuel's voice. "We have to accept every case—it says so on the website. Trouble is Frida, Gaston and I are all booked solid just now. Can you take it? We've got a woman who wants to know if her husband is having an affair."

"And she can't wait till next week to find out? Give me a break, Manuel."

The silence on the line told her he had no intention of doing any such thing. She gave him her most theatrical sigh.

"Oh for God's sake, all right then. But only if you pay for my ticket home. Tomorrow, and not too early either. I've only just landed and the man I love will not be happy if I spend the only evening we're going to have together looking for last-minute tickets online."

"Gunvor, you're a sweetheart, thank you. I'll sort a ticket and text you when it's done. See you tomorrow."

It wasn't going to be nice trying to explain to Kjell that she was leaving the next day. Especially as she had promised him in the spring that she'd fly out in the summer, and it had taken her till the beginning of September to do that. But when she was offered the chance to stay on in the office all summer, working full-time to finish off all last year's reports on the database, she couldn't say no. She was new to the business, and it was a great opportunity to get priceless knowledge by going through a year's worth of cases. Till then she had only worked on short and simple jobs at the agency.

Luckily, she and Kjell had seen each other a bit during the summer anyway. He'd flown to Stockholm a couple of times. And he seemed to like her for who she was and understood how important the work was for her. He was delighted for her that she got this chance to retrain and start afresh in a new career.

The driver took a left at the roundabout and followed the road down to the little square in the center of Arguíneguin. He carried on to the unpretentious entrance of Los Marinos. Despite her earlier bargaining efforts, Gunvor gave the driver more than they had agreed on and he thanked her profusely with a warm smile.

The receptionist was sitting on the sofa, engrossed in her iPhone.

"Hola señora!" She greeted Gunvor with a hurried smile.

To Gunvor's dismay her knee almost gave way as she was walking up the stairs to the first floor. *It's probably due to a combination of sitting still on the plane and lack of exercise over the last few days,* she thought. She stopped halfway up to rest and looked out over the inner courtyard. The building was an atrium with rooms that ran along four sides. At the top she could see the roof, which acted as a sun terrace. Below her was a courtyard filled with every shade of green, in the middle of which the owner had placed a number of bird cages; some with canaries, some with budgerigars and one with a desperately gregarious parrot that responded joyfully to any whistle or call.

Gunvor whistled to the parrot. It responded immediately, going through a repertoire of all the songs and expressions the tourists had taught it during the year. Gunvor smiled and stopped for a moment to talk to the pale grey bird. She knew the long flight and taxi ride would test her knee, and repeating the whole thing tomorrow wasn't going to help. But tomorrow was tomorrow, and for now she was determined to make the most of the few remaining hours she had left of her vacation. She took a firm grip on the railing to lighten the load on her worst knee, the right. She just barely managed, and she was soon on the second floor knocking on Kjell's door.

He was surprised and delighted to see her, though his eyes betrayed sadness when he heard she had to leave in the morning.

"Obviously if I'd known I wouldn't have come at all."

"That's supposed to make me feel better, is it?" His smile betrayed the seriousness of his words. "I know how you are, and you know that's why I love you, but I have to admit I'd feel better if I could spend more time with you. Maybe one day we can agree on a place we both like, but for now let's go to Amfi. We'll have time for a quick swim before it gets dark. Of course, we might fancy a swim after it's dark too."

He smiled mischievously at her then pulled her close and took her in his arms. She leaned her head against his chest, enjoying his warm embrace. He was a handsome man, a head taller than her and strongly built. His head was shaved. It made him look a bit dangerous, but his clear blue eyes had a positive twinkle that more than compensated for it. She sighed with satisfaction.

"I've longed for just this moment. Just to be in your arms again."

"Would you rather we stayed home? I could just hold you all night."

"But I want to look at you too. And swim. If we hurry, we can do both." She slid out of his arms, opened her case and quickly changed into a red sundress and a pair of high-heeled sandals, regardless of the damage they'd cause her. But considering she wasn't even going to be with him for a full day she wanted to look good, whatever it took. But within moments of getting out of the taxi, before they were even halfway down the hill towards Amfi Beach she had taken them off and was walking barefoot.

"Are you hurting?"

Gunvor nodded. "The flight was a bit tough on my body."

"Are you still training as hard as you were?" Kjell looked at her with concern.

"I want to take it easier, but it's hard," she smiles at him. "I've been to my last aikido class now, you know. It's sad, but I just can't do it anymore."

"I know it's hard, and you were good at it, too. But you have to listen to your body." He smiled at her flirtatiously and continued, "I'll happily massage it later. Who knows? Maybe I can wake it up a bit."

She smiled back at him and took his hand in hers.

Amfi Beach had become her favorite place on the island. She wasn't alone, judging by the banks of timeshare apartments, the wonderful sand that was said to have been brought in from the Sahara and the restaurants that lined the promenade. But what fascinated her the most was how the lights of Arguíneguin reflected on the ocean after darkness fell. It was so beautiful. And when the wind was calm and the sea was warm and inviting, she could think of nowhere better.

As always, she felt a comforting tingle when the waves lapped over her toes. A bit further out in the bay she laid on her back and floated, while Kjell went further out in a powerful crawl before he turned and swam back to her with a more relaxing breaststroke. His arms pulled her to him, and he kissed her. His lips tasted of sea salt and she closed her eyes, enjoying the moment and admitting to herself that there was a lot that was quite wonderful about life here. Sometimes she got fed up with herself as she struggled to come to terms with these conflicting emotions. In Kjell's arms life couldn't be better, but she knew that after a few weeks of paradise she'd start to get impatient. That old feeling of being trapped would sneak back in, and before she knew it, she'd be making plans to leave.

The sun had gone down when they took seats at a table in Kjell's favorite restaurant. The waiter tapped him on the shoulder and said something about how happy he looked now that love was in town. Gunvor smiled at him and said in Spanish that she too was happy to be visiting her love. She'd always had a gift for languages, and Spanish was one she spoke fluently. Kjell did his best to keep up with the conversation. Even though he'd lived in Arguíneguin for almost two years, he was still a beginner and found it hard to follow any conversation that dealt with more than ordering food or asking for bills. But he loved speaking to people, so he was always throwing himself into conversations that as often as not ended up in combinations of gestures and broken English.

They had met just over a year ago, when Gunvor had just stopped working as a surgeon. It had been a difficult period for her. She wasn't ready for retirement, but her shaking hands had finally let her down. No beta blockers in the world could hold back the aging process. Everything so nearly ended in disaster. She came close to puncturing a patient's artery in what was a routine operation. She asked a colleague to take over when the shaking wouldn't stop and put in her resignation the same day. They'd have suspended her with immediate effect anyway, she reasoned, just as soon as the hospital management found out about the incident. To some extent it was a relief, but at the same time she was devastated to know that she would never operate again. She feigned illness at her farewell do, and the last time she heard from her workmates was when they sent an enormous bouquet and some fine wines to her home.

Lars had been Gunvor's favorite colleague, but she hadn't gotten back to him despite the long, touching message he left her.

When she found him outside her front door one evening, she broke down in his arms. But when the tears had stopped, she asked him to be patient and not to get in touch again. She explained that she needed time to heal first. Seeing the sadness in his eyes she promised it wouldn't be forever, even though she knew it would be. She said it mainly to calm him down. Deep inside she wasn't sure she would ever be able to spend time with him again for fear of being reminded of her failure.

Her new jobless life was filled for too long with tears and self-pity, until eventually Ciwan told her she had to move on. They came up with the idea of going away on holiday. Ciwan hoped it would inspire Gunvor to enjoy life again. A few weeks later they flew to Gran Canaria and checked in to Hotel Los Marinos. As they went up to their rooms, they bumped into Kjell, who seemed to take to Gunvor immediately. The same afternoon, as Gunvor laid in the sun on the hotel terrace and Ciwan and her daughter took a siesta in their room, Kjell introduced himself. He sat down on the sun lounger next to Gunvor's and began to make conversation. They enjoyed each other's company. She found herself nodding eagerly when he excused himself but said he would be back if she didn't mind. She watched him walk away and admired his well-trained body and attractive looks. When he returned with a bottle of Cava and two glasses, she was even more impressed.

When Ciwan and Tara appeared on the terrace after their naps, Kjell hurried off to his apartment to find some more Cava. Ciwan noticed the warmth in the glances Gunvor and Kjell were sharing. She suggested they all go out for dinner together and asked him to show them the best restaurant on the island. Gunvor was lost. Half-way through the week she moved into his apartment. When they were due to leave, she waved farewell to Ciwan and Tara and stayed for another three weeks.

She'd fallen completely in love with Kjell. It was like nothing she'd ever felt before, but she couldn't stay any longer than that.

She knew she couldn't just run away from what had happened at work. And she couldn't run away from the feeling that she did not want her career to end in failure. So she went back to Sweden, after they'd promised to meet as often as they could.

As soon as she got home, she wrote out a list of detective agencies in the Stockholm area. It was her first step in her search for a new career. She had thought about it and then talked it over with Kjell. They both felt it could be an option for her. It had begun as a crazy idea that greatly amused them both, but after she'd thought about it a bit more it didn't seem quite so far-fetched at all. It helped that she had an analytical mind and was fascinated with the science of criminology. She had also practiced aikido for many years and would have a reasonable chance of defending herself if she encountered any dangerous situations. Even if she hadn't trained for a while because of her knee, she was convinced she hadn't lost her self-defense skills, and she kept up her speed with her gym work. So, she thought she'd give it a go.

It turned out that her instincts were right. She received a positive response from the very first agency she contacted. She had a good feeling about Manuel, Frida and Gaston right from their first meeting and accepted their job offer—even though it wasn't full-time, just random hours when needed.

The wonderful night was going far too fast. In the taxi back to Arguíneguin from Amfi she received a text from Manuel saying he had booked her on a flight at noon the next day. She felt a tingle of excitement and anticipation in her stomach. It wasn't going to be her first surveillance on a suspected unfaithful partner, but the work still felt new and exciting to her. She had certainly not been in the job long enough to feel blasé about it, but it was sad to be leaving Kjell so soon. So, she would do her best to make the most of the few hours they had together.

They fell asleep in the early hours of the morning, and when she woke up, she only had time for a quick shower and a bit of breakfast before leaving for the airport. Kjell offered to drive her there so they could spend one more hour together. They enjoyed the drive, but it was over too soon. Before that hour had passed, she was checked in and alone again. Not that it bothered her. After a 20-year relationship with an extremely controlling man she appreciated having time to herself. Especially now that she had the most wonderful partner who would never get jealous or attempt to control her. A man who wanted her to remain the woman he fell for and now loved.

She resisted the temptation to have a drink or two on the flight as she had promised to take a taxi straight to the office to meet the client when she landed. The time difference meant she would land just before 7 p.m. and the meeting was planned for 8. So instead of killing time by drinking, she leaned back and dozed off after the in-flight lunch. She fell into a deep sleep and didn't wake up until the pressure change in her ears told her the plane was coming into land.

5

Her baggage, which she hadn't needed, took longer to arrive than usual. When she arrived at Arlanda it occurred to her that she might as well have left the bag at Kjell's, full as it was with summer clothes that Sweden was already too cold for. Cursing silently, she rinsed her face with cold water and bought a coffee for an extra kick before going to find a taxi.

It was already quarter past eight by the time she got to the office in Liljeholmen. Despite the late hour Frida and Gaston were still at their computers in their shared office. Gunvor was late for her meeting, but she took the time to greet them with a hug. She worked mostly with Manuel but had gotten to know Frida and Gaston pretty well too, thanks to their regular after-work sessions. During all her years as a doctor, Gunvor had had lots of colleagues. However, after this last year at her new work-place, she came to realize that, apart from Lars, she had not known any of them very well. With her new workmates she had learned to unwind, put her work to one side and simply enjoy their company.

The door to the meeting room was open, so she entered without knocking. Manuel was sitting in one of the armchairs talking quietly with a woman in her mid-thirties with reddened eyes who was sitting on the sofa. She was stylishly dressed in a tight pale cotton dress, a darkish jacket and a pair of brown trainers. Her jewelry was gold and her rings and necklace sparkled with what Gunvor guessed were real jewels.

What use is all this finery if you can't trust your husband? Gunvor thought, appreciating Kjell all the more.

"Here she is," Manuel said to the woman. "I'll leave you to it." Manuel got up and shook hands with the woman, nodded at Gunvor and left. Gunvor closed the door, moved one of several unnecessary cushions from the sofa, and sat herself down next to the woman.

"Gunvor Ström." She held out her hand to the woman and gave what she hoped the woman would interpret as a trustworthy smile.

"Nadja Franzén."

The firm handshake told Gunvor that Nadja was a strong woman who knew what she wanted. Although her eyes were red from crying, Gunvor detected a warmth in them when she offered her the slightest of smiles.

"I heard you had to cut short your trip. I want you to know how much I appreciate that."

"No problem. I'll be spending lots of time in Gran Canaria soon enough." Gunvor reached for the carafe of mineral water and one of the glasses standing in the center of the table.

"Shall I fill your glass too?"

Nadja declined with a hand gesture. "I'm fine," she said

"Okay. I'll have to ask you to tell me your story once again." Gunvor took a few sips of water, picked up the notepad she always carried with her and extracted the pen from the pad's top corner.

"It's my husband. I don't know what's going on. He's just not been himself lately, and he won't talk to me about it. At first, I thought maybe he's having some trouble at work. You know, we both work a lot, and sometimes we get kind of caught up in chasing money."

Gunvor looked up from her notes and nodded.

"But now I'm certain there's something else. He's been staying out really late. He says it's work, but almost every night I can smell alcohol on his breath. He's always been very careful about his health, you know, working out a lot and eating well. Then all of a sudden, he doesn't seem to care. It's like he's changed from one day to the next…

"Anyway, after this had gone on for a few weeks, I'd had enough. So I basically pushed him up against a wall and asked him if he was seeing someone else."

"What did he say?"

"That's what was so strange. After behaving like a shit for weeks, pushing me away and refusing to speak whenever I tried to find out what was going on, he burst into tears. He said he loved me more than anything else in the world and that he wouldn't be able to cope without me. But there was something about the way he said it that made me even more worried." Nadja leaned forward and picked up another tissue from the table.

"How did he say it exactly?"

Nadja blew her nose before answering.

"He said whatever happens, he wanted me to know that I was the best thing that's ever happened to him. But he refused to say what it was that might happen."

"I see. So it could be something other than an affair?"

Nadja thought for a moment, then nodded.

"Maybe. But I don't understand what."

"No, it's impossible to know at this stage. So, let me define my brief. Do you want me to just find out if he's having an affair or would you like me to find out exactly what he's up to?"

Nadja answered without hesitation, "Just whether he's having an affair."

Despite considering Nadja's response remarkable, Gunvor

offered her a nod of understanding. Personally, she'd be much more concerned if he wasn't being unfaithful. *If her husband is having an affair, it's bound to be painful and humiliating, but at least it can go some way towards explaining a major personality change,* Gunvor thought. Nadja looked down at the table and seemed to hesitate before continuing.

"Of course I'm worried, but I also have financial reasons for needing an answer. I've always trusted him, but if it turns out he is being unfaithful and intends to leave me, then I need to address a number of issues to make sure he doesn't disappear with all our assets."

"I understand. Don't worry, we'll sort this out. I'll need your home address and a number I can call you on discreetly. I'll also need his work address and car registration number, his mobile number and a picture of him. What's his name?"

"Mikael Franzén." Nadja picked up an envelope that had been lying on the table since their meeting started and handed it to Gunvor.

"Everything's in here. We live just 'round the corner from Sjövikskajen. Sjöviksbacken 2, third block from the square. The inner courtyard nearest to the jetty. Micke walks to Liljeholmen every morning and takes the underground to T-Centralen. He works at the Riksbank, by Brunkebergstorg. He usually leaves home about eight o'clock. Before all this started, he used to come home between six and seven in the evening. But these days ..." Nadja stopped, and fresh tears fell.

"Sometimes he texts and says he's working late and eating in town, sometimes I hear nothing. But he usually gets home around midnight."

"I'll start first thing tomorrow and I'll hopefully have an answer for you within a week. Then we can meet here again, if that's okay with you. Shall we arrange a time now or do you want me to get in touch nearer the time? Can I contact you if anything turns up, or would you rather contact me so I don't call at an awkward time?"

"We can meet in a week, and it is fine for you to call me if anything happens. Mikael is used to me being snowed under with work calls evenings and weekends."

"Okay. How about next Wednesday, 4 pm?"

After the meeting, Gunvor took the envelope home. She left her suitcase in the hall and went straight to the kitchen table. She made a cup of tea and sat down to examine the contents of the envelope.

6

Just after eight the next morning Gunvor was standing on the platform at Liljeholmen pretending to wait for a train while she looked out for Mikael Franzén. He was heading for the Riksbanken head office, so she expected he'd get on the front carriage. But just to make sure, she stood at the bottom of the escalator closest to the tram stop and what she assumed was his walking route. That way she'd surely spot him when he arrived. And sure enough, here he came, hurrying down the steps to get on the 8:15 train. Gunvor stepped into the same carriage but kept a safe distance and turned her back to him so he wouldn't recognize her if she got too near to him later. She saw enough of him to notice that he was well-groomed and good-looking. A man in good shape wearing expensive clothes comfortably.

The type that thinks he owns the world, Gunvor thought. She was maybe being too judgmental, but she wouldn't be at all surprised if he had two lovers, let alone one.

At T-Centralen he left the station and crossed Sergels Torg. She took the right-hand escalator and walked a few steps down Drottninggatan before turning up towards Kulturhuset. She saw him climbing the steps at the other end of Sergels Torg and turned into the arcade, as she expected. She got there just in time to see him turn the corner. She presumed he was going into the Riksbanken to start his working day. She walked past the entrance and crossed the road to Gallerian for some breakfast where she'd have a good view of the Riksbanken's main entrance.

Most of the day was spent just waiting. She spent the first few hours in the café, then walked to the park with a sandwich and a latte. Thankfully it was a warm September day, so she wasn't the only one sitting in the park. Franzén came out just before one o'clock, but only to buy a wrap and a smoothie from a food stall in Gallerian, just down the escalator from Brunkebergstorg. She pretended to browse the women's clothes in KappAhl but watched him head back towards the escalator after buying his lunch. She managed to get up and out through the glass doors in time to see him return to his office.

The afternoon was longer than she had hoped it might be. Franzén finally came out around seven o'clock and strode quickly down Malmskillnadsgatan. Gunvor's knee protested strongly as she hurried after him. But she managed to just about keep up, at a discreet distance. What felt to her like a power walk took them right down Jakobsbergsgatan and then left into Norrlandsgatan. Franzén took another right at Lästmakargatan, then at Birger Jarlsgatan he crossed the road and disappeared into Sturehof—one of Stockholm's coolest bars for the rich and trendy.

"Shit!" Gunvor cursed. There wasn't a chance in hell that she could blend in unnoticed in a place like that. Everyone would wonder what on Earth some old granny was doing in there on her own. Maybe it'd work if she upgraded her wardrobe dramatically with a bit of Östermalm, lady style, but even that would be dubious. There'd be too much chance Franzén would notice her.

The terrace bar was relatively full, despite the cooler evening. She could make out Franzén in the bar. He seemed to be looking out towards the street, so she moved quickly past, not stopping until she was out of sight from the bar's window. With no idea of how long she would have to wait, she walked towards Svampen—the distinctive shelter that looked like a big mushroom in the middle of Stureplan that people often used as a meeting point. Once there, she could easily pretend to be waiting for a friend.

It was several hours before Franzén eventually came out and Gunvor followed him, again at a safe distance. It was a short walk. He went no further than Riche. Gunvor made a quick decision. She walked back to Stureplan and into Sturehof. By the time she had attracted the bartender's attention, she had adopted a worried expression.

"Sorry to bother you, young man. I was supposed to meet my son here a few hours ago but I got held up. And my mobile's died on me. And now that I've finally got here it looks like he's gone. Has a man been in here—mid-thirties, dark hair, well-dressed? Black or dark grey Armani."

"Yes, there was a guy sitting here who looked more or less like that," the barman replied. "But I don't know if he's the one you're looking for. He was looking for a girl."

"That'd be his girlfriend. She was meant to be coming with me." Gunvor attempted to appear upper class, despite her well-worn coat, jeans and trainers.

"Yeah, but the thing is this guy didn't seem to know the girl very well. He showed me a blurred picture on his mobile and asked if she'd been here."

"A blonde?" Gunvor tried her luck in the hope of keeping the conversation going and eliciting more information.

"Yeah." The bartender nodded but appeared to be thinking. "He's actually shown that picture a few times. To be honest, I don't know what he's up to. All I can say is I hope he's not your son, because he seems to have some serious problems."

Gunvor was of two minds for a few seconds but decided to chance her luck again.

"Okay. It's like this. I'm a private detective and I am investigating this man. I'd be very grateful for any information you might be able to give me about him."

"Really? Christ, I'd never have guessed." A surprised smile spread across the bartender's face. "I can't think of anything else I can tell you. He seems nervous, but I'm not sure why. He drinks a lot, and quickly. He checks everyone out and turns 'round whenever the door opens."

"And the girl, what does she look like?"

"Tall, straight hair and big eyes, blue, I think. Lots of make-up. Full figure, small waist. Gorgeous, if I'm honest." He ended his description with a laugh.

"Have you seen her in person?"

"Yes, a while back. Hard to say when. Time's a blur to me these days. One night is pretty much like all the rest."

"Have you seen the two of them together?"

"I'm not sure. Maybe, but I can't be certain. Lots of people know each other here. And lots of them flirt and sometimes they get lucky. Then next time you see them they're with someone else. It's hard to keep count." The bartender laughed before continuing: "On the other hand, she is incredibly fit, so it's not impossible he's fallen for her and maybe got a bit obsessed without even actually knowing her."

"I see. Thanks for your help. Could you text me if either of them turns up here again?" Gunvor placed her card on the bar.

"Oh, right, cool. Can you tell me what it's about?"

"I'll tell you later, if you give me some information. By the way, what's your name? So I know it's you when you text."

"Fredde."

"Thanks Fredde, you've been a great help," she said, and gestured goodbye with her hand as she left.

Approaching Riche, she saw Franzén coming out and making off towards Nybroplan. She knew it was pure chance that she hadn't missed him. She realized that if she hadn't seen him now, she wouldn't have had a clue whether he was still inside or not. So she thanked her lucky stars and followed him.

Next to Dramaten he crossed the road and disappeared into Berzelii Park. Gunvor had to pick up speed to keep up and just managed to spot him going into Berns.

"Shit." She was delighted to have been given this job, but right now she felt she was the wrong person for it. He moved in circles she'd never feel at home in. She had no other choice but to grit her teeth and wait outside in the growing evening chill.

Her hunger was gnawing at her, and now it was coupled with a growing feeling of exhaustion. Which was no real surprise, it was getting on for midnight and she'd been on the go since early that morning. She should have brought a drink and some sandwiches with her, but when she had dashed out to the park outside the Riksbanken she hadn't wanted to leave her observation point to go back and buy something to eat. It wasn't as if she hadn't lasted longer than this without food before, especially when she was working full-time as a surgeon. But now, when she only worked sporadically, she had developed new habits, like eating when she was hungry.

She sat on a park bench and took out her phone to look busy, but she was fully focused on keeping watch over the entrance to Berns and the people coming and going. She was also watching a disturbingly large number of rats moving around in the bushes on one side of the park. She shivered in discomfort and decided to watch from Hamngatan instead. After all, she hardly looked natural sitting on her own in the park at this time of night.

This time at least she didn't have to wait quite so long. After less than half an hour Franzén came out again. He walked into Näckströmgatan, so Gunvor went in the same direction, struggling down Hamngatan, which runs parallel. At the pedestrian crossing on the corner of Kungsträdgården she saw him cross the road and disappear behind Fridays. She crossed over and walked up the other side of Hamngatan. He suddenly appeared a short way ahead of her, on the other side to the restaurant. She smiled, pleased with her perfect timing, and guessed he was on his way home. This seemed to be the case as his route took him across Sergels Torg and down into the underground station.

Out of the corner of her eye she saw him get off the train in Liljeholmen and decided to go home. There's was no point in following him all the way to his front door. His secrets probably had no connection to Liljeholmen, especially when she thought about how he had just spent his evening.

Gunvor had put in a long day's work, but she felt frustrated. How was she going to find out what was going on if she couldn't blend in at the places he spent his time in? She decided she would follow him the same way tomorrow. If he went to the same places again, she could assume that that was his routine. And if it was, she would need to come up with another plan. Walking across the square in Fruängen, an idea came into her mind.

7

As expected, the next day's surveillance was almost identical. One difference, however, was that this time Gunvor got a text from Fredde a minute or so after Franzén had gone into Sturehof. Gunvor smiled to herself, thinking this was a contact she ought to nurture, even when the case was over. You never know what the next job will bring, or what help you might need in the future. Being so new to this business, she appreciated the importance of building up a network of useful contacts.

As she did yesterday, Gunvor followed Franzén to make sure he went into Riche after leaving Sturehof. Aware of the risk of losing him, she went back to Sturehof where Fredde appeared pleased to see her. Most of the clientele had chosen to sit outside, taking advantage of those last fleeting days of summer while they could. Just one man remained inside, as he stood at the bar with his back to her. He seemed to be concentrating on something else, so she decided it was safe for her to talk freely with Fredde.

"Hi Miss Marple. Your guy's already been and gone." Fredde flashed her a dazzling white smile.

"I know." She grinned back. "For one thing, I got a text from a fantastic new friend, and for another I've been standing outside keeping the whole place under surveillance."

"Of course you have." He took a small glass and filled it with draught Staropramen and placed it in front of her.

"It's on the house. It's the likes of you that keep the rest of us safe." He raised a glass of what looked like mineral water. "Cheers," he said.

Gunvor took a long, slow drink of her favorite beer. She put her glass back on the bar and smiled again at Fredde.

"Thank you. I don't think you realize how much this means to me. The text and this." She nodded her head to indicate the glass. "What did our mutual friend do?"

"Not much. He ordered a few beers and the hamburger deal. May I ask why it is you're following him?"

"If I tell you, I'll have to kill you," They shared a grin. "His wife suspects he is having an affair."

Fredde raised his eyebrows. "Of course. And what do you think?"

"It's clear that something's not right. He's under a lot of stress, and he's looking for that girl. He obviously doesn't have a phone number or address for her, so he goes from bar to bar asking if people have seen her. She might have been his lover, but there are lots of other things that can make people stressed and secretive."

"Drugs?" Fredde dampened his voice, just to be on the safe side, even though no one was really near enough to hear.

"Possibly. Or a gambling addiction. Blackmail. Selling inside information. He works for the Riksbanken, so he knows a lot of stuff that people on the outside aren't allowed to know."

"Yeah, of course." Fredde was clearly excited by Gunvor's work. So she switched track and tried to emphasize the mundane and less glamorous side of it.

"But usually it's just good old-fashioned adultery. And most of the time I have to spend hours standing around and looking for the signs, just to confirm that lots of men still want to have their cake and eat it."

"Steady on. These days there's just as many women that want the same, if not more. Or is it just that men are too tight to pay private detectives to find out what they are pretty certain they know anyway."

Gunvor laughed. "Yeah, you've probably hit the nail on the head. To be honest, it's a shame couples don't trust each other; it's a shame that people live together but can't speak about their problems. It's just…sad."

Fredde nodded.

"And the worst thing is, I know exactly how it is. I spent 20 years with a man I never really knew. Ridiculous. You work and work and keep thinking that later you'll find time for each other. Just as soon as you've sorted *this* out, then *that* out, and suddenly you realize the days have turned into years and you've lost each other. You're standing there wondering who the hell it is living in your flat with you."

"Now you're getting far too serious. Do you want a Jäger-meister with that?" Fredde pointed a finger at Gunvor's beer and smiled at his own joke. "No, seriously, I know exactly what you mean. I've been in the same situation, but luckily I realized and got out before it turned into 20 years."

Their conversation was interrupted by two girls who wanted to order. Gunvor sipped at the rest of her beer and by the time the girls got their drinks and moved away she had finished it.

"Best be going," she said. "Do you want to carry on being my eyes and ears in here?"

"Absolutely. It's fun. I'll text you as soon as either of them shows up and keep an eye on what they do. I don't work on Mondays, just so you know. But I'll be working every night till then."

"Great. Stay in touch."

Gunvor felt satisfaction at a job well done as she stepped out into the street. She had secured observation of Sturehof for the next three nights. If Franzén came back later tonight, Fredde would be fully occupied with his bar work and wouldn't be able to watch him. But Gunvor had had time to come up with a Plan B and it was almost time to activate it. But first, she'd hang around and see whether Franzén met anyone this evening.

She glanced back into the bar, ready to wave at Fredde, but his back was turned so he didn't see. Something else was different in there too. It took a few seconds before she realized that the other man in the bar seemed to have completely vanished. She turned around but she couldn't see anyone, coming out or behind her on the pavement. She shook her head. How cynical she'd become since she started earning a bit on the side as a private eye.

This evening was very much like the previous one in terms of Franzén's movements, though there were a lot more people out and about on a Friday. She decided to wait outside Riche, even though she didn't know whether he was still there or not. But she was in luck again. After half an hour he came out and headed for Berns. Gunvor walked down Hamngatan until she found a place where she could see the entrance to Berns across the park.

To her relief, he set off home at the same time as the night before, even though it was Friday and places were open later. This evening she had decided to follow him all the way home, just to make sure that nothing happened between Liljeholmen and Mikael and Nadja's home. It didn't.

He turned off towards Sjövikskajen. Gunvor crossed the square and went quickly along Sjöviksvägen, before turning into Sjövikskajen. Just in time to see him go in through the door of number 2. She slowed down, strolled past the door and out onto the jetty.

The island lights of Söder flickered from the other side of Årstaviken and got her thinking about the evening on Amfi Beach with Kjell. Three short days ago. It seemed so close that she could almost feel the sand between her toes, yet at the same time it felt like another life. She pulled out her phone and texted Kjell.

— *Love you.*

It wasn't long before she got the same message in return, plus one more word.

— *Forever.*

Forever is a long time, she thought, heading towards Liljeholm-storget to look for a taxi. But she couldn't stop herself turning back again to see the magical, beautiful lights reflected in the water. She saw a man standing exactly where she stood just moments before. *Where did he come from?* It looked as if he was standing there looking at her, but she assumed her tired eyes must be playing tricks on her.

The next day was a Saturday and she had decided not to follow Franzén during the day. According to Nadja, he still spent the weekend days with her; partly in the gym and partly at home, where he went through his shares and investments. Nadja had not elaborated, but Gunvor had the impression that they made most of their so-called 'big money' speculating on the stock market.

Nadja had also said they were going to a birthday party on Saturday afternoon. She'd be leaving the gathering at about 6 pm to have dinner with some friends and she assumed her husband would head off as soon as she had gone. Gunvor had the address and would follow him from then on. But before any of that, she had something else on her agenda, and it might take a while.

*

I see through you.
You, who thinks you are unseen.
Private detective?
Is that what you call yourself?
You're pathetic.
To go unseen in the night requires something more
    than you possess.
It takes darkness and an understanding of darkness
    to overcome darkness.
You are creeping after the scum.
The one who got caught in flagrante.
What is it you want? To save his marriage?
He is way beyond saving.
But carry on creeping, woman.
I'll let you creep on...
For as long as you amuse me.

8

G unvor was up early despite the late night. The plan that had been forming in her head seemed to cohere the more she thought about it. It would, however, require a challenging combination of good timing and skillful persuasion. A conversation with Manuel cleared the extra expenses she'd need. The next step was to look up David's phone number and write a message. She re-drafted it several times before she sent it, so it took a while.

—*To compensate for 'borrowing' your phone I have an offer to make you. 1000 kronor for an evening's work.*

She sent the message and then stared at the phone, nervously waiting for an answer. She didn't have to wait long.

—*Who the fuck are you? What sort of job?*

Gunvor smiled as she replied that he'd find out if he came to Fruängen School's football pitch in half an hour. She'd blocked her number so he couldn't find out who texted him. She hoped curiosity would bring him to the meeting place.

—*Come alone.*

Gunvor believed you can never be too sure. Boys his age tend to move in groups of like-minded friends.

Before she set off, she sent another message to confirm a meeting with someone else, at the same place ten minutes later. She changed into something appropriate in order to give a professional impression. She was aware of the importance of a proper dress code. Her newly ironed jacket felt like the best choice, along with a matching skirt and blouse.

Gunvor was sitting on the steps leading up to the school playground as David came slouching down the path to the right of the school. It occurred to Gunvor that he'd been wearing the same clothes every time she'd seen him: loose jeans that threaten to slide down to his ankles at any second and a worn-out grey hoodie that hid most of his hair and even his face when he let his head hang. He was tall and muscular but his choice of clothes made him seem young, almost childlike.

He walked across the grass to the opening in the fence that surrounded the pitch. It was only after he had taken a few steps out onto the football pitch that he noticed Gunvor. He stopped and looked around. Evidently, he was anticipating meeting someone entirely different. Gunvor got up and walked down the last few steps onto the football pitch. She saw his irritated expression slowly change when he realized she was the woman from the train station. She was the one that stole his phone and pulled the pranks on him!

"You?"

"Yes, me. I warned you, didn't I? I told you to stop or I'd have to do something, and you didn't stop, did you? Now you've got the chance to learn that not everything is as it seems. That it can be worth having respect for other people, even if it's only to stop yourself getting into trouble." Gunvor paused briefly, then continued." But that's not why I want to meet you now. I need your help."

"And why the hell should I help a mad old woman like you?" David made no effort to hide his contempt.

"Did I not mention the 1000 kronor? I'm sure I did. But mainly because I'm offering you the chance of a bit of part-time work as a private eye. And believe me, it'll do wonders for your self-esteem. You'll get a chance to be something other than a loser from the estates for a night." Gunvor knew she was taking a chance, but she was convinced it was the only way.

"A private eye?" David's lip curled. "You mean like some sort of cop?"

"No, I mean like a private investigator. I need help watching someone tonight. He goes to a place where I don't fit in, because like you say, I'm just a mad old woman. But I need someone to be my eyes and ears in this place I can't go. If you agree, we'll go into town right now and get you the right sort of clothes—and you can keep them when we're done." Gunvor spoke as fast as she could in the hope of getting as much said as possible before he interrupted and started complaining.

"Are you having a laugh?"

Despite the harsh tone, Gunvor sensed a glimmer of hope in his eyes. She silently held out her card from the agency, which was called, somewhat unimaginatively, *The Private Eyes*. But in this situation it was more than enough to suddenly transform David's mood.

"Tonight? Who am I going to follow? Have you got a picture? What am I supposed to do?"

"We'll go through everything when you've agreed. And when your partner gets here. But first, we have to get one thing straight. It seems like every other word that comes out of your mouth is "fuck." That has to stop. From this point forward, you are to act like a professional. Not only are you representing the firm, you are my representative. Your behavior reflects on me. So, you have to act like a pro, both in word and appearance. In other words, if you want to work with me, clean up your act, David. Right here. Right now. Do we understand each other? Think you can do that?"

David looked down at his shoes and, after a moment of what

seemed to be contemplation, gave a reluctant nod.

"Your partner should be here any minute." Gunvor turned her head towards the direction she was expecting Elin to come from, and sure enough there she was, walking from the opposite corner of the football pitch. David's eyes followed hers.

"Oh, for fuck's sake. Is this some kind of wind-up?" David asked.

Gunvor immediately pointed her finger at him in a forceful and damning gesture. Realizing his unconscious mental error, he silently acknowledged her veiled threat.

Elin's sudden appearance totally threw David, but Gunvor had no intention of losing control of the situation.

"Forget what's happened. And remember, you were the one that was horrible to her. She's done nothing to you."

"Oh, come on. She's a moron."

"You're not going to hang out. You're not even going to pretend you know each other. I need two young people, one of each sex, so control yourself and you'll soon be 1000 kronor better off. You'll even get a job reference as a private detective. Put that on your CV, they'll love you."

Gunvor was pretty sure she'd managed to persuade David. As Elin got closer to them, she seemed, if anything, even more apprehensive than he was. But she and Gunvor had already begun to develop a friendship so Gunvor was able to explain the situation to her without her interrupting. To Gunvor's surprise, Elin needed little persuasion and, before she knew it, they had all shaken hands to seal the deal.

They left the football pitch at five-minute intervals and made their way into central Stockholm where they would re-group outside River Island in Gallerian.

"Okay. It's Saturday and you're going out in Östermalm, so you need clothes that are a bit more up-market than you're used to. I think a black dress and some high heels for you, Elin."

She looked at Elin and thought that just about anything would be a huge improvement to her current style. Today she was wearing dark tights, black ballet flats and a skirt that's way too big with some sort of grey pattern all over it.

"And David, you can have a look for some chinos or something and a nice top or shirt."

"What the f...,," he said, catching himself. "What are chinos?"

"Trousers that don't hang half-way down your ass. Come on." Gunvor led the way into the store.

"Yes, Mum," David sneered.

"If I was your mother do you think I'd let you use language like that?" Gunvor said. Elin failed to suppress a giggle.

It took a while to find the right clothes—or rather to get Elin and David to accept their new fashion status. For a while she wondered if maybe she had lost her sense for fashion. But when she saw what Elin and David had each chosen, she realized they were stuck in their respective suburban princess and ghetto gangsta styles. And that simply would not work in Sturehof or Riche. Eventually, Elin agreed on a black, low-cut dress and a pair of snakeskin patterned stilettos, and as David looked pretty cool in a pair of black skinny jeans, Gunvor dropped the chino idea. They went perfectly with a tight-fitting purple shirt and a pair of brown boots. Gunvor made another circuit of the store while David and Elin were still in the changing rooms checking out their clothes. She returned with a light-grey bomber jacket for David and a body-hugging, sky blue imitation leather jacket for Elin. All they needed now was a bit of make-up for Elin and some hair products for them both and they were ready.

On the way back to Fruängen they sat in separate carriages. Elin carried the bags so none of David's friends would get the chance to ask why he'd started shopping where the rich kids go. There wasn't much chance that anyone would wonder about Elin. Even when she went to school here she had only a few friends.

Gunvor stopped at Donna Bella and bought three pizzas. They needed to eat well as it could become a very long night. To her delight, she heard David and Elin's voices when she walked in through the main door of her apartment block. They'd gotten there before her and had to wait a bit, but that was no bad thing. In fact, if nothing else came of the evening she had at least managed to help them to relax with each other. And now, as they sat at the table eating pizza and drinking coke, the atmosphere was relaxed, almost pleasant.

The plan was that Gunvor would follow Franzén when he left the birthday party. Starting at six o'clock, David would hang out in the bar at Sturehof and Elin at Riche. They would both watch Franzén and use text messages to keep each other up to speed on his movements.

"If you see him speak to a woman, make sure you hear what they're saying. Or at least watch carefully so you can work out what's going on. If you really think it's necessary to make contact with him, do. But that's a last resort, because once you've made contact the chances are he'll remember you and then you won't be able to follow him if he leaves. And the next time you have him under surveillance he'll probably recognize you." Gunvor took a bottle of white wine out of the fridge while she was talking.

"What do you mean, next time?" David interrupted. "You said it was just one night."

"I know I did, but you can never be sure. That's what's so exciting about this business. Can you get the glasses? You two need to get in the mood."

"Wine? Got any vodka?" David asked. Gunvor shook her head.

"You'll be drinking really slowly later," she replied. "Do you think I'm paying you a thousand kronor each so that I can wipe sick off your stupid faces at midnight while the man we're watching heads off God knows where to do God knows what? This wine is just to relax you a bit and help you blend in."

Elin looked like she was still struggling to understand, so David gave her a little nudge before he got up and went to get three wine glasses.

"We're not going to say no to a thousand kronor a night, are we?"

Elin still seemed confused, but this time Gunvor thought it was more due to David suddenly using 'we' about the two of them.

After they'd had a glass of wine each, Gunvor emptied the bag of make-up and hair products onto the kitchen table. She opened the bag containing eye pencils and brushes and set up some warm, brown shades of powder and eye shadow. Elin closed her eyes obediently when Gunvor lifted the brush she had just circled in the powder to her face. Before she started, she looked at David, "You can get changed while we're doing this, and while you're at it, put some kind of style into your hair with this. And don't worry, you're not going to bump into anyone who knows you on the way there, I've sorted us a lift." She tossed him a bottle of hair gel, and he fumbled it and it threatened to smash on Gunvor's kitchen tiles before he recovered and got a better grip. Elin giggled again, and David pulled a face at her. But there was no malice in it. They shared a smile before he headed off to the bathroom, carrying his shopping bags to get changed. Gunvor began applying Elin's make-up with her experienced hands. She'd always been interested in make-up, going back to her time in upper secondary school when she joined the drama club and ended up doing all the actors' faces. And because she'd always been something of a perfectionist, by the opening night the makeup was so good that she even got a mention in the local newspaper. Since then she had always kept up-to-date with the latest colors and styles and bought the newest products. She seldom used them, apart from very special occasions and big nights out.

Elin had dark hair and green eyes, so Gunvor chose a combination of gold and brown shades for her eyes and dark red for her lips. It was a good choice. Even the mascara looked as good as it did on the poster. Elin was pretty enough as it was, but with Gunvor's make-up a real beauty began to emerge. Her eyes looked seductive as they flickered and shone from behind long, black lashes. And once she put on the new dress, she looked downright sexy.

"You're looking good," Gunvor said, "but a pair of stilettos won't hurt." Gunvor was waiting with the shoes in her hands as Elin struggled to get her legs into shiny nylon tights. She put the stilettos on and looked up at Gunvor who could only hold her breath.

"You were cute before, but now…well, go look in the mirror." Gunvor nodded in the direction of her full-length mirror in the living room.

"Oh, my God! I'm going to be a private detective full time!" Elin was ecstatic.

The toilet door opened and out stepped an attractive, confident young man. His contented expression turned to surprise when he caught sight of Elin.

David let out a low whistle. "Elin, you are gorgeous," was all he managed to say, and Gunvor saw him struggling to take his eyes off Elin. She could also see how Elin was flattered and just a little embarrassed by his reaction and guessed that she was not used to being appreciated. She looked back at him.

"Yeah…likewise," she managed to say. And she was right. David was in good shape and good-looking. With the hair wax, and without his customary hood, she could see his cheek bones, his even white teeth and the twinkle in his blue eyes, in a way she couldn't before.

"This is perfect. But we need to hurry. My friend Aidan will drive us. I will call him now and say that we are ready to leave. Put your jackets on for one final check before we go." Gunvor had lent Elin a handbag and given them 500 kronor each for drinks and snacks. They were both exited but had some difficulty tearing off the mirror. Gunvor nearly had to push them out of the apartment.

Aidan was already sitting waiting in the car. He looked excited to be part of the adventure. Until today he'd only heard occasional stories about her work and in his imagination even the longest, most boring stakeout was filled with drama. It was never going to be difficult to persuade him to give them a lift into town, even though Saturday was his pub night.

"No shots tonight. You need to stay in control and focused. David, drink beer. Order beer with a weird name. Ideally a Singha, it'll make people think you go to Thailand. No cheap crap, OK? You're not in suburbia now. Elin, rosé or white wine, okay?"

David and Elin were excited, even if Elin expressed concern about going into Riche on her own.

"What am I going to do there on my own? I'll look totally weird."

"It's natural. Lots of women go in bars to have a glass of wine by themselves, especially if they're waiting for someone. Try to look engrossed in your iPhone, so no one tries to chat you up."

They stopped close to Norrmalmstorg and let David and Elin out. Then Aidan drove off via Strandvägen and on to Gärdet. It was a quarter to six when he found a parking space on Vallhallavägen. Gunvor gratefully accepted his offer to stay and wait with her. It was a lot easier, and the longer it took for Nadja to appear, the more grateful Gunvor became for the comfort of the car. You can't just stand outside someone's house staring at the pavement indefinitely, and there really isn't much else to do. Not at this end of Valhallavägen anyway.

Forty minutes later Nadja came out of the door and walked towards Karlaplan underground station.

"There she is, another woman who doesn't trust her husband."

Aidan's eyes followed Nadja intently.

"So now we wait for the asshole, right?" Despite several years in Sweden, Aidan was still much happier speaking English.

"Precisely, if indeed he is an asshole. And that's what we aim to find out."

It didn't take long before Franzén came out. He glanced

nervously in the direction Nadja had taken before walking with short, quick steps towards Gärdet.

"There he is. I've got to go and follow him now. Thanks for the lift."

Aidan started the engine before Gunvor had chance to open the door.

"I'll drive you. This is fun."

With a contented smile Aidan drove in the opposite direction to Franzén, looking for the first opportunity to turn around. They saw Mikael cross Valhallavägen to their side of the road. To their relief he hailed a taxi. When it set off, they followed slowly behind.

They found themselves going back the way they'd came. After Dramaten the taxi turned right, as they'd guessed it would, and into Birger Jarlsgatan before stopping outside Sturehof. Aidan pulled up a short distance behind it.

"Thanks again for the lift. Are you staying around or getting off? No problem at all if you need to go, we can get a taxi home."

"I'll see if I can find somewhere to park, though it'll probably be a bit tricky. I'll get back to you when I know. But like I said, I can pick you up later."

"Thanks, Aidan. See you when I see you. Cheers."

Gunvor just managed to catch sight of Franzén going into Sturehof. As she walked towards Svampen her phone sounded. It was a text from Fredde saying that Mikael was in Sturehof.

Gunvor thanked him, then texted David to check if he was on site and watching Franzén. She received a speedy response that yes, he was. He had also texted Elin, who was on her way over from Riche.

Gunvor was delighted that her idea was working exactly as she'd hoped. Despite their shortcomings, David and Elin had so far performed faultlessly. They'd hardly begun, of course, but she had a good feeling about them. All she had to do now was wait, so she looked around for somewhere appropriate she could do so.

9

E lin and David got out of the car in Norrmalmstorg and walked in silence across the square and into Smålandsgatan. When they got to Birger Jarlsgatan, David pointed out Riche to Elin and set off towards Sturehof.

"Good luck. Keep in touch," he said.

"Thanks, likewise." As Elin watched David leave, a tingle of excitement ran through her. Today had already given her moments unlike any she'd ever come close to experiencing before. She was literally out on a private detective assignment. If someone had told her, even yesterday, that this would happen, she'd never have believed it.

During the short walk to Riche, she focused on walking slowly and appearing sophisticated, as if this was the most natural thing in the world to her. It was not just Gunvor's approval that she was seeking now, success had become important to her as well. For once in her life, she had a chance to make a difference in someone's life. She was the only one who could do it, and Gunvor really needed her.

Elin had been told there were two entrances to Riche, and that she was to use the one farthest away from Stureplan. Passing the first entrance, she noticed just how many of the people sitting inside were actually looking at her. Her pulse started to race as she saw another door. She moved quickly towards it and reached out to open it—only to find it locked. After a few seconds of panic, pulling and pushing at the handle, she noticed that it led to a stairway. Confused, she took a few steps further along the street before spotting the second entrance to Riche a few meters on. She walked in quickly, her cheeks burning, hoping to God that none of the customers saw her blunder.

She took the few steps to the bar, but the moment she entered her veneer of sophistication crumbled. She looked nervously around, managing to obtain an overview of the room. Reflections from the beautiful stainless steel bar glimmered on the turquoise walls and the contorted mermaid reliefs on the ceiling. There were some empty stools at the far end of the bar. She headed for the ones furthest away, partly to ensure she had a bit of space but mainly to force herself to walk there at a measured pace when all she wanted to do was turn around and run out. She took off her jacket, hung it on a little hook under the bar, and slid up onto the stool. To stop her hands from shaking, she placed her handbag on her lap and rooted around in it for her mobile. The bartender appeared before she could survey the room any further. She ordered a glass of rosé. He took a glass down from one of the impressive metal gantries that seemed to provide lighting for the bar and storage space for the glasses. While he filled her glass, she managed to steal a casual look around the room. She caught her own reflection in the mirror behind the bar. It calmed her down as she realized that she actually blended in quite well. However lost she might feel, she at least looked like she could belong here. She could be anyone popping in for a quick drink after work or unwinding after a shopping trip.

The place was quiet, just as Gunvor said it would be. It was immediately obvious to her that Mikael Franzén wasn't here, which was no great surprise considering he was due to be at a party anyway. But you could never be too sure. And there's no guarantee that if he were here, he'd be in this particular bar. Riche frequented several bars, but from what Elin understood the Lilla Bar was the one to be seen in, especially if you were young and cool.

She saw a man sitting alone at a small table facing the bar who seemed to be finding it hard to stop staring at her. Her initial reaction was that there must be something wrong. She checked the mirror again, making sure she hadn't smudged her make-up or something. The next time she glanced in his direction he smiled at her, at which point she realized that he had probably just taken a fancy to her. She tried to recreate the image in her mind of how attractive she actually was now and then to transmit that feeling through her whole self.

She cast a shy smile back at the man, who suddenly got up and walked towards her. She didn't know what to do with herself, so she stayed put and battled to maintain an inner calm.

"You are the most beautiful woman I've ever seen." The man, who was a good deal older than her, sat down on the stool next to her without once taking his eyes from hers.

"Thanks, but you're probably exaggerating a little." Elin felt uncomfortable yet flattered. Well, mostly flattered if she was honest.

The man's smile disappeared.

"Why don't you let me be the judge of that?"

"Of course." Elin's first instinct was to put things right. She wanted to avoid causing offense. "I didn't mean to... to... sorry, I didn't mean to..." Elin looked down at the bar and felt like a ten-year-old again—the young girl whose father always told her she did everything wrong.

"I am so sorry, my dear, I didn't mean to upset you." He smiled again, lifting Elin's spirits. "May I suggest a toast?"

"Yes, of course."

The man raised his glass of crimson wine ceremoniously. Elin thought he looked and behaved like a character from one of the old Orson Welles films her mother loved so much. Elin had inherited her passion, often dipping into her mother's film collection on a rainy Sunday. The man conveyed the same aura of ceremonial formality. He seemed a little odd and very different from anyone she had ever met before. She found him rather charming.

"A toast to beauty."

"Cheers." Elin conjured up her most alluring smile before taking a sip of her rosé.

"Can I offer you a glass of my favorite champagne?"

"Oh, thank you, but I still have a drink."

"But I insist. Have you tasted champagne before?"

"No, I don't think so."

"That's it then. A beautiful creature like you was born to drink champagne. It would be a tragedy not to."

"But you don't need to…" She got no further. He silenced her with a gesture and winked at the waiter.

"A bottle of Dom Perignon in the young lady's honor. I believe I have found my princess."

"Certainly sir.' The bartender smiled and rushed off to find the most expensive champagne.

"Just so you know, I have to go soon."

"All the more reason to cherish what few moments we have together." He looked at her with the beginnings of a smile before continuing. "Like a chance meeting of two lost souls. Fumbling in the dark, they suddenly catch sight of one another. They stop and smile, with curiosity at first and then with joy, for they know it is meant to be." Elin didn't understand what he was saying, but she listened attentively. He leaned in closer to her. "As I dreamed." He kept his head close and looked deep into her eyes for a second, then leaned back again and raised his glass. "Cheers."

"Cheers."

"To lost souls who finally find their way home."

She smiled and took a drink at the same time as him, afraid to do the wrong thing. She'd never tasted champagne, she'd never raised a glass in a toast before. Her father's approach to alcohol hadn't been that sort of drinking. But she'd had the occasional drink since she turned eighteen, she'd gone out from time to time and learned to enjoy a glass of wine, although she knew nothing about types or labels.

She really liked the taste, and with every sip, she felt more and more attractive. The man was pleasant enough, and she enjoyed his unrestrained flattery. His looks of admiration and the way he poured her champagne made her feel like a princess.

"Does my lady ride?"

It took a few moments before Elin realized she's the lady he was referring to.

"I do, actually. But I haven't for a few years now."

"Ah, now you have awoken another desire within me."

Elin didn't understand his way of speaking so she just smiled.

"To see the lady riding my favorite Chestnut across my fields in Uppland. Bareback, in a long, white lace dress. Barefoot, of course, and with that wonderful shiny hair flowing free over her shoulders."

He reached out and gently stroked her hair as he said this. He took a lock and let it slip slowly between his fingers. The curl fell softly against Elin's chin, and he brushed it away with his finger and gently touched her skin at the same time. She knew he was too old for her, but she couldn't help but enjoy the feel of his finger, soft as a feather on her face. She couldn't remember the last time anyone had touched her so tenderly. The thought that he wanted to see her riding a horse with a white dress on excited her too. To have someone fantasizing about her in that way, as if she was some remote and desirable princess sent shivers through her.

Her iPhone sounded, which brought her back to reality. She offered a polite apology then read the message.

– *MF in Sturehof. Come now.*

She replied that she was on her way then looked back at her new acquaintance.

"Thank you for the drink. It was lovely, but I have to go now. I'm meeting a friend." She smiled at him, hoping she appeared reserved so that he would assume she was on a date with someone else. But at the same time, a large part of her would like nothing more than to stay here and enjoy this stranger's flattery.

"Everything that is beautiful must end." He smiled a little sadly, his eyes moved down to the neckline of her new black dress. "I pray the gods are on my side, and that I might set eyes on you again.'

"Maybe, who knows?" was all Elin could think of as an answer, but he seemed happy with it.

"One final toast before you leave me?"

He filled her glass without waiting for her answer and looked at her with longing. Before she could pick up her glass, he took her hand and pulled it to his lips for a kiss.

"*Au revoir, mademoiselle.*"

"*Au revoir. Il a été un plaisir, monsieur.*" At last, something she understood and could respond to. He seemed impressed and maintained a firm grip on her hand while they drank. It tasted even better this time, so she finished it before she slid the glass away from her and stood up. Lost in the moment, Elin leaned forward and kissed him on the cheek. He moved his head quickly so that their lips briefly met. He was extremely reluctant to let her go, but when he did Elin left Riche with significantly more assurance than when she had arrived. Swinging her hips as she strolled down Birger Jarlsgatan felt like the most natural thing in the world.

10

David was feeling euphoric as he left Elin and headed off towards Sturehof. This day had been mental so far, and hopefully, it'd get even crazier. He hoped they manage to solve the case tonight, or rather, that he'd solve it. Or at least that he was one of the main reasons for its resolution.

He was furious when he got those bloody stilettos. He thought his friends were never going to stop laughing. And they've brought it up more than a few times since. Not to mention that Facebook shit. It was totally humiliating—and the worst thing was that he wasn't sure whether it was one of his friends that had done it. He'd had a few sleepless nights where he was sure they were all in it together. If he found out they had done it, he'd have to at least beat the shit out of them, one by one. But it was that mad little old woman, and he hadn't even touched her. She'd actually done him a favor. Say what you like, these were cool clothes, and the job was exciting. It might be just for one night, but there'd be more if he played his cards right. He hadn't totally forgiven her but if he got some more work off her, maybe he would.

He shrugged off his affected ghetto slouch and held himself a little straighter as he stepped through the door of Sturehof. He'd never been here before. In fact, he'd never been out in Stureplan before, or even north of Slussen when he thought about it. Everyone in Fruängen hated these rich kids with their privilege and their false sense of superiority. On the handful of nights he'd been out in Stockholm, it was to an Irish or English pub on Söder. But usually, he just went to Parma in Fruängen or to Västertorps Hjärta, one station away.

He saw his reflection in the glass door of Gallerian and smiled. He was looking good. Maybe it was time he started hanging out in places like this a bit more. Get a change of scenery. He'd spent his whole life in the suburbs. Same crappy places with no girls apart from the ones most of his mates had already shagged. Always the same old conversations. He was fed up with hanging around in the center talking crap, but what else could he do? He was starting to really hate his life.

The bar was about half full. He scanned the room carefully for Mikael Franzén. Once he was sure he wasn't there, David went to the bar and ordered a beer. He noticed that there was more than one girl eyeing him up. He tried smiling at one of them, and she delighted him by smiling back. *Shit, I could pull tonight, if I wasn't working,* he thought. Though he reasoned that one doesn't necessarily rule out the other.

He forced down some disgusting designer beer. A Trappistes Rochefort 10, he thought it was. He decided to switch to draft beer, despite Gunvor's suggestion that he try to act a bit sophisticated. It didn't seem to matter. Everyone was drinking beer. He was enjoying the more familiar taste when he saw Franzén come in and order a bottle of white wine, then sit at a table at the far end of the bar near the doors leading to the terrace.

The girl who returned David's smile earlier was sneaking glances at him. Glances that were almost making him forget why he was there. But when he spotted Franzén his adrenaline rose, and he was soon on full alert again. He was not going to take his eyes off him until the case was solved. Franzén's appearance was impeccable. He was wearing a really expensive-looking suit, but his face seemed grey, and his movements were nervous and awkward. David thought he looked worn out.

David saw the bartender pick up his phone just before he took out his own to text Elin. His phone beeped, and he thought it was Elin replying. But it was a text from Gunvor. He replied that everything was under control and that Elin was on her way. Then he turned to look towards the door, which had just swung open, to see if it was Elin coming in. It wasn't, but that wasn't so strange. It had only been a minute since he texted her. He looked slowly around the bar and noticed that the cute girl gave him another of her looks.

Franzén was sitting alone at his table, apparently lost in thought. He was filling his glass a second time, even though he'd only been there for a few minutes. David wondered what was troubling him so much. Because something was, there was no doubt at all about that. The bartender placed a few small bowls of popcorn along the bar, which David guessed were free. As he pushed a fistful of the popcorn in his mouth, he felt a hand on his arm.

11

It was only shortly after six, but Gunvor felt that Friday night had kicked off early this week. She knew she'd fit in perfectly at The Bull and Bear, but she had next to no chance of finding a free window table. Experience told her that even this early it would be standing room only at the bar. But that had to be better than standing for hours on end in the freezing wind under Svampen. "So, when Aidan texted to say he'd found somewhere to park, she decided they could go for a beer there and trust the kids and Fredde to keep an eye on things. Aidan would be perfect company, an Englishman in an English pub. What more could you ask for?

She met Aidan, and they walked slowly down Birger Jarlsgatan; Gunvor took the side of the pavement nearest the road. She told him to talk to her or just look at her or the pavement, so she could glance casually into Sturehof, as if at random.

Even though they walked slowly, it wasn't easy to see all the way into the bar. The doorway was partially covered by a low-hanging blind, and there were more people inside than last night. But she spotted Fredde. Fredde didn't yet know about Elin and David, and they didn't know about him. Gunvor had no experience herself, but Manuel had told her it was good to have more than one source of information—maybe several— who were independent of one another. People always made their own interpretations of everything, so this was a way to ensure a more balanced view when you couldn't be there yourself.

She suddenly saw Elin, who seemed to be intently watching someone sitting between the two exit doors. Someone she couldn't make out from outside. As she walked past the bar, Gunvor realized she needed to start looking in the direction she was walking before she attracted undue attention to herself.

12

E lin saw David as soon as she walked into Sturehof. He looked up, and their eyes met briefly, but neither of them showed the slightest sign of recognition. David refocused on his new and attractive acquaintance while keeping an eye on Franzén on the other side of the bar.

Elin looked around as she went to the bar to order a glass of white wine. As she raised her hand to attract the bartender's attention, she noticed Franzén sitting alone at a table. She immediately turned her head away from him and looked at the bartender. He gave her the wine she had ordered, and she pretended to think something over before walking up to Franzén's table.

"Do you mind if I sit here? It's getting a bit busy for my liking, you know? You can hardly stand up without getting shoved all over the place." She nodded towards the room and smiled at Mikael.

"Oh, of course. But I'm afraid I'm not feeling very sociable this evening." Franzen looked quickly in her direction before looking away again and gazing around the room.

"That's absolutely fine. I'm not feeling particularly sociable myself either."

Elin was seriously questioning the wisdom of her impulsive decision to approach Franzén. The wine and the attention she had received earlier has gone to her head, but that upbeat, confident feeling was disappearing fast. But then her eyes met David's across the bar. She could tell he disapproved of her making contact with Mikael, and somehow her confidence came rushing back. *I'm not going to let that loser sit there and think I've screwed everything up. I'll show him.*

She took a long breath and dug deep, in search of the inner calm she sometimes found when she did yoga. That feeling that arose when the noise of her thoughts was stilled and she felt grounded in the center of her own being. It was a wonderful feeling, although it always seemed to disappear the moment she opened her eyes. Now, sitting there next to Franzén, she attempted to raise her consciousness and find that calm. She didn't completely pull it off, but she felt a little stronger. That was all she needed. She took another sip of wine and turned to Franzén with sorrowful eyes.

"To be honest, I feel just like you. I'm lost in my own thoughts, and I don't feel I can be at all sociable. But I know that what I desperately need to do is talk to someone. Do you think you could bring yourself to waste a few minutes on a stranger? I've done something really stupid, and I need to talk to someone. Preferably someone who doesn't know me."

Franzén looked at her, and she sensed a whisper of curiosity, although she could also see how stressed out and tired he was. He looked exhausted, his eyes were red and bloodshot. And sitting this close, she could see that his skin was bloated and puffy; perhaps because of his drinking. Elin knew she had to keep going now that she'd actually caught his attention.

"I don't want anyone that knows me to find out. My boyfriend's really jealous and judgmental, and most of our so-called friends always side with him. That's why I have no one to talk to."

"Join the club," he raised his glass in a toast and Elin followed suit.

"You too?"

Franzén started into the distance then turned back to Elin and nodded.

"Ah, so maybe it's not good for you to sit and listen to my problems?"

Franzén shook his head, though Elin detected the glimmer of a smile on his lips.

"Your problems are hardly going to be worse than mine, so go ahead."

Elin was feeling very pleased with herself, but she started to panic now that she realized she had to come up with something interesting and believable, and quickly. If she didn't, she'd blow her cover and maybe the case. She took two more mouthfuls of wine, focused on looking devastated and got into the zone. Right here, right now. She was in the middle of a situation that could change the course of her life.

"Really, I'm the faithful type, I always have been. Well, mostly … I didn't really go out with anyone properly till I was quite old. I was never one of the "In Crowd" at school, the ones that were always going with different boys. It wasn't 'til I started sixth form that I started dating. Not that I never wanted to before then, but … I don't know, I somehow didn't let myself."

Elin realized that even though she was well out of her comfort zone, she was actually talking about herself, which wasn't the plan. So she paused a moment and finished off what was left in her glass then threw herself back into her made up and improvised story, "But in college, I really came to life and had quite a few relationships. One was with a married man. I was 17, and he was 43. But God, he was good in bed."

She rolled her eyes and giggled. "How old are you, by the way?" She asked Franzén, somewhat abruptly.

Luckily, he laughed. "Much too old for you."

"Don't say that. The 43-year-old was the best lover I've ever had." She smiled at him, then carried on, "When I met my boyfriend, the one I'm with now, everything felt right, you know? But then it all started moving too fast. I love him, but there are so many things I haven't done yet, and I really want to feel free, so I can do them."

"What is it you really want to do?"

She had noticed that even though he was listening politely to her, he was always monitoring the room. It was only when she said there were things she hadn't done but really wanted to that he finally switched his full attention to her. Suddenly he was looking at her with curiosity. Elin lifted her glass to drink, then halfway up she realized it was empty. Without stopping to ask, Franzén filled it from his bottle.

"There are lots of things I still want to do, but what I need to talk about now is what happened last weekend. Me and Sebastian, my boyfriend, went to Gondolen with a few friends. We hung out in the bar and had a few drinks. Sebastian's friends got a bit loud, and things started getting a bit messy. I joined in and had a laugh, but really, I was starting to get pissed off with the whole thing. I was kind of standing at the edge of the group, leaning on the bar when suddenly I felt a hand on my bum. I span round, feeling pretty offended, and found myself looking into a pair of fantastic blue eyes. He must have been at least 50, with a shaven head and glasses on the tip of his nose, but he had muscles like a body-builder and looks to die for. Or maybe that was just me. Anyway, I know one thing for sure, if I hadn't pushed his hand away, I'd have come there and then. I'd have probably cried out with pleasure, as well."

Elin paused to drink some wine, knowing she had Franzén's full attention, "He basically ordered me to go with him to the cloakroom. I knew I had no choice, I just had to go. For my own sake and, yes, I knew that whatever was going to happen would be worth it."

"What happened?"

"I told Sebastian I was going to the bathroom. I went out into the foyer, and the man was there standing by the lift. He beckoned me over. We stood next to each other in silence, no one could tell that we had anything to do with each other. The lift came, we got on, and then it was crazy."

"Did you have sex?"

"He kissed me, and then everything was a blur. He kissed me like no one has ever kissed me before. Suddenly he stopped the lift, and.. and.. Well, yes. We had sex. He was like no man I'd ever been with. He was.. manly... and dominant."

Elin tried to look dreamy when she paused again. In reality, she was thinking desperately how to come up with a good ending to the story, "It was over quick, but I'll never forget it. He started the lift again, and when it arrived at street level, he just walked out and away. I went back up and went to the toilet, to have a look at myself in the mirror more than anything else. I was certain everyone would be able to see that I'd just had the best orgasm of my life. But apart from a dopey grin, you couldn't tell a thing."

Elin drank some more wine and felt Franzén looking at her, so she turned towards him and looked deep into his eyes, "And what about you?"

13

D avid had gotten himself into a delightful yet frustrating situation. The cutest girl in the world was standing next to him, with her hand on his arm and a most wonderful smile. Her closeness made him tingle all over, but his long-held cynical view of girls told him she would disappear as soon as she realized he was a school dropout from the suburbs. That didn't have to stop him from making the most of it while it lasted, but unfortunately, he kept having to remind himself that he should be prioritizing the evening's work ahead of those hypnotic blue eyes.

They talked about the music that was playing and which drink she was going to choose. Today was her nineteenth birthday, and she giggled as she told him she'd had a few too many. He just smiled as she kept on talking without leaving any pauses where he could come in. Which was fine by him. He certainly didn't want to talk about himself and risk the bubble bursting and her turning around to look for someone more interesting, not yet anyway. So he smiled and laughed and let her conversation flow over him, all the while carefully keeping an eye out for Franzén and Elin.

David was furious with Elin. She had completely ignored their plan by approaching Franzén. And it was obvious he didn't want to talk to her. David shot her a furious look.

Then suddenly Elin was holding court, and Franzén was listening to her intently. David had no idea how, but Elin seemed to have succeeded. He thought it might have something to do with the fact that she looked gorgeous in her new clothes. Sophisticated, too, as if she always hung out here. It's hard to believe she was the same shy, clueless girl who couldn't stand up for herself when he was teasing her a week or so ago.

David's attention swung between his new-found friend and the two at the table. Elin seemed to have everything under control for the moment, so he allowed himself to devote a bit more time to the girl, who had now introduced herself to him as Linnea. Linnea wanted to go dancing. He tried hard to convince her it was too early to move on, but she was determined, flickering her eyes and pouting her lips to try and entice him. When that failed, she simply tried to drag him by grabbing his arm.

David was charmed, and really wanted to go with her, but he couldn't - not yet. Although he sensed his budding relationship with Linnea was on the verge of collapsing before it even started, he hoped he could squeeze a little bit more out of the evening. Franzén was hardly likely to do much more now; maybe they'd carry on the job tomorrow instead. Then he could hang on here anyway, or Linnea could take him somewhere. For her, he'd even go dancing.

David looked across at Franzén and Elin to check that everything was going as smoothly as it was before. But the whole situation had changed dramatically. He cursed himself for not watching as he should have been as he struggled to work out what exactly had been happening.

Franzén had risen from the table, and Elin seemed confused as she watched him walk away. A few seconds later, she caught David's eye and gave him a look that suggested she didn't understand what was going on or why he was leaving. But they immedi-

ately realized when they saw him barge up to a blonde woman
standing with two men by the door. David couldn't hear what was
being said, but he could tell Franzén was really upset, despite only
being able to see him from behind. He was waving his arms about
in a state of agitation, and his face was so close to the woman's
that their heads were almost touching. He was pushed away
quickly and aggressively by one of the men. For a moment it
seemed he would fall, but he grabbed hold of the woman, who he
dragged along with him for a few paces until he regained his
balance. The woman screamed at him so loudly that for a second,
she was louder than the music.

In an instant, a doorman and a waiter from the dining area
were on the scene trying to calm things down. But Franzén didn't
want to calm down, so they removed him to outside. Now David
could see the woman he was shouting at. She was tall with unnat-
urally large breasts. Her beautiful and expertly made-up face was
framed by blonde hair, but as attractive as she was, David didn't
like what he saw. There was something about her appearance that
made him feel uncomfortable. Something artificial and unnatural.

"What's happening over there?" Linnea had only just noticed
the fracas as Franzén was taken outside. "Is he drunk?"

"Yeah, I guess. You'd better be careful they don't throw you
out. You've had loads to drink." He offered Linnea a cheeky smile,
and she responded by sticking out her tongue.

David risked a discreet glance over at the two men and the
woman. One of the men was leaning over and saying something
into the woman's ear. David thought it may be because of the
noise of the music. The woman seemed shocked and took hold of
the man's arm as if to stop him. But he brushed her hand away
and nodded at the other man, who stood up and followed him
outside. To David, the woman had an air of resignation and
sadness about her. She stayed alone in the bar as the men left.

David glanced at Elin. She seemed nonplussed, but at least
noticed his gesture telling her to go outside.

"I'm just going out for a smoke," he told Linnea.

"Can't you wait? I've just ordered."

He didn't wait, despite her pleading puppy eyes. He had to go and see what was going on.

"I'll go and find a good spot." He headed for the exit and pretended he was oblivious to her protests.

14

E lin took her jacket and handbag with her as she left. She
saw the girl who'd been drooling over David paying for her
drink, so she hurried outside to catch him for a quick word. She
walked past the woman Franzén was shouting at, who was
standing alone looking quite blank. Before she had time to think
she found herself putting her hand on the woman's arm.

"Are you okay? You seem sad."

The woman pulled back, looking horrified.

"It's gone too far."

"What's gone too far?" Elin tilted her head to one side and
offered the woman an uncertain smile.

Either Elin had totally misjudged the situation, or the woman
had suddenly come to her senses. Whatever, the moment had
gone, and Elin got only a narrow smile and a few words in
response.

"Sorry, it's nothing. I was just thinking about something. I've
got to go to the loo."

The woman marched purposefully away, and Elin went
quickly out to catch David before his new friend joined him.

There were about a dozen people standing smoking outside the restaurant. Elin went right up to David and asked quite loudly if he could give her a cigarette. He produced a cigarette and passed her a lighter too. He was surprised when she inhaled deeply then let the smoke come slowly out. He had expected a coughing fit.

"What happened?"

"I pretended I needed to talk to a stranger about how I'd been unfaithful. I made up a story that he got really into, but then he started talking about his guilty conscience and suddenly went quiet and just sat there staring. Then two seconds later, he virtually jumped up and went … and you saw the rest."

Elin suddenly realized she was drunk. She had drunk much more wine than she was used to, and the sudden nicotine kick had made her head spin.

"Did you see which way he went?" She looked around to see if she could see Franzén anywhere.

"No, I was thinking of going to look for him now, but I'll text Gunvor first."

David looked down at his phone; meanwhile, Elin noticed that the girl he was talking to inside was on her way over.

"Thanks for the ciggie," she said, loud enough for the girl to hear, then walked slowly towards Svampen. She needed fresh air to clear her head, which had begun to spin. Her legs were beginning to feel unsteady too. She didn't know what to do now that Franzén had disappeared. What she should have done was wait in Sturehof for Gunvor to get back to them. Anyway, Gunvor had a cell phone too, she could easily call and tell Elin what to do. And she hadn't, so what was wrong with Elin using her own initiative, looking around for Franzén while she was clearing her head?

She walked slowly along Sturegatan. It felt really nice out there in the fresh air. There was a hint of autumn in the air, though it wasn't that cold. As she approached, she saw two men coming out of the Humlegården Park. They were both tall and well-muscled. They were big and bulky. Elin could tell, even from this distance, that one of them was really good-looking even though she didn't usually fancy the muscular gym type. He had short, cropped hair and a nice body under his black jeans and green Adidas jacket. The other had longish blond hair but was not as attractive as the first. The handsome one was looking at one of his hands as if it was hurting him. But it didn't seem to be anything serious as they were now both looking at each other and grinning.

That's when she realized they were the men at Sturehof, the ones who had been standing with the blonde girl. She suddenly felt a twinge of panic set in. She willed herself invisible as the two men got closer to her on the pavement. They were right next to Stockholm's liveliest nightlife area but out here on the street they were alone, the three of them. What felt like an adventure earlier now felt like a bad dream. She was terrified they were going to hurt her or that she would somehow give herself away.

When they were a few paces away from each other, she couldn't resist the urge to look up. The good-looking one turned his head at just that moment, and for a second, their eyes met. For Elin, it felt like an eternity, he had a way of staring that made her feel even more threatened.

Then she felt his hand. He turned around at the exact moment they passed her, and from behind, he pressed his hand up between her legs. It was soon over, and the men continued on towards Svampen laughing. Elin carried on without turning back and straightened her skirt as she walked.

Bastards, she thought before hearing a hysterical scream from the park. She stopped dead and tried to peer into the darkness beyond the junction. It was impossible to make anything out, but the screaming hadn't stopped. It changed into cries for help, and then it stopped. It was a woman's voice, and there was obviously something really bad going on over there in the park. She was terrified but knew she had to do something. She was a private detective and felt that part of her job was to keep others safe. If she hadn't still been feeling so dizzy, it would have been easier to think. She was at least alert enough to fire off a text to David and Gunvor.

—*Come Humlgdn - NOW!!*

15

G unvor stared at her iPhone, "What …?"

She had just gotten a message from David saying they'd lost Franzén and she had replied that one of them should go to Riche to see if he was there. Then Elin's message arrived.

Gunvor looked up from her phone and saw that Aidan was waiting to hear what was happening. She was grateful that he managed to find a parking space and was here as a potential backup now that events have taken such a dramatic turn.

"Trouble. Let's go."

They put their glasses down and rushed out. While they were walking – jogging almost – the short distance to Sturehof, Gunvor explained why they had to hurry to Humlegården. Then her phone sounded again. This time it was from Fredde.

— *The guy you're following started a fight. Got thrown out.*

She called David, who rejected her call. She grunted to herself. She now regretted giving them such strict instructions about not speaking on their phones for fear of giving themselves away and how all communication had to be by text. But David was at least smart enough to send a message.

— *You check Elin? I'll stay here. Talk later.*

As much as Gunvor was grateful she had the kids' help, she was now really frustrated. She had lost control and had no idea what was going on. But she was lucky that David was so smart. He realized they didn't all need to run to the same place. Hopefully, it was enough that she and Aidan could rescue Elin on their own.

From a distance, everything in the park looked calm; but as they crossed the road, they started hearing shouts and then the sound of an ambulance approaching. Someone appeared from nowhere, out of the darkness, and ran towards the street. Gunvor thought it might be someone on their way to flag down the ambulance, so they headed in the direction he had come from. It turned out to be an accurate assumption. They came across a man lying on the ground, with three people kneeling round him trying to help. A short distance away, a woman was using a tree for support as she threw up. Gunvor realized it was Elin. She asked Aidan to deal with her while she went to the injured person. Although his face was masked in blood, she saw straight away that it was Franzén. He moved his head slowly and groaned in pain. Gunvor was hugely relieved he was alive. She crouched next to a woman who was holding his hand and placed her own hand on her shoulder.

"How's it going? Do you need help?"

The girl was gasping heavily but managed to say between gulps of air, "He was just lying there, covered in blood. I thought he was dead. How can anyone do that to another human being?"

"Do you know him?" Gunvor kept her hand on the girl's shoulder. She could feel her shivering.

The girl shook her head. Gunvor leaned forward, over Franzén, and managed to make eye contact.

"What happened? Who did this?"

What she saw in his eyes caused a knot to tighten in her stomach. It took him a long time to respond.

"I fell," he said, then closed his eyes.

She heard footsteps approaching quickly. The ambulance crew pushed people to one side and crouched down to deal with Franzén. They checked him for signs of life, they tried to talk to him. Eventually, they moved him carefully onto their stretcher and carried him back to the ambulance. The siren started, its sound dwindling to nothing as it headed for the hospital.

Her phone beeped. David had shown himself to be way more useful than she could have ever imagined. He sent her three photos in quick succession of a smiling girl. The images were blurred. David tried to zoom in on the background. Gunvor realized immediately who it was, despite the crowds in the bar. The girl was blonde and pretty and the men by her side looked like human bulldozers. She texted him back:

— *Perfect. Don't lose them.*

Once she had sent her message, she went over to Elin, who seemed to have composed herself a little. Aidan was holding her handbag while she tidied her make-up with the help of a pocket mirror and a powder brush.

"Are you OK?" Gunvor thought at first that Elin was throwing up at the shock of seeing Franzén and all the blood, but when she smelled the sour-wine stench of her vomit, she realized it was probably more than that. "It's the drink, isn't it? How much have you had?"

"Too much, sorry." Elin looked up from the mirror with sad eyes that suddenly lit up again. "But I spoke to Franzén at least. He was actually about to tell me everything when all this happened."

Elin described the whole evening in detail. But when she got to the point just before Franzén ran off she became unsure.

"It was like he wanted to tell me something, yet he didn't want to... He started to talk, but stopped as soon as he saw those people."

"What did he say? Think. Try to remember. It might be important." Gunvor struggled to hide her impatience.

"Something about how even your dreams can be dangerous. About how I should keep my dreams as just dreams. And that if you try to make a dream come true, you can mess up everything. You can ruin your life. That's what he said. That your whole life can be destroyed."

16

David and Linnea stood outside in the little group of smokers. They shared two, then three cigarettes. David saw Gunvor and Aidan walk quickly past. They both glanced into the bar, but they didn't notice him, even though they were at most two yards away when they went past. David thought about how easy it was to miss things that are right in front of you, just because you weren't expecting to see them.

A few minutes earlier, the two men who had been with the blonde returned and went back inside. Just after Gunvor and Aidan walked past, Linnea pulled David by the arm. She wanted to finish her new glass of cider. He allowed himself to be guided back inside but told her he needed to go to the toilet before joining her at the bar. On the way, he tried to make eye contact with the woman Mikael had shouted at. She noticed him but ignored his attempt to lure a smile from her.

When he went back to the bar, Linnea had already downed her cider and thought it was high time they went dancing. She'd already waited far too long. David realized their time together was almost over, so he went outside with her. No matter how hard he tried to think of an excuse, he just couldn't come up with a good reason for not moving on with her. He had managed to delay disappointing her so successfully that she was convinced he was about to go dancing with her, and then who knew where the night would end. He clutched at his last remaining straw and persuaded her to have a cigarette with him before they parted. This way, he was even better positioned to see if the two men and the blonde decided to leave.

Linnea told him it was a total waste of time to stand there when they could easily smoke on the way, but in the end, she went along with it. Just as they lit their cigarettes, the woman and the two men came out of Sturehof. Suddenly the woman looked straight at David. She gave a little blink of her eyes, placed a finger in her mouth, then looked down towards his crotch. Thankfully, Linnea didn't notice. In a second, the moment had passed, and he noticed that the woman and the two men were getting into a taxi. There was no other taxi nearby, so David had no choice but to stay where he was and watch them disappear along Sturegatan. He texted Gunvor.

"God, you spend half your life on your phone," said Linnea, pretending to be annoyed but smiling.

"It's my mate. I've got to answer."

"And what about me?" She rolled her eyes upwards. He knew she was putting it on and was still assuming tonight was all about her.

David found it hard to stay composed. He leaned towards Linnea and kissed her. She returned his kiss willingly, so he put his arm around her waist and pulled her closer. They stayed like that until his mobile beeps.

— *Time to go. Come Humlgdn.*

"I've got to go."

"But …" Linnea was not expecting this.

"I'm sorry." He tried to work out what to say, then decided he would tell her something close to the truth. "I'm actually working this evening. That text was from my boss. I've got to go and meet her and a couple of others."

"Oh ..." There was a hint of curiosity in Linnea's eyes but, to David's dismay, she was more disappointed than impressed.

"But maybe we could see each other another day? Like tomorrow? Here?" He gave her a hopeful smile.

"Maybe. I'm not sure I can tomorrow, but we could say about seven, and I'll come if I can."

That was a lot better than nothing. David wasn't going to ask her for her number, but he dared to kiss her again before leaving. She tasted of apple cider and cigarettes, a combination which had just become his absolute favorite flavor in the world. He felt weak and dizzy when he let go of her and set off to meet the others.

He saw them as he neared the park. Elin was sitting on a bench that encircled a tree trunk next to the pedestrian crossing, and Gunvor was standing a short distance away talking on her phone. He saw Aidan walking towards them carrying two McDonald's bags and realized how hungry he was.

"Oh, wow, great! Is there something for me?"

"Course there is."

David sat down by Elin, who was staring at the ground and looking distant.

"How're you doing?"

"Kind of still pissed. Puked like a dog a bit back," said Elin.

"The food'll do you good then. Always the best cure."

Aidan handed them the burgers and chips, and they dived into them ravenously.

Gunvor hadn't started eating yet, she had just finished her call. "That was Franzén's wife. I had to tell her what's just happened. Not very pleasant."

She took a bite out of her burger before continuing. "She promised to ring and tell me how he is as soon as she knows. He took a real battering there."

"Is she likely to report it to the police? We can testify. We saw them arguing, and I saw them come out of the park when Franzén was lying there all beaten up. It's obvious it was them."

"Nadja wants to talk to him first, so we'll have to wait for now. First I want to hear everything about this evening."

Half an hour later, they had gone through the evening's events, devoured the contents of the McDonald's bags and were all sitting in Aidan's car. David looked for Linnea as they drove past Sturehof. He saw her straight away. She was standing and smoking with a guy who had his arm around her, and he could see she was laughing. David's face showed none of the hurt he felt. He said nothing, but he knew Elin could see her too. He glanced in her direction, and she quickly looked away and out through the opposite window.

17

Gunvor awoke early as always, even though it was a Sunday and it had been pretty late by the time she finally got to sleep last night. They had dropped David and Elin off just after midnight, but Aidan was in the mood for a chat, and neither of them felt the slightest bit tired. So they opened first one, then two, bottles of Portuguese red from the makeshift wooden wine cellar concealed in the little store cupboard on Aidan's balcony. They went over the evening's separate incidents in the hopes of making sense of the situation. But the more the wine flowed, the more philosophical their conversation became. Discussing Nadja's claim that she didn't recognize her husband's behavior led them to wonder if you could ever really know another person. They eventually agreed that you could learn more or less how someone close to you feels and thinks—perhaps enough to predict how they would react in different situations—but more often than not they would suddenly do something that was the complete opposite of what you'd expect. And this so often happened just when you think you've truly got to know them. Infidelity, divorce, and financial crises could all massively affect a person, with no warning given to their partner.

They also worked out that this could be an exciting character-istic. In the small hours of the morning, they gradually came to the shared conclusion that life would be incredibly boring if people were predictable, even though this meant it was almost impossible to ever properly get to know anyone. Not even yourself.

In the middle of the discussion, Fredde rang and reported what little he had seen. His description supported David and Elin's, apart from his analysis of Franzén had changed. During the call Gunvor went to another room, pretending it was Kjell that had called. She wanted to keep Fredde secret for a little while longer, mostly for the sake of the youngsters. She knew, however, that it would be much harder for her to keep him secret if Aidan knew.

"It seems to be exactly as I said. He's obsessed with her. There's something really screwed up about that guy, the way he's following her. They don't even know each other." Gunvor remembered clearly what Fredde said. And how, in contrast, he hadn't been certain whether he had ever seen them together. Not a word about Franzén following the woman. But they'd ended the call without her commenting on this. She was used to people changing their positions in response to changing situations.

When Aidan had finally gone upstairs to his flat, Gunvor forced herself into bed but lay awake thinking for what seemed like ages. They were missing several pieces of the puzzle, and she had no idea where to begin looking for them. If she was honest—and it was easier to be honest when you were alone at night, they were still missing most of the pieces of the puzzle. For a good time now and on a nightly basis, Franzén had been looking for a particular woman. When he finally found her, he shouted at her, got thrown out of a bar, and then beaten up. What had made him so angry was still a mystery. She hoped that he had become wiser since the beating and would now see the wisdom in looking for help; from his wife and from Gunvor and her little crew. But there was absolutely no guarantee of that.

She had only slept six hours but felt too restless to stay in bed. In her dreams, she tried to solve the riddles they were acing, but her thoughts were dimmed by darkness and the absence of logic. She got up and made herself a latte with her Italian espresso machine. She flavored the milk with cardamom before heating and frothing it. Her morning routine included a protein shake, which she drank standing up before sitting down at the kitchen table with the latte and her iPad. She took a drink of her latte and switched on her iPad. The phone rang.

"Hi, Gunvor. Sorry to call so early on a Sunday but I need to know what the hell you were up to last night." Manuel sounded excited and irritated.

"What do you mean? What's happened?"

"I was rather hoping you'd tell me that. Our – or should I say your – client has withdrawn the case she gave us. If it turns out that you've done something to damage our reputation, I promise you …"

He got no further before Gunvor interrupted, "Stop!"

Gunvor felt like a drill sergeant, but she knew from experience that when Manuel got his teeth into something you had to bring in the heavy artillery.

"We did nothing wrong. In fact, Mikael Franzén got himself beaten up last night, so he's got himself into a mess. If they have called off the investigation, it's probably because they've been threatened or they're scared of something. Not because we have screwed up. Is she refusing to pay?"

It took a moment for Manuel to respond.

"No, she has just deposited the sum we agreed on."

"The whole amount? As in, something approaching a week's wages?"

Manuel's silence was explanatory.

"And you've got the nerve to ring and shout at me? You

dragged me back from my holiday for this case, remember? And I might have only worked here for a year part-time, but I am pretty sure we're dealing with a case involving extortion. Am I wrong?"

Manuel delayed his response and cleared his throat, but still failed to come up with anything clever or face-saving.

"Well, it sure looks like that. But we don´t know and now it´s not our case anymore, which is annoying. We want to solve every case we get. That's always been our policy."

"Okay, let's do that then." Gunvor suddenly had an idea. "Let me continue working on the case with Elin and David. If we solve it, you pay us, and you can put it on the agency's CV. If we don't solve it, we can just blame ourselves. And then there's no link to the agency."

Dead air. That's all she could hear at the other end of the phone.

She stopped herself from going on. She wanted to convince him but didn't want to overplay her hand. He understood exactly what she meant, and any more dialogue from here on in would merely be to her disadvantage as she would be disturbing his thought process. It was almost a minute before he replied.

"Okay. You'll get 10,000 kronor each, plus expenses if you solve the case. But it'd better be a good story, something we can splash across the website."

"It's a deal," said Gunvor, smiling to herself as she ended the call.

She drank her latte, jotted down her reflections, and planned the next stage of their surveillance work. They were on their own now, and she would have to assume full leadership.

A couple of hours later, she had done her thinking, had a shower and prepared for the day. With another round of lattes underway she texted Aidan.

—*Time for work. Coffee almost ready. My balcony or yours?*

18

"So, we're going to work without knowing if we'll get paid?" David summed up the situation perfectly, but there was no irritation in his voice, only curiosity.

"You've got it."

It was already late afternoon by the time Elin and David made their way to Aidan's balcony on the third and highest floor. It was pleasantly warm in the sun, and there was room for all of them around the little white plastic table. Aidan came out with a jug of elderflower juice and four glasses. He filled each in turn and placed one in front of each guest.

"Okay. Fine by me." David seemed delighted, despite having just agreed to potentially work for free.

"Me too, but I'll need money for the drinks," Elin added. "I can't afford to pay for them myself."

"Try not drinking so much." David grinned at Elin, who raised her eyebrows before deciding to ignore him.

"Sorry if I'm making you uncomfortable, but I agree with David. He's winding you up, but for your own sake, you really shouldn't get too drunk. Neither of you. You need to be focused and ready to think quickly if something happens. And if all hell breaks loose, you really have to be ready to run for your lives." Gunvor attempted a stern look, to be sure they understood she was deadly serious.

"I can be a driver and help you with the planning, but I'm off to Manchester on Tuesday, and I'll be away about a week." Aidan was incapable of hiding his joy at finally having an official role in the mission.

"Okay, but we can keep in touch on Skype." Aidan hadn't been promised any form of payment and hadn't asked for any. But he and the others felt that he was an important member of their little team.

Gunvor allowed her gaze to move from Aidan to Elin and David.

"So, now we really are a team. We certainly couldn't have imagined that a week ago. It's going to be fun working with you," said Gunvor, and she really meant it.

"Yes, you're right. And now that we're working on our own we really should have a name. A cool, detective type of name," Elin said.

Gunvor couldn't stop herself from smiling at Elin's enthusiasm, and David soon followed suit.

"You're right, we should," he said, wrinkling his forehead, deep in thought. Then after a few seconds, his eyes lit up.

"The Fruängen Detectives? Fruängen Fighters? The Fruängen Bureau?"

"Fruängen Fighters sounds more like an ice-hockey team. I like The Fruängen Bureau, even if it does sound a bit old-fashioned."

And so it was agreed. David held out his hand and looked determinedly at Elin and then Gunvor and Aidan. They all placed one hand on David's as if they were members of some sort of sports team.

"Fruängen Bureau. Are you ready?" David shouted.

"Yes!" The others roared as one and raised their hands to the sky in a victory salute.

19

The hours passed, and soon it was time for David and Elin to ready themselves. They had the clothes they bought yesterday, which they had hung and aired on Aidan's balcony during the afternoon's discussions.

"We need to get more clothes. We can't wear the same stuff every night, or they'll see us for the poor and not-at-all-trendy kids from the suburbs that we are," Elin said.

David nodded in agreement, and Gunvor realized they were right. She had expected it to be a straightforward case that she would solve quickly when she engaged the youngsters' help. But it was now clear that the case was anything but straightforward and they'd have to adapt to the new circumstances. They wouldn't be getting a krona from the agency until the case was solved, so Gunvor would have to cover all the costs herself. Not that that was a problem for her. She did well out of the divorce settlement, with her ex buying her share of the house in Djursholm.

"We'll sort it out tomorrow. Let's meet in Gallerian at about 3 o'clock. Does that work okay with your schools and everything?"

"Yeah, it'll be fine."

It worked for David too, so the time was agreed upon.

A timer bleeped in the kitchen.

"Dinner's ready," Gunvor said.

They were all hungry and dug into the vegetarian lasagne with gusto. Despite her reservations, Gunvor didn't protest too much when Aidan opened a bottle of wine with the meal. The Mediterranean tradition of wine with dinner every single night had long since become embedded in her routine. And although she was a little worried about Elin's excess consumption the night before, Gunvor also appreciated that a glass or two of wine brought her personality out from beneath the shell of shyness she had hidden under for too long.

When they had all finished eating, Elin turned to David.

"Would you mind starting off at Riche today, and I'll go to Sturehof? There was this creepy older guy who tried to chat me up yesterday, and he might think I'm interested in him if I go back tonight, especially if I'm on my own. I say older, I reckon he was maybe around 30."

Before continuing, Elin noticed Gunvor roll her eyes.

"Well, maybe he wasn't that old, but he just kind of acted a bit old-fashioned."

David looked into Elin's eyes, but he couldn't tell whether she really meant what she was saying or if she was making it up for his sake. She couldn't possibly know that he had arranged to meet Linnea, but he was certain that she saw Linnea with that other boy when they passed her on the way home. So maybe she understood that he was feeling a bit awkward about going to Sturehof again tonight. Because it probably would look like he was going there for Linnea. Linnea who had forgotten him so quickly.

"Sure."

On her way home last night, Elin had felt sorry for David when she saw Linnea flirting with someone else. Even though she was preoccupied with her own concerns, she still noticed how happy talking to her had made him. In Fruängen, David walked around looking completely sure of himself, which was her own experience of him. That's why it was such a surprise to see him so bowled over by this girl. Elin had thought to herself that maybe everyone would benefit from David meeting a girl who could smooth away his rough edges. But the fact that she seemed to have gone off with someone else so quickly might end up having the opposite effect and make him even colder.

She was not being totally truthful when she described the older guy she'd met the night before. Not about his age or style, but about her finding him creepy. He was a bit weird and definitely very forward, but her strongest memory of him was of how much he seemed attracted by her. Of how he treated her like a princess. Something no one else had ever done before. In fact, she was pretty keen on the idea of meeting him again, perhaps a little too keen. The idea scared her, but fascinated her at the same time. It would be awful if he didn't treat her the same way, but if he did, she had no idea where it could end. He'd been so different. A real gentleman. Whereas she was just a lost soul, hardly even an adult and with zero self-confidence.

"If anything dodgy happens this time, get out or call me. Do you understand?"

The severity of Gunvor's voice roused Elin from her reverie. Gunvor obviously thought Elin took too big a risk yesterday when she went off on her own looking for Franzén. If she'd got to the park earlier, it could have ended really badly.

"It was you that gave me this job, wasn't it?" Elin felt annoyed, though she understood Gunvor's concern.

"Yes, but I want you to be careful. I ..."

"I know. I promise I'll keep in touch." Elin cut short Gunvor's lecture before it even began.

They let go of the subject. Gunvor wasn't sure why, but she was worried about Elin. At the same time, Elin was right. Gunvor had involved Elin in this, and she needed her help. So who was she to be sitting here lecturing the girl?

This time Gunvor let Elin do most of her make-up herself,

though under her guidance. Even Gunvor and Aidan made real efforts to do themselves up. As Franzén had been to Berns on both the nights Gunvor had followed him, they decided it was best to go there rather than to some English pub he was unlikely to ever set foot in. The nights they'd watched him he had looked in three places, and tonight they were going to keep all of them covered.

They all went in Aidan's car. After dropping David and Elin off at Norrmalmstorg, they parked in the underground city parking. As most days, finding a space in the inner city parking structure took a few minutes, but luck was with them today. Aidan parked near the entrance, and he and Gunvor took a leisurely stroll in the direction of Berns.

"Do you reckon we're going to end up feeling like parents on patrol?" Gunvor had really gone for the aging swinger look, with a black skirt, dark red lipstick and high heels.

"This is Stockholm. Anyone can go out here, however old they are."

"Well, yes, it's definitely easier here than in the rest of the country. But we do segregate the generations here in Sweden, at least a lot more than they do in the Canaries. Over there the whole family, from the oldest to the youngest, sticks together no matter what they're doing."

But when they got into Berns, it felt fine. She hadn't actually been there since the early 1980s when she used to hang out there three or four nights a week. It was the year she finished her medical practice and started to specialize as a surgeon. A colleague had introduced her to Röda Rummet, and she had fallen in love with the place. What attracted her most was the slightly bohemian feeling of freedom and wildness she sensed in the other regulars, many of whom went on to become writers, artists, or actors. In those days, originality was the key to gaining attention. After years and years of long hospital corridors, it felt so liberating to come across this watering hole. It was like a grown-up playground. A place where you could show people who you really were. You'd get some people there emphasizing how artsy and cultural they were by having something like a single-lens reflex camera or Dostoyevsky's *Crime and Punishment* on the table next to their beer.

She smiled to herself at the memories and told Aidan how you could get the best *pyttipanna* in the world here 30 years ago. Aidan smiled politely, and Gunvor wondered why she chose to tell him that when Aidan had been a vegetarian for years. Not to mention that he used to go to pretty wild festivals and raves himself. In fact, he might have been more impressed if she told him about the guy who bit the waitress's leg or the three jugglers who once ended up on the same table and spent the evening trying to see who could juggle the most empty beer glasses.

The interior of her red room came back to Gunvor when she saw the long balconies on the first floor and the large mirrors along the walls. The furniture was still red, but it was different now. What was once a room full of young art school socialists, fully made-up glam rockers and a smattering of post-punks, all filled with excitement as they started out on their journeys through life, was now a room half full of more low key clientele. No one seemed to be playing marbles between the tables, waving to friends across the room or reciting Strindberg. She did, however, see quite a few people her own age, or close to it. Most of them were sitting in small groups eating from the Asian menu while others were perched at the bar looking more interested in their phones than in finding someone to talk to.

Then they sat down, Gunvor with a dry martini and Aidan with a beer. It felt good. Gunvor slowly surveyed the room, but she saw no one that looked like the blonde girl or her companions. She looked down at her phone and saw that she had missed a message. It was from Elin, who was watching one of Franzén's assailants. Gunvor smiled and raised her martini for a toast before the strong drink warmed her throat.

20

S turehof was heaving, but Elin managed to find a space at the bar. As she ordered a glass of rosé, she spotted the better-looking of Mikael's two presumed assailants, the one who had groped her between the legs. He was standing at the far end of the bar, deep in conversation with the bartender, so she took the chance to send a text and let the others know she had one of the attackers under surveillance.

When she got her drink, she went over to the long counter near the entrance to the arcade, where she could study him discreetly while enjoying her wine. As well as the 300 kronor Gunvor gave her for drinks, she had 200 of her own. Even if she wound up getting too drunk by the end of the night yesterday, the alcohol had worked well for her for most of the evening. She had drunk wine and beer before, of course, but yesterday it seemed like she was really appreciating it. For the first time in her life, it reinforced this new feeling of being attractive and sexy. Well, it kind of reinforced it. She had never felt beautiful before, but yesterday someone thought she was lovely enough to be offered champagne. And interesting enough for Franzén to actually listen to her. Even if she had mostly told him lies, at least her imagination had got him going.

The only part of the story that was true was the bit about having an older lover when she was in upper secondary school. He wasn't particularly good in bed, even though he was married. She still wasn't really sure why she'd gotten involved in that relationship. It was maybe a mixture of wanting to lose her virginity, an urge to have a more experienced lover and the need to be important to someone.

He was her chemistry teacher. He looked her in the eyes carefully a few times before making his move. She responded by smiling and moving a little closer to him. Then he touched her cheek. His kiss tasted of old tobacco but was still quite pleasant. And when he then touched her breast, she had felt butterflies in her stomach. But everything that followed from there had taken place without any real emotions.

Elin drained her glass quickly and ordered another. The tension within her eased, and she slowly started to feel more comfortable again. Comfortable enough to look around the bar. She enjoyed the fact that quite a few of the men looked back at her. Even the man she was there to watch had noticed her now. She sensed recognition in his eyes, and he smiled a little flirtatiously at her. She half-smiled back before pretending to be occupied with her phone. She was then aware of him getting up and moving around the bar towards her. She felt his hand on her backside and looked up at him. He released his grip but stood where he was, smiling provocatively at her.

"Am I so addictive?" Elin was pleased with how she had pulled herself together so quickly.

Being this close to him, she saw how he had nice blue eyes under his pronounced dark eyebrows. His expression was much friendlier today. His tight, short-sleeved, sky blue collarless shirt helped emphasize the color of his eyes.

She could clearly see the contours of his muscular chest under the light material and when she looked at his tattooed biceps her first thought was that she probably wouldn't even be able to span them using both hands.

"Yeah, you've got a lovely little ass," he said, whilst looking shamelessly down at her cleavage. "And it's not the only nice thing about you. Are you new in town? I haven't seen you before. Or have you just got old enough?"

"I've been away studying in Paris for a couple of years."

The four of them had devised background stories for Elin and David during dinner, so they wouldn't have to improvise in situations like this. Luckily, Elin was pretty good at French, so anybody would believe she had lived there. In secondary school, she was lucky enough to have a French woman as a teacher. She had shown both interest and talent, so her mother arranged for her to have private lessons, and she became fluent in conversational French. Despite them sitting in an empty, bare classroom with a blackboard as the main teaching aid, it really captured her imagination, and she dreamt of travel and exotic places. She imagined going to elegant cafés and dark Paris nightclubs and walking along the Seine with some irresistible Frenchman.

"Can I get you something? Some wine? Seems appropriate if you've spent time in Paris."

He did his best to appear worldly, but Elin was certain he wasn't born with a silver spoon in his mouth. He was too similar to some of the guys she knew in Fruängen.

"Sure. Rosé, please," she responded with a smile, hoping she looked seductive.

Before ordering, he held out his hand, "Christoffer Ståhl, but everyone calls me Chibbe."

"Elin Canborn."

They shook hands and Elin was pleased she had such a beautiful surname, even if it was just for one night. As part of her new identity, she left Svensson at home in Fruängen.

Chibbe then kissed her politely on the hand, but as he did so, he took the opportunity to lick her fleetingly between her index and middle finger. Elin felt violated, in the same way she had when he squeezed her between the legs. But she did her best to make it look as if she liked it. The outer sides of his fingers were slightly scratched and bruised. When he didn't release her hand, she raised it and turned it around so she could look at it more closely.

"What's happened? Have you hurt yourself?"

Chibbe's smile straightened for a moment, and he hesitated. "I got a bit drunk last night and fell over."

"Poor you. I'm sure a few beers will help."

He appeared relieved and winked at her as he went to the bar. When he returned with a glass of rosé and a draught beer, he slipped his arm around her and held her slim waist firmly. Her job was to watch, so she felt obliged to go along with it. She saw no way out other than to drink her wine, keep her eyes and ears open and not think about it too much.

"Come on."

They chinked glasses in a toast, then Chibbe suggested they go to a room a bit further in. It seemed to be a restaurant area, but only two of the tables were occupied, so Elin allowed herself to be guided to a chair. A waiter soon appeared. He looked at Chibbe, apparently waiting for a food order. Chibbe shook his head.

"Strictly speaking, you should order food when you sit here, but it's okay when you're with me."

Elin nodded at Chibbe and attempted to smile. Her smile started to fade as she found herself trapped in conversation on topics ranging from martial arts and cage fighting to weightlifting. Chibbe was obviously in a good mood, and Elin tried to keep up with things even though it wasn't easy considering the forced nature of the situation and her proximity to someone she found threatening.

They were both drinking quickly, so their glasses were soon empty. Before ordering another round, Chibbe demanded a kiss.

Elin succumbed after unconvincingly feigning resistance. She had a quick internal conversation and decided she would play along as far she could, just to see where it would lead. So when Chibbe's lips came closer, she gently parted hers and told herself just not to give it any more thought.

But when their lips met something totally unexpected happened. Remembering it later, she compared it to someone putting wood on an open fire that was about to go out; they position the wood and blow until the embers begin to glow, and hot flames start licking all around. For a few seconds, she forgot who she was kissing and allowed herself to be swept up in the moment. Passion and lust rose to the surface. An intended peck on the lips became a deep and intense kiss. When their lips eventually parted Chibbe looked surprised and not a little shaken.

"I think we'd better take ourselves off to a hotel." He squeezed her thigh firmly, underneath her short skirt.

Elin was shocked by the strength of her own feelings and did her best to regain her composure, but when more wine arrived at their table, she was unable to say "no" to either Chibbe or the wine. She tried to convince herself it was just for the sake of the work, but deep down, she knew that some pretty strong desires had awakened in her. The wine made her feel more and more relaxed about Chibbe's overactive hands that were making her tingle inside.

"Alright, Chibbe."

All of a sudden, the man that was with Chibbe last night was standing by their table.

"Alright," Chibbe replies. "How you doing?"

The two men shook hands. Chibbe introduced his training buddy and workmate Lars Kronlund, or Lacke as he liked to be called.

"Aren't we supposed to be working?"

Elin saw Chibbe discretely signal to Lacke to be quiet.

"Where is …?" Lacke got no further before Chibbe interrupted him.

"We'll talk about that later." His voice was firm and decisive, but in the next moment, he flashed a big smile. "We don't want to bore my little diamond here with work talk."

He put his hand around the back of her head, pulled her towards him, and kissed her on the lips.

"Can you take charge of things here for a bit?" Chibbe asked Lacke. "I'll be back soon."

"Is that such a good idea?" Lacke looked dubious.

"Come on. I'm just going to the office for a minute."

"But there's no one there now …" Lacke seemed confused.

"Exactly," said Chibbe with a little wink to Lacke, for whom the penny finally dropped.

"Ah, okay, sure. But hurry up."

Chibbe got up, patted Lacke on the shoulder and guided Elin to her feet.

"Come on."

Elin briefly feigned non-compliance, but followed him to the door, partly because Chibbe was pulling her by the arm and partly because she wanted to. The kiss had triggered something she didn't want to end. Whether it was a good or a bad idea wasn't important at the moment.

As they came out onto the street Chibbe took her hand, and they walked quickly towards a door that only seemed a few paces from Sturehof.

"Where are we going?"

"You'll soon see." Chibbe kissed her then entered a code that opened the door.

"What sort of work do you and Lars do?" Elin tried to refocus on her mission, despite being almost totally consumed by her feelings.

"Oh, different things." Chibbe led her through the door

towards a lift. He pressed the button to summon the lift and tried to kiss her again. But she drew away with a smile.

"Hold on a minute. I want to know a little bit more about the man who is kidnapping me."

"You've got twenty seconds."

"What do you do?"

"Security, of a sort."

"What, are you a doorman?"

Chibbe laughed.

"More like bodyguards. But our clients are paranoid, so I can't really speak about it."

As the lift arrived, Elin looked around at where she was and caught her breath. The beautiful staircase was like something from a fairytale. She guessed the floor and walls were marble, and the stairway was illuminated by a glittering chandelier.

"Your 20 seconds are up."

As the lift rose Chibbe kissed her, and she forgot about the stairway and her mission. She only felt his lips, his tongue, and his warm hands on her skin. His hands managed to explore a lot of her during the short journey to the third floor. Elin hurriedly straightened her clothes as the lift door opened onto the beautiful stairway. He unlocked the door closest to the lift and pulled her into what appeared to be an office.

She was soon lost again. Before the door swung shut, she was back in his arms. His lips and tongue didn't leave her as he pulled off her clothes. It was not until she was totally naked that he held her away from himself and looked at her. He unbuttoned his own shirt and jeans before lifting her and carried her into an adjoining room. It had a high ceiling with incredible stucco. She somehow managed to admire the burgundy-colored velvet curtains and the ornate office furniture as Chibbe laid her down on a desk. But when he pushed himself inside her she forgot the beautiful room and just gave herself to the moment.

21

D avid was relieved he had taken Riche and managed to avoid Sturehof. But just as he walked into the bar, his heart stopped when he saw the back of a girl who looked just like Linnea. To his immense relief, he almost immediately realized that it wasn't her. It would feel really awkward bumping into her tonight. And a bit painful – it would have meant that she had gone here to avoid him too. He decided there and then that from now on, if he was going to hang out in places like Riche and Sturehof, he was going to have to change his attitude and act like he'd been there before and that he was used to chatting to beautiful women. So used to it that he mixed them up and had to scour his memory to remember their names.

He got himself a beer and sat down at a table inside the bar. They were projecting clips from old films on the wall. Someone who worked there then changed the music on the sound system at the far end of the bar. David thought it was ridiculous to have films on with no sound and music playing that had absolutely no connection to the films. It must be something cool and trendy, Östermalm style.

If he was brutally honest, he found the whole place a bit much, with its garishly-painted walls filled with mermaids, or whatever they were. But there were some pretty tasty girls in there, so he made do with keeping half an eye on them while playing some kids' game on his phone.

After about an hour, one of the men from last night turned up and went up to another guy at the bar. They talked quietly so David couldn't possibly make out what they were saying. But he could recognize the apologetic gestures and expressions the one who'd just turned up was making. They were the same as the ones he and his mates in Fruängen did all the time. Saying, "It wasn't my fault," was the immediate reaction in almost any situation where there was a chance, however slight, your accuser wasn't totally certain what happened.

David texted Gunvor and then Elin.

— *The other bruiser's here. What's happening where you are?*

It was ten minutes before Elin replied. Long enough for him to start getting worried. He wasn't really sure why last night had ended so violently. It felt like anything could happen.

— *Sorry. Couldn't text before. Spoke with the other guy - Chibbe. He's gone now. I'll stay here.*

When David read the text, he felt stupid for being worried. And he was bothered that again it was Elin that had made contact and moved the case along. *Shit.*

Suddenly, Chibbe entered the room and went up to the two men. The older one still seemed to be really pissed off, but it didn't seem to bother Chibbe very much. He patted him sympathetically on the shoulder and smiled, then left with his accomplice from the previous night.

A moment later they were back, and the blonde woman was with them. David, who had just reported the men leaving together, picked up his phone to text again. But when he saw the blonde approaching him, he quickly put Finance Sweden's website up on his phone and pretended to be studying the unintelligible figures and diagrams.

"What are you going to get me?" The blonde sat next to him and looked at him hungrily.

"A Sapporo, to get in the mood for a trip to Tokyo?"

He'd had no idea what Sapporo was until a few hours earlier. To be honest, he hadn't really known where Tokyo was either. Geography, like most other school subjects, was not really his forte. He'd never imagined there could be a beer called Sapporo, but the little crash course in world beers that Aidan gave him was already proving useful.

"What's wrong with some champagne?" The blonde leaned towards him slowly and seductively until he felt her firm breasts against his arm. For some unfathomable reason, he was more put off than turned on.

"Because that's sooo 2014," drawing out the "so" for emphasis.

The blonde laughed.

"Isn't Sapporo a bit "1970s"?"

"Yeah, but it is obscure enough to be cool." He winked and gave her his most charming smile, "But honestly, I don't imagine they have it here, it's not really a place for beer aficionados."

"You're a beer nerd? I'd never have guessed."

"Well, not exactly, but I'm really not into Swedish beer."

Her phone sounded, and she looked at it at once.

"Sorry. Sapporo another time. Duty calls."

She was about to disappear as quickly as she had appeared, but David managed to stop her by taking her arm. She looked at him.

"What about a date then? I don't even know your name." He loosened his grip on her arm and let his hand slide gently down to hers.

"Alice." She smiled and squeezed his hand for a moment before getting up and leaving. He thought he noticed a flicker of sadness in her eyes, but he couldn't be sure. The more he thought about it, the more he felt he probably imagined it, so he decided not to tell the others.

Neither of the men were still in Riche. They must have dashed out during the short time he had been busy with Alice. He texted his report, but after that, there wasn't much else for him to do apart from order another beer and go back to his game.

22

E lin was back in Sturehof and trying to understand what had just happened to her. Her head started to spin, so she ordered a Ramlösa water. Whether it was due to alcohol or passion, she wasn't entirely sure. What she did know was that she had been completely thrown upside down. Everything had changed, and nothing would ever be like it was before. Not that this was a problem in itself; she had been hoping for something in her life to change for so long now. But now that passion had apparently revealed itself to her, she had no idea how to deal with it. She didn't have a clue whether he was satisfied with the few minutes they had together or whether he too wanted more.

Chibbe had seemed just as caught up in the moment as she had been. The sex was intense, almost violent, over in just a few minutes. Afterward, they kissed passionately until they were interrupted by his phone. He disappeared into another room in the office, so she didn't hear any of the conversation, but she could tell from his voice that he was annoyed. When he came back out to her the spell between them, if not completely broken, was certainly nothing like it had been minutes earlier.

While he was speaking, she locked herself into the toilet and cleaned herself up. She fixed her hair and make-up. Her cheeks were scarlet and her hair tousled, but she managed to make herself look fairly respectable, she thought. When she came out, Chibbe was standing in the hall with his hand on the handle of the outer door.

"I've got to go."

Elin nodded and followed him out into the stairway and then into the lift. Once inside, he softened a little and kissed her tenderly as the elevator made its way down.

"Can I have your phone?"

"What for?"

Reality hit home hard. There she was, standing in a lift with a man she knew had viciously beaten another man the night before. It was very likely that this was merely the tip of an iceberg as far as Chibbe was concerned. It occurred to her that she was doomed. He'd probably known all along who she was and now he was going to look through her phone to confirm it.

"Just give it to me."

She stood as if paralyzed, while he took the phone from her bag. She tried to think of some sort of excuse or explanation, then started to panic even more when she couldn't come up with anything. Then he handed her the phone back.

"You've got my number. Call it."

He kissed her again, and they stayed for a moment in the lift, though it was already on the ground floor. Then he was gone. When Elin stepped out of the door, she saw him walking quickly past Sturehof and onwards down the street.

After replying to David's text and sending one to Gunvor, she headed for Sturehof, trying to let these recent events sink in. She was also trying to devise a story to cover what had happened between her and Chibbe.

23

G unvor and Aidan had ordered some Dim Sum and more to drink. Gin and tonic didn't really go with Asian food, so she moved on to white wine.

— *Blondie and friends just left Riche. Her name is Alice. Shall I stay here?*

Gunvor contemplated for a moment then replied that he should stay where he was until she contacted him again. She asked Elin to stay in Sturehof too. After all, it wasn't that late, and the evening could yet have a good deal more to offer.

"Isn't that …?" Aidan started to say, but stopped himself and focused on the bowl of newly-arrived Dim Sum instead. He chose one, dipped it in the soy sauce, and placed it in his mouth.

"Yes, they are fantastic. I'm not really into spicy food, but these are wonderful."

Gunvor sensed that someone was walking past behind her back, so she kept on chatting about nothing in particular. When Aidan gave her the all-clear with a gentle nod, she looked casually around, as if in search of the waiter, and saw the backs of three men and a woman walking up to the bar.

"That's her, isn't it?"

Definitely. Gunvor recognized Alice when she saw her profile. She even recognized the two men that David had managed to capture in his photo last night. They stood by the bar, either side of Alice, while the third man sat down at a table a little further away. Gunvor thought that the third man had nothing to do with the others, he just happened to walk into the bar at the same time. But she asked Aidan to keep an eye on him just to be sure. Aidan was allocated the job of watching them all as he happened to be facing in the right direction, but nothing much happened except that the man at the table was joined by someone else. Another man, around the fifty mark, wearing a smart-looking suit and tie, sat down at his table for two. They shook hands in a way that told Aidan they didn't know each other, at least not very well. They then ordered drinks and started talking, softly but intensely. Aidan saw them both – especially the new arrival – shooting glances at Alice. Whether that meant they were talking about her, or that her appearance was simply causing the men to stare at her, he couldn't say.

About half an hour passed during which nothing much went on. Aidan and Gunvor had finished off the Dim Sum and had even managed a chocolate truffle each and a coffee before things began to happen.

Gunvor saw Aidan suddenly freeze. His eyes widened. "Aidan, don't give yourself away." She raised her glass towards Aidan in a toast. "What's happening?"

Aidan filled his glass with the last of his low-alcohol beer and tapped her glass in return. "The guy who came in last has just given the other one an envelope." Aidan drank from his glass and lowered it to the table. "And now the woman is leaving. Suddenly everything's happening at once." Aidan's eyes were shining with excitement. "Her friends are staying at the bar."

"And the men at the table? Are they staying?"

"The one who came last is getting up now. It looks like he's going to leave." Aidan tried to make it look like he was looking for the waitress. "Yes, they're shaking hands. And now he's off."

"And the other?"

"He's just waved at the waitress. It looks like he's going to pay."

Gunvor tried to think quickly about how they should proceed. What was bothering her now was that she had no experience in leading surveillance operations. She should obviously have anticipated that someone might need to follow Alice. It couldn't be David, as she'd seen him, and Elin was too far away.

"Explain fairly loudly now why you have to leave early and thank me for dinner. Then follow her, if you can."

Aidan looked at Gunvor with surprise.

"Shame you have to go already, but that's life. It was great meeting you again." Gunvor spoke clearly and tried to look like she was being sincere.

"It was lovely. Thanks for a nice evening. Sorry, but I've got to dash, my train is leaving soon." Luckily, Aidan took to his role with ease.

"Go on then, off you go. Don't miss it."

Aidan shook her hand quickly and hurried from the restaurant. Gunvor texted David and Elin, then paid the bill. She wanted to know whether Alice had headed down Birger Jarlsgatan. But in the meantime, she decided to wait a while outside Berns to see if the two thugs had gotten up to anything else tonight. She was fairly certain they wouldn't remember her if they saw her when she left the bar, but she realized the risk would be greater if she left at the same time.

But before she left, she had to go to the toilet. She took her time to put on more lipstick and to soften her hands with the moisturizer she had brought on the flight. Then she returned to the bar.

"What the …? Oh, shit."

The men weren't there, not even the one who was at the table. She swore at herself for being complacent, then left as quickly as she could without drawing attention to herself. The park outside was almost deserted. The couple who were walking silently along the gravel path was of no interest to her. Of course, there was activity on Hamngatan, but there wasn't anyone she recognized there either. She swore at herself again then went back inside, just in case the men had gone to the toilet as well. But it was wishful thinking, to say the least, and Gunvor soon realized she had lost them. Despondently, she left the bar for a second time, just as Aidan came walking back towards her through Berzelli Park. He raised his shoulders and held out his hands, presumably indicating he has no idea where Alice had gone.

"Shit!"

"Sorry." Aidan looked embarrassed.

"No, it's okay, it's my fault. I didn't mean to sound like that, I've messed it up. Crap, amateurish planning." Gunvor felt totally incompetent. She'd pulled in three people who all trusted her to organize things, and she'd let everyone down.

"It's no problem, we'll find her another night. She seems to be out often enough. We can just concentrate on the others tonight," said Aidan, nodding in the direction of Berns.

"I lost them." It hurt Gunvor, but she had to own up.

"Oh," was all that came from Aidan.

Gunvor had heard him say that a million times before and knew it could mean absolutely anything, from 'Oops-a-daisy,' to 'What the hell have you done?'

She looked at her watch. It was already nine-thirty.

"Maybe it's time to gather the troops and retreat homeward. If none of them turn up in Riche or Sturehof, that is."

Aidan and Gunvor sat themselves down on a bench in the park and contacted David and Elin again. After a half-hour, when there hadn't been a single sighting of Alice or the others, they met up with David and Elin and walked silently towards the car and drove home.

*

I am so close, yet you still cannot see me.
But I see you.
I see your disappointment. I see your failure.
You really aren't as clever as you think you are.
Or as you want to be.
Think very carefully. Think of the risks you are
    taking.
You play with the tail.
Do you not see the lion?
Now I will play with you.
Just a little.
Will you notice me?
Before it's too late?
Dear old lady detective.

24

They ran through their respective reports in the car on the way back to Fruängen. Elin told the others an edited version of her story and convinced them she had done a good job. The fact that Chibbe flirted with her and gave her his phone number, which she had now passed on to Gunvor, gave her the chance to keep working on him and hopefully squeeze some more information out of him. At the very least, it gave her the chance to see him again. A worm of desire crawled through her lower belly.

Everybody felt positive about how David had made contact with Alice too. In fact, their reactions were a lot more positive than David expected so by the time he was dropped off on Kata Dalströms gata he was feeling very pleased with himself.

Elin was pleased too, not least with the way she had managed to get out of telling them everything she'd done. At the same time, she was worried about how she was going to manage the situation from here. But she put that to the back of her mind along with the vague hope that things would take care of themselves.

Aidan and Gunvor felt slightly less positive about their own performances, but they decided to sleep on it before talking about it anymore. They agreed to meet early the next morning and make a list of the people they suspected could be involved and discuss whatever theories they had. With that, they bid each other goodnight and went to their respective homes.

25

O ne of the few things they knew for certain was that one of the men that assaulted Mikael Franzén was Christopher Ståhl, or Chibbe as he preferred to be called. He'd had a couple of run-ins with the police, but nothing particularly serious. In one, he was charged with assault but not convicted and in the other, he was found guilty of making violent threats and fined.

Lars Kronlund, a.k.a. Lacke, had no police record, and there was no trace of him in the local phone directory. There were no relevant hits about him on Google. They only knew Alice by her first name, and they still didn't know if the third man was involved in any way at all, or if he had just happened to go into the bar at the same time as the others. The two men had certainly made some sort of agreement. But whether it had anything to do with Alice was uncertain. One of the men seemed to match David ´s description of the man he saw talking to Chibbe and Lacke at Riche. But his description was so vague it could be almost anybody." But if he did have some connection to the case, then he was a person of interest, as he clearly made some sort of deal in Berns. Gunvor said it was probably some kind of dodgy deal as an envelope was handed over in a public place, which may well have contained cash. Perhaps it was payment for the assault they had witnessed – in which case it would be extremely important to find out who had paid for the attack and why he would want Franzén beaten up. On the other hand, it could be absolutely anything, from protection money to a stamp collection or theatre tickets. Businesses like Blocket had driven growth in person-to-person trading in recent years. It could also have been two old friends who didn't have much to say to each other anymore and the highlight of their evening was one of them handing the other copies of some photographs from when they did national service together or some unforgettable journey they took in their youth. And the recipient put them in his pocket so he could look at them in peace later.

No matter which way they looked at it, they kept coming back to the conclusion that they should just ask Franzén directly, if for no other reason than to see his reaction. They were confident that he knew they were watching him, otherwise, why would Nadja have canceled the investigation?

"He might not say anything, but his reaction could tell us a lot."

"Couldn't that cause problems, seeing as they don't want us to work on the case anymore?" Aidan felt uncomfortable about it, even though he knew the case had now become important to them all.

"If they get angry, it's because someone's pressuring them. There's obviously something odd about all this, but we're not going to give up. If we don't get anything definite, we'll just carry on watching Mikael."

Aidan let it go, despite still not being convinced it was a good idea. Gunvor was concerned that going to see Franzén could lead to things spiraling out of control, but the more she thought about it, the more convinced she became that it was worth the risk. They had to know what type of monster they were chasing. How else could they catch it?

Gunvor felt they had no time to waste, so she decided to

squeeze in a visit to the hospital to check on Mikael Franzén before going out to spend more money on clothes for her young sidekicks. Feeling emboldened, she rang up the surgery department at Södersjukhuset pretending to be an aunt of Mikael's. She gave the receptionist his social security number, and found out that he was in Orthopedic Ward 32.

She didn't feel comfortable about conning her way into the hospital. Partly because she had lied to a presumably hard-working nurse who did her best to protect the privacy of patients, and partly because she risked bumping into Nadja. Even if she was lucky, she worried about what Nadja would do when she found out she had been there. She was sure that Nadja would find out sooner or later. But she'd cross that bridge when she came to it. Soon she was sitting in Aidan's car on the way to Söder.

Gunvor knew Aidan had a lot to sort out before his trip to Manchester, but he was determined to drive her there, and she couldn't be bothered arguing about it. It was up to him. She was happy to be avoiding public transport as it was now gone lunchtime and she had a tight schedule.

They said little. Gunvor was deep in her own thoughts, though her eyes followed the shapes of the outer city, bathed in the gentle rays of the late summer sun. She could see from the little flow of people walking to and from Coop Forum in Västberga that today's temperature was a few degrees lower than yesterday's. Just a week or so ago people were wearing short sleeves, but now they had taken their jackets and coats out of summer storage.

Going over Liljeholmsbron, her gaze traveled across the water as Aidan drove over the bridge, and she smiled to herself. Her thoughts went from the jetty outside Mikael and Nadja's apartment and on to the day with Kjell in the Canaries. She sent him a short but loving text and thought that she ought to ring him soon.

Their journey continued, from the bridge, up Hornsgatan and then right into Ringvägen. Soon, Aidan turned right again, drove up the little hill to Södersjukhuset, and stopped the car a short distance from the main hospital entrance. He turned around and looked thoughtfully at Gunvor before she got out of the car. "Do you want me to come with you?"

"I really appreciate your help, Aidan, but remember that I work as a private detective. I chose to do this work. It is me that's gotten you all involved in this and it ought to be me that takes responsibility for you."

"Okay, but promise you'll call me if things get tricky?"

"I promise. Now you promise to go straight home and sort out everything you have to sort out before your trip, so I don't feel guilty for wrecking your new career."

Aidan smiled and nodded. "Okay, okay, I promise too."

Gunvor waved him off and headed for the main entrance. It was a long time since she was last there, but the memories came back, cutting into her. Luckily, she never worked at Södersjukhuset for any length of time, just a few years at the start of her career. That career had ended when she left Huddinge hospital for the last time. She had vowed she would never set foot in either Huddinge or Karolinska again. At least not of her own accord. She was aware that never is a very long time, but she was fully prepared to stand by her decision. If the ambulance had taken Mikael Franzén to either of the university hospitals, he would not have had a visit from Gunvor. This was precisely why she was convinced it was to her and his advantage that he was lying here in Södersjukhuset.

When Gunvor rang Nadja straight after the assault, Nadja had been horrified to hear what had happened but was also sincerely grateful that Gunvor had rung. She had texted later in the evening to let Gunvor know that the doctor had said Mikael had a severe concussion. To Gunvor's relief, Nadja also informed her that most of the blood had come from a broken nose.

After that, Gunvor heard nothing more from Nadja. However, Manuel said that although Nadja had called him to call off the case, he'd managed to get her to tell him that Södersjukhuset had decided to keep Mikael in for a few days in order to determine why he had difficulty breathing.

As Gunvor entered the corridor leading to Ward 34 her unease grew. She was actually beginning to feel physically sick. It was all too familiar. All hospitals might be different, but those long corridors are all the bloody same. Like walking the road to Calvary to be given confirmation of fate or liberation. The abrupt end of a glorious career, a career she would rather not talk or even think about. The pain was all too recent.

She might be nervous about visiting Franzén, but she was relieved when she reached his ward. It felt better to have something to do, anything rather than face those cruel reawakened memories. She didn't actually have a plan; instead she was trusting in her years of experience of gaining the confidence of patients.

She opened the door to the ward as quietly as she could. She let out a sigh of relief upon finding that the ward was as deserted as she'd hoped it would be. It was the time the staff usually had lunch, and the nurses made their reports. Assuming not too much had changed since her time, it should be quiet for another quarter of an hour or so until they returned unless one of the patients decided they needed help. It seemed like luck was still on her side when she saw Franzén in the second single room on the right-hand side.

She stood in the doorway. Franzén was awake, lying partly upright with the back of his bed raised. He was looking through the window though he didn't appear to be looking at anything in particular. He seemed far away, lost in thought. His face was swollen, and he had purple bruises under his eyes. His mouth was open, so she imagined he had trouble breathing through his nose.

He didn't see her until she entered the room. Franzén noticeably jumped with surprise and stared at her. "Who are you?"

Gunvor decided to be completely honest. "I don't know if Nadja has told you." She paused to see if there was any reaction.

"I'm a private detective." He hid it well, but she could see that he understood.

Franzén nodded but said nothing.

"I was there when you were beaten up."

"I fell," he said, quick to correct her.

Gunvor walked silently toward the window. She could see a helicopter landing pad and Mälaren's waters glittering beyond the trees. "Up till about a year ago, I worked as a surgeon. I worked in the health service for over 30 years, and during that time, I saw a lot of injuries." She turned around and looked Mikael in the eye. "There is absolutely no doubt whatsoever that you were beaten up."

Franzén was the first to look away.

"I am here to help you."

"You no longer have an assignment, am I right? I would like you to leave. Now."

"Mikael, I don't know what it is you're involved in, but most things can be sorted out. You seem to be a good man."

"What the hell do you know about me?" He stared at her again, and Gunvor could almost make out the fire in his eyes. "You don't know me."

"I've met your wife, who has been incredibly worried. For her sake …"

"For her sake, I'm keeping quiet," Franzén cut her off again, "Get out of here. Can't you see you're ruining everything?"

"What do you mean?"

"Go!" He stretched his arm out towards the buzzer and pressed it forcefully.

Gunvor made a quick decision to leave before any of the nursing staff saw her. Franzén's words seemed to follow her down the corridor. She tried to work it all out but she couldn't. The fear of worsening the situation in some way for Nadja or Franzén had triggered something in her that reminded her of that awful moment when she was forced to let someone else take over her operation. When she had almost caused someone's death because she refused to see her own failings. She allowed her own need to feel she was a good surgeon to take precedence over all the warning signs that she should stop.

Am I about to make the same mistake again? Is all this just about me and my desperate craving for recognition? I convince myself that I am doing everyone a huge favor, but maybe I'm just screwing things up for them all. Giving them false hope and putting them in danger.

The corridors seemed never-ending. She picked up her pace, trying to ignore the fact that it felt like someone had stuck a knife in her knee. She kept her head firmly pointed towards the floor to minimize the risk of eye contact. When she finally got outside, she slumped her shoulders then walked even faster, terrified that she would break down crying in the middle of the pavement. She concentrated on trying to breathe calmly, but tears were welling up in her eyes. No matter how hard she tried to smother her inner voice, which had been silent for months, it carried on, drowning out all reason. She was not good enough. She only thought of herself and cared nothing for anyone else. She was exploiting Elin and David, using them as underlings who followed her every instruction. But the truth was that she was leading them all to disaster. It was her that was going to destroy everyone's dreams.

The panic had hold of her throat, and she was finding it hard to breathe now. Her field of vision was narrowing, and she was struggling to orientate herself. But she saw a bench and made her way to it. She felt the cool wood through the thin material of her dress and remembered the method she'd used before to help her through these feelings before. So she did what she had learned to do—focus on the present, to force the demons from her past to release her. She said quietly to herself, "Breath. Don´t fight it. Just breath." She tried to stop the thoughts of self-accusation. But it was hard. "Breath. Don´t fight it. Just breath."

She sat for a while as the panic slowly subsided.

*

That stubborn woman is sure she can outsmart me.
　If she knew how many lives she is risking she
　would never carry on.
But she doesn't know. Not yet.
After all, the game has only just begun.
It must take what time it needs.
She looks tired. Exhausted.
She still can't see me.
She is lost in her own thoughts. Trapped in her own
　hell.
When she has passed, I will go back to her tracks.
I've been there before and did what was needed.
I got tired of his attitude.
No pain, no gain.
Even for him.
As soon as he sees me, he is overwhelmed by
　pathetic self-pity.
"I haven't said anything, honestly. I told her to leave
　and called for the nurse. She was only here for a

couple of minutes, and I said I fell and I didn't
want to talk to her."
"Never forget, I see everything you see. One single
mistake, one betrayal, and you are gone."
I stand by the window, pretending to look outside,
while my fingers feel their way along the curtain
rail where I discretely attach a state-of-the-art
listening device. A tiny, tiny little bug that hears
every word that is said within ten meters.
"I know. And I promise."
I turn and leave, not deigning to give him the
slightest glance.

26

E lin went out onto Gunvor's balcony and closed the door
behind her. She didn't want to be disturbed if Chibbe rang.
Partly so he wouldn't hear that she had company, but mainly so
the others wouldn't get an inkling of how intimate they had been.
She couldn't even be sure he was interested in seeing her again.
But if he did ring, she had to be ready to step back into the role
she was playing yesterday and carry on from where they left off –
if it could be called a role, that is. In one sense she felt like nothing
had ever been as real as that moment, there in the office.

Elin was sitting on the balcony now, absently running her
hand across the shiny surface of her new imitation red leather
skirt. She'd seen it in River Island the first time they went there,
but at the time it had seemed too dramatic. Two days later it
seemed the obvious choice, along with a white silk top and white
high-heeled sandals. David had settled for a tight T-shirt in shades
of grey. He was so happy with his new jeans that he decided the
new T-shirt was all he needed for tonight.

After they had finished shopping, Gunvor invited them for a
latte in the café outside Gallerian, where she told them about
visiting Franzén. Elin thought Gunvor sounded a little shaky.

There was an air of seriousness about her that was different, especially when she asked them if they were sure they wanted to carry on. If Mikael Franzén was terrified, maybe they should be too, she'd said. But David and Elin both agreed that they were determined to get to the bottom of whatever was going on, so they made their plans. They had already made contact, so they decided to leave first. David would move between the three bars and look for Alice, while Elin's mission was to agree to meet Chibbe.

It wasn't long before she received a reply to her text.

— *Of course, I want to meet—Stureplan an hour?*

She felt a tingle in her stomach. She longed to be in his arms again, but she tried her best to focus and remember she had a job to do. It was vital that she sniffed out as much information as she could, even though she had no idea how things would actually turn out. She'd leave that problem for later. For now, she went in to tell the others she had a date.

27

D avid obviously had something on his mind. Walking with Elin towards Gunvor's car, he finally let it out.

"Sorry about being such a dick before."

He told her it'd been bothering him a while, and it was a relief to let it out. Elin was surprised but also pleased. She reached out and took his arm.

"It's okay. That's all behind us now, and I'm happy that we're doing this together. I'm not sure why, but it feels like we're friends, and that feels good."

"It does, doesn't it?"

They didn't mention it again. Like Elin said, it was behind them now. They had both been aware for a couple of days now that David would do anything within his powers to protect her.

They were getting used to being dropped off at Norrmalmstorg now. As they crossed the square, they agreed to get in touch by 10 at the latest. Elin emphasized that she'd be switching her phone off when she and Chibbe meet for their date. If she was to gain his trust, she couldn't sit there texting all night. She needed to lull Chibbe into a sense of security and to do that she'd need to give him her undivided attention. David had no problem understanding this, but he told Elin that if she just left her phone alone at the start of the evening, Chibbe would hardly be bothered if she checked it once, at around 10 pm. Or better still, she could go to the bathroom to look at it in peace. At least that way she'd have time to call if anything had happened and they needed to talk.

When they separated, David went towards Riche and Elin headed towards Svampen. She felt butterflies in her stomach now. Chibbe was just a few steps away, but her sense of longing seemed unbearable. In her head she struggled to come up with a plan for getting as much information from him as possible. She felt it was up to her to find out what happened to Franzén and why. Walking the final few steps towards Chibbe, who had his back to her, the waves of desire washed all other thoughts away. She touched him on the shoulder. He spun around and pulled her into his arms. She felt a rush of joy as she realized her longing was reciprocated. His arms were warm and strong, and it seemed like he would never let her go.

"Shall we have a drink in East?" He didn't wait for an answer; he simply took Elin across the road. In order to stay in control of her thoughts and feelings Elin had prepared a speech about how she didn't drink on weeknights, and how she'd rather have a cranberry juice. But before long she had a glass of rosé standing in front of her. A whole bottle in fact, in an ice bucket.

"Have you been protecting anyone today then?" Elin smiled and tried to look like she was making chit-chat.

"Nah, it's been really quiet today. Anyway, I've had more important things on my mind," he said with a suggestive grin.

"Was that your office we were in yesterday? It was really nice."

"I sometimes go there, but it's not mine. A couple of friends own it. Well, sort of friends. People I work with."

"The man you're guarding?" Elin twinkled her eyes as best she could, to make him feel special and keep talking.

"Yeah, that sort of thing. But like I said, I can't really talk about it."

Chibbe's voice was still gentle and amiable, but it was quite clear that he was not going to talk about his work anymore.

"But I've thought of something we can do in the office – and that's something I'm happy to talk about. Maybe we can go there a bit later, eh?" Chibbe glanced hopefully at Elin.

"Can't we go back to your place instead? Doesn't it feel a bit strange being in someone else's office?"

"But they're not there."

"No, but why can't we go to yours?"

Chibbe looked uncomfortable. He stayed quiet for a moment. Then he appeared to make a decision. "I live with my mum because she can't really look after herself all the time. She wouldn't leave us alone if we went there. Sorry." He suddenly seemed almost timid and insecure.

"Ah, that's so sweet. You're really nice."

Elin showered him with flattery and a couple of quick kisses, watching as he relaxed again. She decided not to ask any more questions for now. She would keep him in a good mood and give him nothing to be suspicious about. It seemed to work. He asked her about herself, and she replied that she was no nice Östermalm girl, she grew up in Fruängen and still lived at home with her mother. She also told him that she hadn't seen her father since he moved out. He wanted to see her, but she refused. After seeing him hit her mother so many times she couldn't bear to see him any longer.

"I haven't seen my old man for years either. He left when my mum got ill, so I had to take over."

"Sounds tough." Elin couldn't resist stroking his neck. She pondered on her dramatic change. Yesterday she had looked at him like he was a lowlife thug. She had even been a bit scared of him. But now she felt real warmth and attraction towards him.

"And to top it off, we've always lived in Östermalm, but we've never had any money. We've lived in the same scruffy two-room flat in Fältöversten for what seems like forever. At school you were nothing if you didn't have a Canada Goose coat and all the other crap with three- or four-figure price tags on them."

"I know what you mean. Fruängen was all about acting like a little ghetto gangsta, which is about as far from what I'm like as you can get." Elin smiled, a touch sadly.

"It's not you, you're too lovely," he said, stroking her chin, "But I'd have fitted in perfectly."

"I can imagine, but it was hard for me. I didn't fit in, and it was obvious that most of the people at school knew it."

She was surprised by the strong feelings of injustice and sadness that came back to her when she talked about her school-days. Despite trying her very best to stay on full alert so she could pick up any potentially useful information about what might have happened to Franzén, she felt she had revealed herself to Chibbe completely. It was because of her feelings for him, of course. Now, as they sat here talking so openly and honestly, she could feel the old resentments rising up again inside her. Part of her realized that she was incapable of stopping the demons that were making her fall for him, and part of her realized that she'd never talked properly about the pain of her schooldays before. Not that she was letting much out now, but it felt like she had unlocked a door and her feelings were lined up and ready to flood out. Chibbe looked into her eyes, and his own were filled with tenderness. His hand trembled slightly as he took hold of hers.

"Then your classmates must have been complete idiots because you are one of the most beautiful women I've ever seen." Chibbe leaned forward and kissed Elin. Then he filled their glasses. "Drink up now so we can go to our little place again. Sorry … I mean … we don't need to go there if you don't want to … I just meant … you're so lovely … but if you'd rather not…"

When their eyes meet, he let out a long sigh. All of a sudden, her eyes were bright again, and her hand was moving inside his T-shirt touching his lower back.

"Of course we're going."

28

D avid spotted Lacke as soon as he walked into the bar. He pretended to be concentrating on replying to a text he'd just received as he moved slowly along the bar and sat on a vacant stool next to him. He didn't even glance at him; he kept looking at his phone. Then he looked up and ordered a drink. This time he didn't wonder whether he ought to order some sort of trendy, expensive drink, he simply asked for a draught beer. After taking a few sips, he looked up and pretended to recognize Lacke.

"Hi. I saw you last night. Aren't you friends with the best-looking girl in town?"

Lacke looked inquisitively at David, who was struck by the sudden, uncomfortable feeling that his cover was blown and Lacke knew exactly who he was and what he was up to.

"That's right. Do you fancy some?" Lacke smiled.

"God, yes. Who wouldn't be interested in her?"

"It depends on your tastes. Alice isn't just any old girl."

"That's exactly what I was saying; she's the fittest girl in town."

"Hmm." Lacke seemed to be weighing something up, but he said nothing.

"Is she coming here tonight? I owe her a drink."

"I don't really know. I've not spoken to her today."

"Are you close? Good friends or something more?" David raised one eyebrow inquisitively, and Lacke nodded but did not reply immediately.

"Nothing more."

"Honest? It must be hard having such a hot friend."

David gave a cheeky grin and hoped Lacke didn't think he'd gone too far.

"Not really," Lacke took a drink of his beer then continued, "She's in a totally different league."

"Have you known each other long?"

"She's been a friend of my mate since they were kids. I work for her in a way."

"Oh, right. What sort of business are you in?"

Lacke peered at David before responding. "She likes it rough, really rough."

"Oh, right…" David was taken aback. That was beyond unexpected. And what it meant wasn't exactly clear either.

"You interested?"

"What? It'll cost me? Is that what you mean?" David couldn't hide his confusion. Meanwhile, in his head, some things were starting to add up. So, Franzén is that sort of bloke. He liked to dish it out but at least managed to spare his wife.

"Course it costs. All the good things in life do."

"Hmm," David didn't know what he should say, but he realized the ball was in his court now. And this was probably the only chance he'd get. It wouldn't help Franzén – it might even do the opposite – but after all it was Franzén's wife who had contacted them, not Franzén himself. And if she was married to a sadistic scumbag, it's probably just as well she found out. But for them, it was now not about Mikael and Nadja; it was about a crime. And the crime was obviously prostitution.

Lacke looked at David, clearly waiting for a response. David took a slow drink, preparing an answer that would hopefully take him deeper into the eye of the storm without putting him into too much danger.

"I'm kind of more into watching, you know? As long as no one really gets hurt or forced to do anything they don't want to." As he said the words, he realized he was starting to feel ashamed of himself. Either way, he managed to pull it off with a sufficiently convincing creepy smile.

"Ah-ha, a voyeur." Lacke grinned. "I have to confess I'm a bit like that myself. It's perfect. I get to keep an eye on the whole thing."

"You watch her while she's at it?"

"Sure, I do. Someone has to make sure everything's in order. There's always a danger someone'll go too far. You know what I mean? You get people who've waited their whole life to live out a fantasy like this."

"I see what you mean, but I don't hit women. What can you offer a man who likes to watch?"

Now Lacke had stopped holding back. David felt pleased with how he had managed to convince Lacke he was genuine – but at the same time he was really uncomfortable that he was coming across like some kind of pervert.

"Alice is wild like I said. She likes men to dominate her and treat her rough, but she has limits. It's like a game – and believe me, there are plenty of people desperate to play it," Lacke grinned. He finished off his beer and raised his empty glass towards the bartender. "And she likes it when other guys watch too. She's mad for it. And what she likes just happens to fit in perfectly with other people's fantasies. Like yours, for example." He laughed and patted David on the shoulder. "I've got something lined up that you might be able to watch. Do you fancy it?"

David nodded, "Too right. When, where, and how?"

"You'll find out when you've made up your mind and paid. Ten thousand."

"But when is it?"

"I'm not saying any more till you've paid. And if you don't pay, I never told you anything, OK?"

Lacke took few sips of the beer the bartender had just placed in front of him. He seemed to be thinking about something and turned to David again. "You know, it's a bit risky for her. Partly because she's so beautiful and partly because she fulfills a lot of blokes' fantasies. Sometimes they can get a bit obsessed with her." He shrugged his shoulders. "It takes all sorts; you know what I mean?"

Before David could think of anything to add, Lacke's phone rang. David fiddled with his own mobile, but he was watching Lacke carefully.

"I'm in Riche having a beer," Lacke said.

David couldn't hear what the person on the other end of the phone was saying, no matter how hard he tried.

"No, he's got something else on tonight." Lacke listened then spoke again, "He'll more than likely nip up to the office again, the dirty bastard. All he can think of just now is shagging that girl again."

Lacke laughed at his own crudeness and David tut-tutted silently to himself. He had hoped to hear something a bit more interesting, but Lacke was not stupid enough to say anything David shouldn't overhear while he was sitting right next to him.

Lacke finished the call and wrote a phone number down on a napkin. "Text this number when you've made your mind up and got some money." He patted David firmly on the shoulder, then headed off to talk to two girls sitting at a table near the entrance.

29

T hey were soon on their way up to the office again. Like the last time, the moment they entered the lift, their passions were released. They kissed, and their hands searched for skin. Elin felt as if she had lost contact with both herself and the world, but she managed to memorize the company name on the door before Chibbe stood in the way as he unlocked it. Before her clothes were completely removed, she extricated herself from Chibbe's grip and with an apologetic smile hurried to the tiny toilet and locked the door.

She sent a quick text to Gunvor, hoping she would understand what it meant and that she hadn't time to write more just now. She flushed the toilet and took off her skirt and top so Chibbe would forget she'd locked herself in there and not get suspicious. She came out wearing only her Victoria's Secret Total Sexy set, which she'd bought in a rash moment about six months ago and hadn't dare wear before today. Chibbe let out a long sigh and held her at a distance, though all she wanted was to get close. It wasn't because he didn't want her, because that was all he wanted; it's just that his eyes demanded their gratification first. But it was impossible, the more he saw, the more he wanted. He'd always thought that Alice was one of the most beautiful women he'd ever seen, but she couldn't compare to Elin. Alice's eyes were hard and provocative, but Elin's reflected a mixture of shyness and longing. Her eyes were alive and innocent and filled with warmth. There wasn't an ounce of evil in her. That, in combination with a fantastic body and sexy underwear gave Chibbe tunnel vision.

He hadn't looked at her enough yet, nowhere near, but he could not hold back any longer. He laid her on the desk and kissed her along the inside of her thigh. Basically, he just wanted to push himself inside her, but he knew he'd probably come as soon as he did. He wanted to prolong the pleasure.

Last time, Chibbe had simply ravished her. Elin hadn't experienced anything like the intensity of it before, but now, as his lips made their way up her thigh it felt like she was going to faint with pleasure. When he finally entered her, he put her feet onto his shoulders. They both moaned loudly in time with his thrusts. Elin, whose eyes were closed at the beginning, now looked up at Chibbe. She thought she saw a movement. She turned her eyes towards the adjoining room. Everything was still, but something was different. Wasn't that door closed before?

Chibbe was lost in the moment and didn't notice that Elin was distracted. Although she tried to get back into the moment, she couldn't stop herself peering towards that other room.

The outer door banged. Both of them stopped suddenly, and Elin screamed in surprise. Chibbe withdrew and turned around, but they couldn't see the door from where they were.

"Hello?" Chibbe entered the hall with his jeans still around his ankles and tried the door handle. He made sure it was locked then shuffled back via the adjoining room.

Elin sat motionless on the desk. She was frozen in the moment.

"There's nobody here. Someone must have accidentally hit the door or something."

"But I thought I saw someone in that room."

"What? Who?"

Elin walked into the room and saw that if someone had been there they could have gone out through the main door without being seen. In addition to the door between the two office rooms there was also a door that let out into the hall.

"I just sensed movement out of the corner of my eye. But when I looked, it was gone. I suppose I could have imagined it, but then the door slammed straight afterward."

"But what the...? He said they were going out to the country house!"

Chibbe looked puzzled.

"Chibbe? Who are you talking about?" Elin was suddenly scared.

"No one; relax." Chibbe went back to the main door and put the security chain on. "Look, now no one can get in."

Chibbe gently but forcefully pulled Elin down from the desk and turned her around. At first she didn't comply, feeling uncomfortable after what had gone on. But when he slid inside her again, she quickly forgot about the rest of the world.

30

G unvor was sitting on the balcony, wrapped in a soft throw to keep out the autumn chill. She was holding a generous glass of red wine. Upstairs, Aidan was packing, watering plants and tidying the flat before his trip to Manchester.

— *D & A Hamrin, Legal Services*

When Elin's text arrived, Gunvor immediately googled the firm's name but found nothing. Strange. Normally, her next step would be to draw up a list of all the names beginning with D and A on her writing pad. But although she was feeling quite restless, she was tired and contented herself with listing the names in her head so as to avoid having to get up and move.

Then it suddenly came to her. Alice. Of course. The tiredness disappeared immediately, and she got up and fetched her laptop from the living room so she could more easily search for Alice Hamrin. Too much reading the small screen on her phone was destroying her aging eyes.

She hoped with all her heart that it would be straightforward. She could do with a following wind to push her in the right direction and blow away the clouds of doubt that were gathering over the case. She realized that none of the others knew that she was very near to dropping the whole thing, not even Aidan, she suspects. She had been agonizing all evening over whether to let him in on her thoughts, or whether to just text him with the news that they were dropping the case when he had landed in his other life in Manchester.

Gunvor wrapped herself in the blanket and sat down again on the balcony. Before heading out into cyberspace, she tilted her screen downward and took a sip of her wine, then looked out over the little square the building enclosed – a courtyard with trees, benches and a few tables which were now in darkness. Her plan was to calm down and summon her energy. It worked well. The fact they now had a name was a big step forward. Was their luck about to change? Was the end in sight? She felt hope slowly returning.

To her delight, she found lots of information on Alice Hamrin. She grew up in Östermalm, with wealthy parents and one brother, Daniel Hamrin. So, a family firm then. Daniel was the qualified lawyer, as far as she could make out. She hadn't managed to discover exactly what Alice did, except that she was a partner. There was something familiar about Daniel, but Gunvor couldn't put her finger on where she might have seen him before. Despite the circumstances he seemed quite ordinary. It was incredible to think he had a sister as beautiful as Alice, and even more difficult to believe that he was only two years older than her. Gunvor guessed Alice was around 30, but in the pictures she saw Daniel looked more like he was in his mid-forties.

There didn't appear to be any scandals connected with the company, and a credit check didn't turn up anything. But it didn't show the kind of turnover Gunvor would expect from a law firm in Östermalm. When she dug a little deeper, she discovered that neither David nor Alice declared particularly high annual salaries, despite being registered as residents of Strandvägen. There was definitely something not quite right about it.

An hour passed as she searched for clues on the internet. She

was building up her own picture of Alice and Daniel. Aidan
popped out now and again to ask if she had found anything then
went back to doing his own stuff. It was starting to get chilly, but
she was enjoying the fact that she could still sit outside. After
finishing off the last few drops in her glass, which Aidan had filled
more than once, she looked out over the deserted courtyard. She
was lost in her own thoughts about how she ought to have a few
wine-free days, maybe even weeks, when she suddenly noticed
something in the darkness. At first it felt almost like an illusion as
she'd been staring at the screen for so long that it's hard to focus.
But the more she looked, the more noticeable it appeared.

What the ...?

Even though it was some distance away, she could see a figure
staring up at her from the footpath that ran behind the two apartment blocks directly opposite, looking up at her through the gap
between the buildings. By the body shape she guessed it was a
man. No matter how hard she tried to peer into the darkness it
was impossible to make out details. Not even the color of his
clothes.

And then he was gone. The silhouette took a few steps backward and was consumed by darkness. It was as if nothing had
ever happened. Her stomach knotted up and there was suddenly a
bitter aftertaste in her mouth that had nothing to do with the
wine.

*

Can you see what I see?
Or do you still think you're invisible?
Who is chasing whom now?
Are you afraid?
Do you know what is coming?
The inevitable?
Your downfall?

31

When the moment of passion was over, and Elin began to return to reality, the first thing she wanted was to get out of the office as fast as she could. That horrible feeling came back to her, along with the images in her head of what she might have seen. After a while she couldn't separate reality from her overactive imagination. Perhaps Chibbe was feeling the same because he suggested that they go and sit down in a quiet café first. While they were dressing and getting ready to leave, Elin noticed that her wallet was visible in her bag and was opened out. She closed it quickly and put the bag down, glancing nervously at Chibbe as she did so. He was either a first-class actor, or he hadn't noticed that she had a different surname to the one she'd given him. One thing she was absolutely certain of was that someone had been through her bag. But who—and why? It was obviously not something she could bring up with Chibbe, because if it wasn't him, then he would still think her surname was Canborn, not Svensson as it said on her ID card. And if it wasn't Chibbe there must have been someone else in the office, someone who wanted to know who she was. Elin shivered, then noticed her shawl was missing.

"What's going on? Somebody must have been here; my shawl's disappeared." Elin was really freaked now. Chibbe placed a hand on her shoulder and tried to look calm, but Elin could see in his eyes that he was worried.

"Of course, no one was here. Someone just banged against the door. And you must have left your shawl in East. Let's go back there and have a look."

"But I saw something…"

He interrupted her with a sudden bluntness. "Stop it now. No one was here, I'm telling you."

That ruined the mood between them, but they both tried to act as if nothing had changed. Her shawl was not in East, but they dropped the subject. They stayed in the restaurant for a coffee, but apart from exchanging banal pleasantries they sat in silence.

"I have to go home soon," Elin said, taking the initiative and releasing some of the tension.

"Yeah, me too. Can I walk you anywhere?"

"I'll be fine. I'll go to Central Station."

Before they parted, he took her hand and pulled her close. "Sorry I snapped before. I was a bit worried, you know, with the thought that someone was in the office while we were there. That someone was watching what we were doing."

"It's okay. I got a bit mad too maybe."

Elin was pleased he apologized, but had her wits about her and saw a chance to dig a bit more. "Do you think it was the owner? Who owns the office anyway?"

"Let's talk about that another time. But if it was the owners, I've known them for a long time. They can be a bit weird. If it was one of them, you could be sure it was me they were trying to get at. They are always playing weird pranks on me. I've never understood why. It's mainly just the two of them, but sometimes they also involve others and try to wind me up. They just love being the center of attention. Anyway, forget it now."

Chibbe leaned forward and kissed Elin. She returned his kiss and slid her hands under his shirt, feeling his chest. They remained standing like that for a few moments before they parted.

32

Gunvor and Aidan sat out on the balcony. They were on their second cup of coffee, attempting to sober up as best they could when Elin and David turned up outside the flats. When Elin had texted that she was on her way back, Gunvor told David to get back to Fruängen too. Gunvor tossed her keys down to them, and soon they were all sitting at the kitchen table. They took a sandwich each and something to drink from the little evening buffet Gunvor had prepared, then Gunvor took over and began to structure the conversation.

"I suggest we introduce a new routine. We'll go through the evening's events in chronological order. I want all the details. Where you've been, who you've spoken to, what you've seen, and so on. And tell me everything you remember, because the minutest detail—even if it seems completely unimportant and irrelevant—could be the key to unlocking this case."

Elin decided she would tell the truth. Partly because things would just get too complicated if she lied, but mostly because she was scared about the course the evening's events had taken. She wanted the others to know and tell whether she should be worried or not because she didn't know. It felt to her as if more things had happened in the last few days than in the rest of her life. She had no idea how she was supposed to react. She had no track record that could tell her whether it was normal for someone to spy on you while you're having sex on a desk in an office. Maybe it was just someone who happened to be there at the wrong time. Perhaps when they saw what was happening, they panicked and didn't know what to do. They might have watched to make sure no one was going to get hurt. Maybe they looked for some ID in case they needed to report it to the police later. They could have meant to sneak out, but the door accidentally slammed.

Gunvor pulled out a pad and paper, ready to take down all the details. Elin attempted to start, to get her part of the evening over with, but Gunvor invited David to begin. He seemed pretty satisfied with his evening and how he connected with Lacke.

"If we could just come up with the money, I would go there, and the case would be solved. Wire me up and shit, bingo, we've got Lacke and Alice for prostitution. Sorted. And I reckon they've been squeezing Franzén for money, or he just ended up obsessed with Alice, just like Lacke said. Beautiful women driving men crazy is nothing new."

"Well done David, great work. But we'll wait a bit before drawing conclusions, just reports for now. Elin?"

Elin took a deep breath before beginning as if she was really about to throw herself into something. After all, she wasn't really sure how the others were going to react.

"I've got something I have to say first. I hope you won't be angry with me."

David was about to take a big bite of his sandwich, but hearing Elin's words, he stopped with his mouth open.

"I was with Chibbe in an office. Yes, Gunvor knows." She looked at Gunvor, who nodded in confirmation. "But I haven't said what I was doing there. And I haven't said that I was there another time before too."

David, Gunvor, and Aidan appeared mystified. Elin wanted to get the rest of the story told quickly before she changed her mind. "We ended up there last night as well. I'd drunk too much, but there's something else. However much of a criminal he is, I've fallen for him."

Elin looked at the others, who were still struggling to comprehend exactly what she was saying. They were all dumbstruck, just staring back at her.

"I know, but I haven't given myself away at all. Not as far as I know anyway, but ..."

"But?" Gunvor repeated Elin's last word, though in a questioning tone.

"But we did it. There in the office. Yesterday, and today."

"What the...?" David's face showed a mixture of surprise, hurt, and mystification. Elin suddenly seemed to be the total opposite of who he thought she was.

"No accusations now, David. We are a team." Gunvor gave him a stern look.

"But I didn't mean it like that. I'm just in shock."

"I couldn't say anything on the underground, because we're not supposed to sit together." For some reason, Elin was mostly worried that David would be mad at her.

"No, okay."

"And what you probably don't know is that the office you were in belongs to Alice and her brother."

Gunvor's contribution startled Elin.

"Brother? Who's he?"

"That's something we don't yet know, but I'm working on it. I'm going to check with Manuel when I've got a bit further."

"There was one other thing," she said, remembering what was in fact probably the most important thing of all, "I think I saw someone in the office while we were ...."

Despite not completing the sentence, the others had no difficulty deducing what Elin meant.

"Did you see who it was?" Gunvor's forehead was lined with concern.

"I didn't even see if there was anyone; it was just a movement in the corner of my eye. When I looked it was gone. Then suddenly the front door slammed."

"That's weird." A sudden shiver passed through David.

"And when I was going to leave, I realized my shawl had disappeared." Elin realized something else. "Chibbe said something about how they used to wind each other up in there or something. But I had no idea what he meant."

"Can you remember exactly how he said it?' Gunvor's instincts told her this was important.

Elin thought for a while before answering, "It felt like he was trying to calm me down. He said he'd known them since they were small and that they were always playing one kind of prank or another. Some sort of game. He said if it was one of them that had been in the office, it was probably just to get at him."

Gunvor had decided much earlier on not to mention the person she thought had been standing between the two blocks of flats watching her. The more she thought about it, the more likely it seems that the person in question was probably just out with their dog and had maybe stopped for a bit while the dog was sniffing around by the edge of the wooded area on the other side of the footpath.

"Okay, I think we can go with David's idea. I'll get the money in the morning. When I've done that, you contact Lacke. You, Elin, can lie low for a while, in case there was someone spying on you. It doesn't feel good that it happened in the brother and sister's office. If Alice is involved in prostitution, her brother is most likely involved too. The main thing now is that we manage to prove it. So don't go tempting fate."

33

The following morning Gunvor was still lying in bed when her phone buzzed with an incoming text message. She smiled to herself, assuming it would be another of Kjell's nice little romantic messages.

– *Something terrible has happened. I need to speak to you. Café Umbrella on Sjöviksgata at 10?*

The message was from Nadja. Gunvor raised her eyebrows, wondering what could have happened. She'd thought this particular communication channel was closed forever. Something really unpleasant must have happened to cause Nadja to turn to her again. Something she couldn't or perhaps would rather not, take to the police.

According to her phone, it was a quarter past nine. She texted 'OK' to Nadja, and started speeding up. Now she was in a hurry. Breakfast could wait, but she could squeeze in a quick shower. On the way out of her flat she noticed she had another message.

– *Pretend you are my aunt. We haven't seen each other for a while, and it's your birthday.*

Gunvor sent another quick 'OK' and hurried off.

She took her car, to make sure she got there in time and so

that she could be mobile if necessary. She managed to find a parking place on Sjövikstorget and had just sat down at a window table in Café Umbrella when she saw Nadja approaching. She was moving quickly and looking nervous. In fact, she looked scared. The stylish, composed woman she had first met was now completely transformed. But she at least attempted a smile when she entered the café and saw Gunvor.

"Aunty G! Oh, lovely to see you." She almost threw herself into Gunvor's embrace. Gunvor, in turn, hugged her tightly and did all she could to play the doting aunt. When they finally released each other, she stroked Nadja on the chin.

"And it's lovely to see you again. It's been too long, sweetheart. What a wonderful birthday present!"

Gunvor thought it odd that no one seemed to be paying them any attention, and at least as far as she could make out nobody was following Nadja. But she waited until Nadja had bought her standard black coffee and sat down at the table out of earshot of the other customers.

"So what's happened?"

Nadja looked nervously around before beginning to speak, "I was at the hospital yesterday visiting Mikael." This thought alone brought a few tears to her eyes. Gunvor passed her a paper napkin.

"Try to compose yourself first. If you want people to think you're happy to see your old aunt, it's probably best if you don't start crying."

Nadja nodded and took a sip of coffee while Gunvor spoke loudly about an imaginary road trip to England in the summer, where she and a couple of friends traveled around visiting gardens. Soon enough, Nadja managed to get back into the homely spirit of things and even managed a few vague smiles at the imaginative stories Gunvor was telling. Gunvor tried to bridge to the real reason they were here, "Good, now try again and tell me what happened."

Nadja looked around again, a little more calmly this time. First, she scanned the street outside, then the inside of the café. "Mikael told me something absolutely horrible."

As a result of yesterday's surveillance, Gunvor knew what was coming, but she would still like to hear it from Nadja. "Something Mikael has done?"

Nadja nodded silently. "You think you know someone. He's the love of my life. He has been ever since the day we first met. But now, after this, I have no idea who I am married to. No idea who Mikael actually is. It's one of the most awful things I've ever heard."

"Tell me." Gunvor saw that Nadja was hesitating. It was impossible to say whether it's shame, disgust or simply an inability to accept the truth. It was probably a mixture of all three.

Finally, she managed to form and then utter the words, "He has raped a woman."

Nadja looked at Gunvor and seemed to be waiting for a reaction.

"But he was role-playing, yes? Living out a fantasy? It was planned and agreed, wasn't it?"

"You know?"

"I suspected, but only since late last night. I still don't know the link between that and Mikael's behavior. And now he's being blackmailed, am I right?"

Nadja nodded again, then added, "There's a tape…a film.'

As Nadja spoke, everything was suddenly obvious as all the pieces fell into place. If Franzén had paid to be rough with Alice, she would be pretty stupid not to film it. She probably liked money just as much as she liked being 'raped' for an audience. It was probably not her sexual desires that were the main driving force behind this setup, despite the way Lacke chose to describe it to David.

"Mikael told me I had to go away, to hide. He said there were some very dangerous people looking for us, but I refused to leave.

I told him I was going to the police. Then he started crying. It looked like he couldn't breathe, so the nurses came running in and gave him something to calm him down."

Nadja sat in silence. Gunvor used the time to think about what she had just heard. It was obviously hard for Nadja to discover these horrible secrets Mikael had been keeping from her, but it did not fully explain Nadja´s nervous behavior.

"Have you been threatened?"

Nadja gave a start, almost as if Gunvor has slapped her.

"If you've been threatened, it's best if you tell me. If you want me to help you, I really need the full story. You understand that, don't you?"

Although Nadja was radiating a look of fear, it wasn't difficult to persuade her to start talking. Gunvor was touched and relieved by the trust Nadja clearly placed in her.

"I heard my doorbell ring this morning. I was expecting a delivery, so I opened the door." Tears well up in Nadja's eyes again and her voice started to shake. "Everything happened so quickly. Before I knew it, this guy had forced his way into the flat and pushed me down on the floor."

Gunvor handed Nadja her last clean tissue. "Take all the time you need. If someone is watching you now, it is essential they don't see you cry. If they do, then we will both find ourselves under threat."

Gunvor took over the conversation again, narrating another quirky anecdote from her imaginary trip to England, this time about a restaurant visit. Nadja did her best to get into the spirit, blinking away her tears and laughing at the story.

"He had a gun," Nadja's voice was little more than a whisper when she finally interrupted Gunvor's monologue about struggling with language mix-ups on the trip.

"A gun? What did he do? I appreciate this is difficult, but you will feel better when you've let it out."

"He sat on me for a long time. I couldn't move, and it was hard to breathe because he was so heavy." Her lower lip started to tremble, so she picked up her coffee cup and took a sip as Gunvor talked about how wonderful the weather was even though they were well into September.

"He rubbed the gun backward and forward over my body."

When she eventually collected herself sufficiently to continue her testimony, Nadja whispered "When he finally got up off me, he pulled me up by my hair. I thought he was going to kill me."

"But he didn't, and you're sitting here now, aren't you?" Gunvor made an attempt at calming and comforting her.

"He pulled me into the kitchen and pushed me down over the table. He pulled up my skirt and tore off my pants. Then I felt something hard between my legs, about to go in me. I thought it was him, but then I realized it was his gun."

Gunvor shuddered, this time unable to mask her reaction, "God, Nadja. Did he hurt you?"

"No. He just frightened me. Looking back now, I realize how he was actually extremely cautious. It was just the feeling of having a gun almost pushed inside me that totally freaked me out. At that moment, I didn't have a clue as to what was going to happen until he started whispering. Next thing I knew he was gone."

"What did he say?"

"He said next time he'd do it for real. He'd push the gun as far into me as it would go and then he'd pull the trigger. He told me to keep my mouth shut."

"I don't suppose you saw who it was? Would you recognize him again?"

"He had a sort of hood over his face, and I guess I was in no state to remember any details about his clothes, or anything. I've really tried to remember."

"Okay, Nadja. Thank you so much for telling me all this. I want you to know that we are on to them. We have a plan. And if it all works, then we'll get them put away without needing to involve you or Mikael. It'd be best if you get away for a few days, and hopefully everything will soon be sorted."

With that, they ended their conversation. Gunvor walked out onto the street with Nadja and told her how lovely it was to see her on her birthday, thanking her again for dinner out in Waxholm she pretended Nadja had promised her. She linked arms with her, and they walked down to the quayside. As they walked, she saw nothing untoward, but she was confident she'd notice if someone were following them. *It takes one to know one, as they say.*

Part-way through a tender farewell, she saw a familiar face. It was Fredde, just walking past. He didn't seem to see them, and she left it at that. There was no need for him to know any more than he already did. She wondered if he lived around here or if he was out on a walk before work. Not that it mattered to her, the important thing was that he was there if she needed more help. But they most likely wouldn't need any more help in Sturehof; now that they had such a good plan. She would just have to clear it all with Manuel before they began.

E lin sat and stared at her mobile. After their date last night, Chibbe had sent her lots of texts, and she'd replied to all of them. But this morning he had suggested they meet again. She told him she was in school, despite the fact she had actually called in sick today. She got up as usual and had breakfast with her mum after she came home from her night shift. When her mum went to bed, Elin decided she would use the day to rest and think over everything that had happened to her over the last few days.

Thankfully, her mother didn't seem too worried about her staying out late anymore. From what Elin could gather from her questions, she was quite relieved that Elin had been acting more like a typical teenager of late. Her mother was quite strict, but Elin knew that she worried about her. And, although Elin was over eighteen now, she had been able to look after herself for some time. But her mother still felt guilty over the number of times she'd had to work on nightshift and sleep during the day, leaving Elin on her own to essentially fend for herself. But more than anything else she was concerned about how Elin had had so few friends over the years and had spent most of her free time alone, locked in her room, avoiding the constant arguing that went on before her father left. Her mother had on more than one occasion asked Elin to forgive her for ruining her life by exposing her to years of fighting, drunkenness, and violence. It had clearly affected Elin; in fact, it had shaped her, leaving her with a serious mistrust of people. But she never said that to her mum.

It was comforting to Elin that because she looked happy, her mother was happy. Her mum asked her if there was a nice young man on the scene. Elin responded with a smile. She was happy for her mum to think there was, although as far as Chibbe was concerned, *nice young man* was hardly the first thing that sprang to mind. Elin would rather spare her the details, for now, at least.

Her mother was still looking hopefully at her, so she decided to give her some titbits, but absolutely nothing more—just the most important things she needed to know.

"He is really nice."

The fact that he was most certainly not the typical nice boy next door could be left unsaid for now. Her mother was happy with the answer and stroked Elin on the cheek before going to bed.

"You deserve the best, my love."

Elin poured another cup of coffee and picked up her mobile, which she'd left on silent, to check if she had any new messages. She had. Chibbe had sent five more texts, imploring her to meet him, even though she had now told him several times that she had to study. He said they could sit in a café where she could do her schoolwork. He would be happy just to sit next to her while she did it. He could help her practice for the tests. She wanted nothing more than to meet him, but it was too complicated. For one thing, she promised Gunvor and the others that she wouldn't meet him just yet, and for another, if she was going to meet him again she wanted it to be as herself. Without the secrets.

She wondered whether to agree to meet him and come clean and tell him who she really was. She wanted to tell him why she contacted him in the first place and ask him to tell her everything he knew. She was certain he couldn't possibly be involved in that awful sex and violence business. In the unlikely event that he was involved, she could maybe persuade him to admit it and put an end to it all before anyone else got hurt.

But she wasn't sure. The chances that she'd ruin Gunvor's plans were too great. Imagine if Chibbe was involved and he actually was a cold-blooded, calculated killer who only wanted her for sex. If his true loyalty was with the people who did these awful things, he would probably warn them that Elin was helping Gunvor, who was trying to find out what really happened to Mikael Franzén.

Different scenarios occurred to her. In the worst ones, Chibbe was a direct danger to her and the others. So in the end, she told him she was on her way to a French lesson and would get back to him but not till later. This did not stop him from bombarding her with further messages.

35

I'm in. *How do I make the payment?* David sent the text message to Lacke in accordance with Manuel's recommendations.

It was late afternoon, and they were all sitting around Gunvor's dining table again. In a few hours, Aidan had to go to Arlanda for his flight to Manchester, but nothing would keep him from this meeting. To be honest, he really didn't want to go. He couldn't face leaving this new team he now felt he really belonged to or the chain of dramatic events they had recently become embroiled in. He was really proud of getting his new position and enthusiastic about starting the project in Manchester, but just now it felt very hard to leave Stockholm.

After this morning's quite emotional meeting with Nadja, Gunvor went to the office to see Manuel, who had listened patiently to her questions and concerns. It seemed to awaken Manuel's fascination with conspiracies and now, contrary to their original agreement regarding this case, he wanted to do everything he could to help. They were keeping to the same agreement on pay and expenses, but from this point on Manuel wanted to be kept updated on events and involved in operational decision-making. Furthermore, he had now done checks on both Alice and Daniel Hamrin.

According to his research, Alice and Daniel's parents both died when Alice was 17 and Daniel 19. A neighbor discovered their bodies in the father's office. The reports Manuel found on the internet said the office door was ajar and the neighbor had decided to look inside to check that everything was okay. It was anything but. The father was sitting in the chair at his desk, and the mother was lying on the floor. The room was covered in blood, and the mother and father had several deep knife wounds. The brutal murder received a great deal of media coverage at the time, and there was speculation over the father's clients. He was, after all, a criminal lawyer. The killer, or killers, were never found.

As Alice was only a few months shy of eighteen, the authorities let her carry on living with her brother in the large apartment on Strandvägen they inherited from their parents. As far as Manuel could see, they still lived there. They also inherited a large country house and a substantial amount of money. The house was no longer registered in their name, and their bank balances had been diminishing year on year.

It took only a few minutes before David received an answer to his text.

"Lacke has answered. It's just some numbers." David was confused.

"Let me see."

David handed the phone to Gunvor who quickly found that it was an account number. She looked at David. "When I send this number to Manuel, he will pay Lacke and you are expected to witness a rape. Admittedly, it is settled. But still. It can be brutal. Are you ready for this?"

"I am ready. We need to solve this." David looked convincing.

"Okay."

Gunvor forwarded the message with the account to Manuel,

who immediately transferred 10,000 kronor into the account. After watching the transfer go through, he quickly informed them that the agency would cover it. The agency had a confidential account for making transfers, thus avoiding Gunvor having to connect her own bank account to the case and risk exposure.

The mood around the table was nervous and restless as they waited to see what was going to happen next.

"Let's hope they don't just take the money and run," said David, voicing everyone's silent fear.

After ten extremely long minutes where different members of the group tried but failed to break the tension, he got a reply.

— *Clarion Sign Hotel on Norra Bantorget. 10 pm. Come alone.*

Gunvor breathed out. She had been worried that David would have to go to some gangster's house, which would have made the whole operation much riskier. She didn't yet know if they were going to be inside the hotel, but as soon as David read the message out to her, she realized how they were going to work it. Lacke, and whoever else was involved were, in face, pretty smart. Those who were going to watch the rape would check in to their own hotel rooms, unaware of how many others were also going to watch. A group of men, and maybe some women, would each sit alone watching something forbidden. Gunvor tried to imagine what the technical setup would be. Private screenings via the hotel room's TV set or a laptop in the room that opened a link to the evening's live show where the sender's identity was hidden? Not that most of their users would care about that, but none of them would want to be linked to someone that would almost certainly become part of a police investigation. Maybe this was the one time that they would live out their fantasy, and for the rest of their lives they'd be able to look back on this most special moment. Maybe some would dream of experiencing it again. What none of the punters would do was work out ways of catching the people who had made their dreams achievable.

Gunvor shared her thoughts and then described the possible

scenarios. The worst one was that the crime had been so well planned that they failed to find anything they could connect to the people who were behind it. But they did at least know that Alice Hamrin and Lacke were involved, so they could be thankful for small mercies. Gunvor also wanted to know more about Chibbe's and Daniel's roles before they handed the case over to the police.

When it seemed they were as prepared as they could be for the evening ahead, David went to get changed. Aidan helped him attach the listening device to his body while Elin went with Gunvor to the wardrobe as a style advisor. When Aidan was satisfied the wires on David were secure, he went up to his flat to check the windows and collect his bags. He'd have to go to the Arlanda airport in about half an hour, but he had promised, or rather, insisted, that he would give Gunvor a lift to the Clarion en route. Once there, she would be able to sit with her laptop and a coffee as any seasoned business traveler would, while observing the comings and goings in the lobby.

Before Gunvor and Aidan set off, they tested the listening device with Manuel, who was in his own apartment ready to record everything. Gunvor gave David a hug.

"Manuel and I will hear everything the whole time. If you need help at any point at all, just say so immediately."

"I know. You've told me about ten times now." David smiled a touch condescendingly, but at least he was showing some appreciation for her concern.

Just before she left, Gunvor held up her spare keys.

"Elin, you take them."

"I'll keep him company till it's time for him to go."

"And stay away from Chibbe, whatever he's suggesting; no matter how much you like him."

Elin said nothing. Gunvor was not sure how she should interpret the look in her eyes, but she didn't have time to bother with that now. If Chibbe was involved, he wouldn't be able to meet her tonight anyway, and she was sure Elin wouldn't be so stupid as to say anything that would give them away.

Aidan's excitement at the thought of how they might solve the whole case tonight was tempered by worry that things could go wrong. He was not happy that he would soon be on a plane for more than two hours, not knowing whether things were going well or not. He found it stressful that he would soon be too far away to help—in any hands-on practical way, at least.

Gunvor didn't want to repeat that it was she who was the private detective. She didn't want to dampen his enthusiasm or his sense that his role was important; it was. She'd miss being able to try her ideas and theories out on him for the coming week too. She told him so and promised to keep him updated by text.

Gunvor felt somewhat alone when she got out of the car and waved goodbye. She was fully aware that she bore the primary responsibility for this case, but with Aidan being so keen and willing, it had felt like he had shared the load. And that made it feel even worse to be standing there alone. Manuel was on board now, but although he'd be following David the whole time, he was not exactly a friend in the same way as Aidan.

Standing and waiting to order a drink at the bar in the hotel lobby, it occurred to her that Aidan saw her as a super sleuth whereas in Manuel's eye's she was an aging beginner. Maybe that was what she was missing most now, someone who really believed in her and her ability to make the right decisions. Her inner doubts were starting to eat away at her. How could she expose those kids to the risks they were facing? But she packed those thoughts away and tried to focus on the evening's operation. She made herself comfortable on a fashionable Arne Jacobsen chair with her laptop and an alcohol-free cocktail by her side.

36

A t first, it felt strange for Elin to be sitting alone with David. Admittedly, they had had moments on their own over the past few days, but not many, and they had always been brief. This one began with a rather uncomfortable silence that lasted quite a few minutes as David fiddled with his iPhone and Elin sat looking down at her hands. She watched with curiosity as David got up and walked to the fridge. He opened it and looked around, then took out a bottle of white wine.

"I'm sure it'll be okay with Gunvor. Do you want a glass?"

"Yes, please. You soon get used to the Östermalm lifestyle, don't you? And it must be about time for the first drink of the evening," said Elin, grinning at her own joke.

David agreed. "Yeah, funny how people are different. Here in Fruängen, they'd call you an alky if you had wine every day, no matter what vintage it was."

"Yeah, maybe—apart from all the ones here who do drink every day, like your old mates at Karlavagnen, for example." Elin meant it as a joke but realized it came out a little sarcastically.

"It's called Parma now, actually. But you're right."

"I wasn't meaning…," she hesitated, unsure how to continue.

David rescued her. "It's okay, no worries. I've started to realize quite a lot of things over the last few days. You know, since all this started?"

"I know; me too." Elin paused, in search of the right words, then went on. "Suddenly you see the world isn't so small. Or it doesn't have to be small. You just have to get out there. Or … what do you think?"

"More or less the same, yeah. It just feels mad that I'm sitting here, all wired up like James Bond or something. Imagine being able to tell my mates that I actually am a private detective." David smiled a broad, dreamy grin.

"It's OK for you; you are really brave. I've been so scared sometimes these last few days. At times I felt like I was going to die or something. But other times I feel proud of myself too."

David looked thoughtful as he slowly nodded. He picked up his wine and took a sip before asking: "That bloke, that Chibbe. Do you really like him?"

Elin nodded.

"I think Gunvor is worried about you, and perhaps she should be. You never know with men. Some are like the hardest bastards out with their mates but then really gentle and nice with their girlfriends. But some are the opposite. Maybe it's not such a good idea to risk it, considering the situation."

"Mmmm."

Suddenly Elin remembered something, "But if—and I mean, if —I ring him now and he can meet me, then he can't have anything to do with it, can he?"

Seeing the look of optimism in Elin's eyes scared David. He wasn't sure why, but all of a sudden he got a feeling that this could go horribly wrong. Elin didn't seem to see danger when it was staring her in the face. At the same time, he reckoned her theory was probably right.

"I think you should take it easy for a bit."

"But if I make a date with him, even if I don't actually go, that'll still prove he's not at the hotel, won't it? Or maybe I could just keep him talking on the phone all evening."

"Or you could just leave him alone. If he's involved and he suspects something's going on, they might just pull the plug on tonight's show. And then our whole plan's ruined."

Elin's smile faded, but the idea lingered.

"I don't want to be a pain, Elin, but we really ought to do what Gunvor says. She's the one giving us the work. If we pull this off, we'll maybe get more. And admit it, it's cool. If that Chibbe isn't involved then you can see him as much as you like later. But if he is involved, then it won't look good if you're with him. And it could be dangerous."

"Okay, okay. I was just thinking, that's all."

Neither of them wanted to show it, but they both felt that the mood had become a little awkward. To their relief, David's phone rang. It was Manuel. He wanted to test the listening equipment, so he asked David and Elin to sit and talk nonsense to each other until he was sure the wire-tapping was set correctly. And so they did. It was done quickly Then it was time for David to go.

David closed the door behind him, and Elin returned to the kitchen. She didn't need to rush home, and there was more than half a bottle of wine left. Of course, Gunvor would give her a lecture if she drank it all but right now it was a price she was prepared to pay. She filled her glass, and her phone rang. It was Chibbe. This time she answered.

"There you are. At last."

"I've told you why I couldn't answer before."

"I know, sorry. It's just that I've been really wanting to speak to you."

"Me too."

"What are you doing?"

"Revising. I've told you a hundred times. What are you doing?"

"Missing you."

"Aren't you working?" Elin decided to take her chances and dig a bit.

"I might be later."

"What do you mean, later? Tonight?" Elin felt a chill inside. It couldn't be true.

"Maybe. I'm not sure yet."

"How can you not know yet? Tonight's already begun." Elin was so desperate to hear that he didn't have anything to do with it that she pushed him more.

"I've told you before; I can't speak about my work. It's like this sometimes. I was told earlier this week I might be needed tonight, but now I haven't heard anything."

Elin was trying desperately to work out what she should do at the same time as she was talking to Chibbe. "Who were you supposed to be working for?"

"God, you're very interested in that tonight. Forget it. I don't want to talk about it." Chibbe raised his voice ever so slightly.

"Sorry, I didn't mean to be a nuisance. I just thought maybe you should check with whomever it is first before you go to meet me. So I'm not left standing there if you have to go to work."

"So you can meet me?" Chibbe sounded happy again.

"Yes, if you can. But not till 10, after my mum goes to work."

The words fell from her lips, and she couldn't but stop herself. It was only when she heard herself say the words that it occurred to her that showing a possible criminal where she lived was maybe not the brightest of ideas. But she so wanted to be close to him and didn't want to go back to that office.

"Great. It's getting late already, where shall we meet?"

Elin was feeling part euphoric, and part terrified when she ended the call. Soon enough she'd be in Chibbe's arms again. And he was not going to be at the Clarion getting filmed or caught.

37

A t two minutes past nine, Gunvor saw David through the hotel's large picture window. As he approached the entrance, she allowed her eyes to look out and across the park in Norra Bantorget. Not that it would look particularly odd for her to look at him. People watching was quite a popular pastime, after all. But even if no one would be likely to suspect any connection between the two of them she still wanted to avoid the risk of anyone even following her line of sight towards David. In dramatic situations people could remember the tiniest of details. Right now, it had no significance, but as they had no idea what could happen, she'd rather play as safely as possible.

Before David reached the entrance, he turned and looked towards the hotel's reception and took a quick glance at his watch. To the casual observer, he looked as if he was waiting for someone. Out of the corner of her eye she watched him walk over to a small set of sofas on the far side of the reception and sit down on one of them. He wasn't so far away from Gunvor, but he was facing away from her. A man came out of the lift and walked towards him. David got up.

All of a sudden, her earpiece started crackling. She knew

Manuel had been listening for half an hour already, but he had so far spared her the sound of David's breathing, people talking and shouting on the underground and all the other noises the device must be picking up. Now she could hear voices as clearly as if they were standing next to her.

"Here's the key to the room. You're checked in as Lars Larsson, and the bill is already paid, as long as you don't use the mini bar. That you can pay for yourself. But if you do, pay in cash, so there's no need for you to show anyone anything that can identify you. There's a laptop on the desk in the room. Click on the link on the screen, and it'll take you straight to tonight's show. It might take a minute before it starts up. Text this number when you leave, and I'll check you out. Have a good evening."

"Cheers."

Gunvor had slowly moved her chair around while she was listening in on the conversation. So now, facing the other way, she was unable to see which way the man went. She didn't see him outside though so she assumed he was still inside the hotel. Then she heard David on the earpiece again.

"Okay, that was Lacke. Now I'm on my own in the lift on the way up to room 809. You heard the rest. Gunvor, I'm presuming you will cover the bill for the minibar." David waited a moment before carrying on. "It's OK, I'm joking."

Gunvor heard a ping and guessed the lift had arrived at the 8th floor. She could hear his footsteps, dampened by what she assumed was a plush hotel carpet. After a short walk she heard another familiar beeping sound.

"Nearly in, stop talking now."

Gunvor would have gladly gone with David but Manuel was certain that someone capable of rigging up a live show like this would be keeping an eye on David too. For the same reason, he instructed David not to speak unless for some reason it might appear natural to be talking to himself.

"Okay, let's see. What was it he said? Switch on the computer."

Gunvor was impressed by David's casual yet informative muttering.

"Yes, right, look. Click here. Hmm."

Gunvor listened in silence and realized she'd taken her mind off her own situation. She couldn't just sit there, staring in concentration without any reason. She couldn't fiddle with her mobile either, which was usually a good tactic, as she needed to keep monitoring the lobby. She had to see if Lacke appeared again and perhaps talked to anyone else who'd ordered a view of tonight's show.

38

As the room door closed behind him, David took off his coat and sat down at the desk. The laptop came to life when he moved the mouse. He adjusted the screen by slowly moving it backwards and forwards until Manuel said stop. Because, as well as the listening device, he had a tiny camera pinned to his shirt, concealed by the shirt's logo. The logo was a yellow and blue shield, and David prayed it fully hid the camera in case he was being watched too.

He sat for half an hour looking at film of an empty street somewhere with nothing happening. The windowless red brick buildings and the deserted street seemed to belong to some sort of industrial area. When a cat suddenly appeared, it startled him, and then he found himself laughing aloud at his own reaction. He didn't explain it as he couldn't think of a natural way to do so. Manuel and Gunvor would have to think what they like.

The thought of starting on the minibar was never far from his mind, but he had decided to resist as it was surely not a good idea to be presenting himself at reception. The best thing was for him to leave the hotel as if he'd been visiting someone who was staying at the hotel—or if he'd just been in the bar, which seemed to be on the same floor as his room anyway.

He only got involved in this thing a few days ago. If someone had told him last week that he'd be going on a mission all wired up with a hidden microphone and camera, he'd have laughed at them. But in many ways, the biggest surprise was that he was one of the good guys. No matter how hard he tried to keep himself high in the local pecking order, he'd always really thought of himself as a loser. It never seemed like he'd get a chance to escape Fruängen. It wasn't even worth trying. But over the last few days he'd started to believe that maybe he wasn't a particularly bad person—and maybe he wasn't totally stupid.

He sat up straight when someone appeared on the screen. A woman emerged from the shadows and walked slowly down the desolate street towards the camera. He couldn't tell if it was Alice, but even from a distance he could tell that she was putting on a sexy walk. She was wearing a short skirt and high heels. As she neared the camera he saw that it was Alice. Her jacket was open, revealing a thin and extremely low cut blouse that was almost transparent in the light of the single street lamp close to the camera.

Then he caught sight of another figure further down the street. He assumed it was whoever had paid for Alice's services tonight—or who was paying for her adventure. The figure was dressed in dark clothes and followed her as she walked past the camera. It was as if she was looking right at David as she winked at the camera and made the same gesture she made outside Sture-hof. She nibbled the end of one finger and closed her eyes for a second. Then she disappeared from the screen. David wondered if this was something she did often, or if she knew it was actually him sitting there watching. He winced at the thought there were probably other men in other rooms in the hotel thinking that she was making the gesture just for them, too.

The screen flickered off; then after a moment, he saw Alice again from a different camera. She was close to the entrance of what looked more like a building site prefab than an apartment. She walked up to the door and appeared to be searching for her keys. It took her a while, but she found them, unlocked the door, and stepped into a hallway. Then it happened. Although he was fully aware of what was due to happen it was still a shock when the person that was following her suddenly forced their way into her apartment and slammed the door shut. The intruder was much closer to the camera now, but David couldn't make out any recognizable details. He was sure it was a man but not much more. He had a mask on his face, and he was wearing baggy clothes. Alice screamed, but not particularly loudly. The camera picked up the sound well, and he heard Alice ask the man not to hurt her. He could tell she didn't really sound that scared. If anything, she sounded a bit sexy.

It was clear that everything was staged. The apartment was lit by several small lamps, so it was fairly dark but still light enough to see everything that happened. When the door closed, they switched to another camera inside the flat. David wondered if it was Lacke choosing cameras to catch the best views, just like live sports on TV.

The room was simple, with a sofa, an armchair, and a desk. The walls seemed cold, although there was a big mirror on one and a few of those mass-produced paintings you get in IKEA on another. Even though he was concentrating on watching events he couldn't help but think that this couldn't be where Alice lived. It seemed much more like a young guy's place, except for the mirror, maybe.

To begin with, her assailant didn't seem particularly aggressive. He was holding her from behind with his arms around her neck. Alice was standing passively as if she was waiting to see what would happen next. The man stepped into the living room with Alice still in front of him and turned, so both of them were facing the camera. At first, he seemed to be doing it deliberately, but when the camera angle changed you could see that he had positioned himself in front of the mirror. Soon the view changed again, this time to a camera apparently placed directly above the mirror.

Still wearing his gloves, the masked man slowly pulled up Alice's blouse and forced one of his hands under her red lace bra. She shuddered when he took hold of a breast, then he lifted his hand and began to remove her jacket slowly. And suddenly he had a knife in his hand and was stroking it along her throat. Alice leaned her head backward and groaned. Either the knife had really turned her on, or she was an excellent actor. He slid the knife under her blouse, using the blade to cut through the thin material. The torn blouse slid downwards, revealing her bra and a well-toned stomach. He had to use a little more force to cut through her bra, but it didn't take him long. Her breasts were large and firm, and she had obviously been sunbathing topless. He slid the knife across her body then sliced off her skirt and panties with ease.

Alice seemed to be watching herself in the mirror as she parted her legs and arched her back, so her breasts pushed further forward. His hands rubbed across her body and down between her legs towards her vagina. Everything down there had been shaved. Alice moaned loudly and started to move her hips backward and forward in sync with the steady friction of his gloved hand.

His other hand held the knife against her throat. Alice appeared comfortable with this as she caressed and squeezed her breasts while watching herself and the man in the mirror.

Then he leaned in close and whispered something in her ear. Whatever it was he said had changed the mood. An uncomfortable-looking Alice attempted to free herself from his grip.

"What the hell are you doing?" she gasped. There was genuine panic in Alice's voice.

Still holding the knife against Alice as if to threaten her to stay still, the man´s right hand appeared to tighten his one-handed grip on her throat. Hard. Alice sounded like she tried to scream, but David could only hear a desperate gurgle of air escape her throat. Alice acted like she knew her life was about to come to an end if she didn't do something quick. With both hands, she grabbed the hand that looked like it was squeezing the life out of her. She tried to pull it off her throat. But the attacker was too strong. Instead she started throwing her head from side to side, her hair flying, in a vain attempt to free herself. She began kicking wildly as her body thrashed about, but the man's grip held.

David jerked bolt upright in front of the screen as Alice appeared to be in a struggle for her life. *Good God! Is this just a show?* David thought to himself as he watched the horrific scene in front of him unfold. The man and Alice now seemed to be in a real-life death struggle. And, Alice didn't look like she was faring well at all. He had been expecting it to be brutal. Just not this brutal. *They are doing it for the money,* he tried to assure himself. *Damn!*

David blinked his eyes hard. He tried to reason that this was how these people did it; it was meant to look like a brutal rape. It was meant to look real. But, it damn sure didn't look like Alice was acting. It looked real. Too real! But, in these short few seconds, maybe the man and Alice were playing the scene of their life, David continued to convince himself it was part of the rape fantasy. He imagined that men who wanted to play at raping a woman didn't want them to act like they were enjoying it as much as Alice had been. Rape was more about power than sex, so if she was enjoying it, what's the point? Especially if you've paid for it.

It wasn't until the man cut her across her cheek that David realized something was going terribly wrong. As if struck by a bolt of lightning, David realized everything about this scene, the smothered screams, the fear in Alice's eyes, everything. Everything was for real now. There was no longer any doubt; Alice was fighting for her life!

With one hand in a death-grip on her throat, and a knife in the other, the man looked intent on killing her. As if she knew this might be her last chance, David watched Alice explode in a violent effort to loosen the grip enough to let a silent scream escape her lips. But the man didn't lose his grip and visibly exerted his deadly hold even more. She grabbed the hand with the knife, desperately trying to push it away. Her face had turned dark in the soft light of the room, and her eyes seemed to budge out of her eye sockets. She was losing the battle for life. She was fighting with all the strength she had, but David could tell her movements were weakening. Her strength was waning, right in front of his eyes.

Then in a sickening flash, the man brought his knife hand down and slashed across her chest. A red ribbon of blood appeared from her left collar bone to the center of her ribs. As she weakly struggled for life, blood began to gush from her wound, soaking her in her own dark red liquid of life. In shock at what he was watching, David saw the man bring his knife hand up and savagely plunge the knife again and again into Alice's now seminaked chest.

"Help! Come here! It's all fucked up!" David screamed, as he jumped out of his chair, sending it crashing to the floor, calling out to everyone, anyone who would listen.

On the monitor, the man was still holding Alice tight. Her body was jerking as her lifeblood pumped out of her chest. As the body stopped moving, David heard it glide slowly to the floor. The man lifted her up by the hair for a moment then muttered something before throwing her body back to the floor in what seemed like rage.

A moment later, he was gone. What was seconds before a brutal killing scene was now tranquil. It could even have been described as peaceful if it hadn't been for Alice appearing to stare straight at the camera, her death face frozen in a look of fear and panic.

David vomited.

39

Elin was standing inside the entrance of the underground station. A train pulled in. She hoped Chibbe was on it, but she wasn't really expecting him to be. He should have arrived a long while ago, even though he phoned and said he'd be late. He told her he'd promised to sort something out for a friend. What it was that was so important for him to do at this time of night he wouldn't say, but he'd said it wouldn't take long. So, Elin had invested all her faith in this being just some little ordinary thing, something totally different from whatever David was involved in. Chibbe would come soon. So, he couldn't possibly be involved in the business with Alice.

But it was now nearly eleven o'clock in the evening and, according to Chibbe's calculations, he should have been on the train before this one. There weren't that many people catching trains at this time of night, so she quickly worked out that he wasn't on this one either. She let out a resigned sigh, and the cold feeling in her stomach got colder. Then her phone rang. Chibbe.

"Hello?"

"It's me, sorry. I am on the way to the hospital. They called about my mother. I don't know what's happened. I'll call you later."

"Which one are you going to? Shall I come?"

It's too late, Chibbe had already hung up. She'd just had to go home on her own. In one way she was relieved, but in another she was feeling sorry for herself. Her plan had achieved nothing, which was not so good, especially as she had gone against what both Gunvor and David had told her to do. On the other hand, the idea was to prove Chibbe was innocent and if he were at the hospital with his mother then he would be free from suspicion.

She was feeling a bit bad about Chibbe too. Here she was, feeling sorry for herself and hassling him when his mother was ill. She hoped it was nothing serious. Actually, maybe this could be a good thing, the doctors might see they needed to provide proper care. Chibbe was a grown man, he had the right to have his own life, and he shouldn't be tied down by his commitment to his mother. Elin texted him saying she hoped everything was okay and that she was thinking of him.

Back home, her thoughts switched to David and Gunvor. She hoped David was able to be a hero tonight and that everything would fall into place so they could tie up the case and hand it over to the police. Then she'd have the time and energy to get back to doing her normal schoolwork and maybe even start seeing Chibbe under more normal circumstances.

40

Gunvor heard David's shouts and headed straight for his room without hesitation. She cursed herself because she hadn't prepared herself for this. She had no idea what had happened, but she knew something had gone horribly wrong. And it was only now, right when something was happening, that it occurred to her that they had no back-up plan whatsoever. She and David were on their own in the city. Manuel was in theory following what was happening to David, but he was at home in Årsta. Meanwhile, Aidan had probably just boarded his plane on his way across the North Sea. She didn't know if Lacke was still in the hotel or not, but she couldn't afford to waste time thinking about that. All that mattered right now was that she had to help David.

As luck would have it there was an empty lift in the lobby. She took it to the eighth floor. Inside the lift she realized how fortunate, or perhaps well-planned, Lacke's choice of rooms had been. It was on the same floor as the hotel spa and bar, so it was the only floor you could get to without needing to use a room card in the lift. Pleased as she was by the coincidence, she also felt a pang of unease for not having thought to check up on that earlier.

The lift's ascent felt like an eternity. To top it all, it stopped on the second floor for a rather overly excited couple who couldn't decide whether to go up to the rooftop bar or down to the one in the lobby. After about two seconds of watching their process of indecision, Gunvor told them she was in a hurry and immediately pressed the 'Close Door' button. They stepped back to let her continue while they decided, but not without one of them mumbling something about "...that miserable old bitch." The comment dug deep, for it was exactly how she'd been feeling in recent weeks. Her somber inner voice kept going on about how she really shouldn't be doing the job she was doing if she couldn't even run up a few flights of stairs.

The corridors were well signed, so she was outside David's door in next to no time. The door was slightly ajar. She peered carefully inside the room and saw David was alone, so she walked in and closed the door.

"What's happening?"

The laptop she had heard Lacke talk about earlier was there on the desk. It was on, but all she could see was a background image with some kind of forest logo. There were no files or folder icons on the screen as far as she could make out. David was sitting on the bed, staring down at the floor. There was an awful smell in the room. A few steps further in, Gunvor noticed that David had vomited in the wastepaper basket. By instinct, she took the basket out to the bathroom and quickly rinsed it under the shower. In the bathroom, it occurred to her that there were probably more important things to be doing right now. She left the basket and went back into the room where she sat down next to David and placed her arm around his shoulders. He sat upright, his eyes full of tears.

"He killed her. He *murdered* her."

Gunvor could only look helplessly at David, who stared at the floor once again. Inside she was in turmoil, her thoughts swirling. *What have I got him involved in? What in God's name am I going to do now?* The sound of her phone ringing snapped her out of it. It was Manuel.

"I heard. Now we have to move fast. Is the link still visible on the laptop?"

"No," she said and turned to David, "What happened to the film you saw?"

"It disappeared before you came. I don't know what happened to it."

"Okay, I heard. Wipe off everything you've touched and get out of there. Stay calm. Pretend you are a mother and son and leave the hotel as if you are going out for a walk or a drink somewhere. Hurry! I'll stay on the phone while you clean the place up."

Gunvor pulled out two handkerchiefs and gave one to David.

"Wipe off everything you've touched."

To her surprise, he did what she said straightaway. He looked a bit manic as he rubbed away at the computer. Gunvor had kept a couple of handkerchiefs with her since she started at the agency for exactly this reason. She tried to think what she'd touched then went into the bathroom to get the wastepaper basket and wiped the shower tap. When they were ready, Gunvor lifted the phone to her ear again. "We're done."

"OK. Can I speak to David before you leave?"

Gunvor silently handed the phone to David. He nodded and muttered agreement in response to whatever Manuel was saying. When the conversation was over, he handed the phone to Gunvor and looked at her.

"Let's go. I'm your youngest son and we've just been here for a drink to celebrate me getting a job. So now we're in a good mood and on our way home. I'd appreciate it if you could hold me. I feel like I'm going to faint."

Gunvor nodded and put her arm under David's, then placed her handkerchief over the door handle before opening it. She wiped the handle on the outside of the door and then they walked to the lift. She was grateful for her ability to waffle on about anything as she went into a monologue about the pros and cons of building a sauna, hoping that David's mortified expression could be mistaken for that of a young man who had been politely listening to his mother for far too long.

41

"Why didn't we just call the police?" They watched the film three times, and David finally got the chance to ask the question that had been bothering him ever since he witnessed the terrible events. It had been troubling him the whole time they were walking to Central Station and then in the taxi to Manuel's apartment.

"Because we'd be in trouble ourselves," Manuel replied. "Accessory to murder? Conspiracy? How'd you fancy that hanging around your neck? You arranged and paid to watch a film involving a violent attack on a woman. We really should have spoken to the police long before now. But we all wanted—you included, as far as I recall—to solve the case ourselves, because we all had something to gain from it. Am I right?"

David nodded but didn't really understand. "But, can't we just tell the truth? If we'd called from the hotel, maybe they could have caught the murderer."

"What? We don't even know where it happened, do we? It was a live stream from some unknown location. You have no idea where it was, and you were the one who saw it happen. We've watched it over and over, and we're still no closer to knowing where it took place." Manuel didn't want to sound overly critical, but he was determined to show David he was serious. David listened and understood. "And you aren't qualified. You're not even employed as a private detective. In the eyes of the law, you're just some young scumbag who paid to watch a rape. Or maybe they'd be able to prove that you'd paid to watch a snuff film in real-time."

David was horrified as he took in what Manuel was actually saying, so Gunvor quickly intervened in an attempt to calm him down, "The police won't be able to connect you to any of this, as long as we don't say anything. The people behind this are hardly going to give you another thought now. They've got their money. And they'll know that you'll want to keep a low profile, just like them. Don't you think, Manuel?"

"We don't even know if there is anyone else behind this apart from Lacke. Chibbe is probably involved, but we've got no proof of that, just indicators."

"Indicators? What's that supposed to mean?" David wasn't following anything very well. The vision of what he'd seen was going around and around in his head.

"We're as good as certain that Chibbe is at least an accomplice to the assault on Mikael Franzén, but we have no proof, as Franzén refuses to talk. As regards Alice's unusual sex life, you've had a conversation with Lacke, no more."

Manuel was pensive, "Maybe we should speak to Franzén again. He knows something we don't, and perhaps Alice's death will encourage him to cooperate."

"I don't think it's worth me trying to speak to him again. His mind was made up when he told me to go. Maybe you could try? Maybe not right now at this time of day, of course," said Gunvor, looking at her watch, which told her it was just after midnight.

"I wonder how she is."

Manuel and Gunvor forgot what they were speaking about and looked at David with concern.

"She is in a better place now." Gunvor's attempt at offering some sort of solace was by no means convincing.

"It's quite strange, I've heard nothing on police radio yet."

Manuel was wearing an earpiece and had been following the police radio ever since David called for help.

"Lacke, or whoever it is that's behind all this, probably wants to get rid of the cameras and any other evidence. He'll probably just leave the body where it is for someone else to discover, some poor neighbor or someone out walking their dog."

"Now," Manuel said, clutching the earpiece. "The police have got a call-out to a 24."

Gunvor explained quietly to David that a 24 is police jargon for a murder or manslaughter.

Manuel looked confused, "What? Hang on a tick..."

David and Gunvor looked at Manuel, who was listening intently.

"Very odd." Manuel looked up at them. "Exactly as you described, a woman in her thirties stabbed in the heart."

"What's odd about that?" Gunvor wondered what Manuel was talking about.

Manuel sat quietly for a moment listening to the radio, then he answered her, "She was found outside, in a car park near Häger-stenshamnen."

"It must be someone else." Gunvor found it hard to believe that someone could walk around on their own carrying a dead woman covered in blood.

"Wait," Manuel held up his hand, listening carefully again. "There's a fire in an industrial building somewhere in Örnsberg. That's the same area. It looked like an industrial area on the film, didn't it?"

David nodded.

"Then it is her," Manuel was certain. "They've moved the body and torched the evidence."

"But shouldn't we check to make sure?"

"Yes, of course. I'll listen to the radio to see how it all pans out. I might have to be patient though. Considering she was murdered, they'll do an investigation of the scene first. Go and make yourselves something to eat. Just try to rest. Go and lie down," he said to try to distract the two while he thought of what their next move should be. "I'll follow developments and let you know when something happens."

Gunvor nodded in grateful agreement, but neither she nor David rushed to leave the room. They were deep in their own thoughts, and Manuel was focused on the police radio.

Gunvor struggled to push the image of someone sticking a knife into Alice's heart from her mind. Despite being a surgeon herself, a doctor who had inserted countless knives in countless people in her time, this image was worse than anything she had seen before. When she had cut into someone, it was under controlled conditions and harsh theatre lighting. And she'd been trying to save or improve the lives of the patients she was cutting. What she had just seen was the exact opposite. To cold-bloodedly take someone's life with one accurate lunge was something else entirely. Perhaps the situation was made worse by her surgical memories. The clean and calculated surgical incisions contrasted so strongly with this brutal stabbing. Gunvor, who had seen quite a few things in her life, was taking this very badly, and she realized David must be in an even darker place. He'd paid to see a rape. Perhaps it had been a put-up job with actors, but in some way he'd helped set up a violent attack that had gone beyond what anyone had been expecting. She looked at him, poor kid. He'd seen it happen right in front of him. She looked at him and felt a wave of maternal concern. Wishing she could save him from all the horrible crap the world dished out. Wanting to comfort him, to take him in her arms and tell him to let it go, get rid of the images, the sense of shock, everything. But right now, she couldn't manage much more than to stroke his arm.

"Come on," Gunvor wanted to drag herself and David out of

this hopeless place they were drowning in, but all she could do was take him to the kitchen and get him something to eat. In some ways, food managed to offer comfort when emotions were running high.

Although Manuel was still relatively young and single, he lived in a spacious two-bedroomed flat, and his fridge was surprisingly full. Gunvor pulled out a chair for David and got butter, cheese, and ham. Glasses, plates, and cutlery were easy to find. And, after a bit of searching, she found a baguette that looked quite fresh. They ate quickly and in silence, then lied down, side by side, on the large double bed. In a few minutes they were both asleep. The last thing that occurred to Gunvor was that she should have called Elin, even though it was late.

42

E lin couldn't sleep. She wondered again whether she should call or at least text Gunvor or David. She'd gotten a feeling things weren't right with them either, and she really wanted to know that everything was okay. But she decided to wait until they made contact first. After all, that was the agreement. Unless something changed, Gunvor would call her at 7.30 tomorrow morning and give her an update on the situation, in good time before Elin's mother came home.

Elin of course still wanted to be totally sure that Chibbe was not involved in Alice's dark and sleazy world. She still couldn't believe how completely she had fallen for him. A man who thought he had the right to grab a woman he didn't know between the legs, and not just once. Right up until the moment they first kissed, she had only seen Chibbe as some sort of desperate loser. And it wasn't just an irresistible sexual attraction she felt for him now either. As well as the overwhelming passion, over the last few days she had gotten to know his warm and tender side. She knew that he must have been involved in the attack on Franzén, and he obviously knew Alice, but she was still hopeful that there would be a good explanation for everything.

When she met him the evening before, her fear that he wasn't interested in her began to slowly vanish. And now that he had been hassling her all day to arrange a meeting, she was even more certain of his feelings towards her. Amid all this worry about whether or not he was involved in this shitty business, she still felt tremors of hope and happiness. Her difficulty in trusting men was not surprising, considering the fact that she'd grown up watching her father abuse her mother. Not all the time, of course, but there were enough pushes and shoves and punches and, above all, a constant fear of making him angry. Chibbe was big and apparently not afraid of using his fists, but now that she'd seen how shy and meek he could be, she couldn't for a moment imagine him ever raising his hand to her.

Even though he didn't reply to her last message, she decided to send him another before trying to get some sleep. Seconds after sending the message her phone rang.

It's Chibbe, "Hi. I was going to call before but thought you might be asleep."

"I can't sleep. How's it going with your mum? Is it serious?"

"No, it was nothing. It's just…weird."

"What?"

"Someone called and said there'd been an accident and that I should get to A&E. But she wasn't there. I panicked and thought for a minute she'd died. So I had a go at them in the hospital. In the end, a security guard came and started to drag me away. But he was cool and it got me thinking. He said I should ring my mum and check before carrying on anymore. I hadn't actually thought of that. I just presumed she was there in the hospital."

"Did you get hold of her?"

"When I called, she was home. Nothing had happened except she was pissed off that I'd woken her up."

"God, that's mad. Who'd do something like that?"

"Exactly. And why?"

Elin tried to imagine how Gunvor would interpret this. She

would definitely suspect Chibbe of lying and that he was trying to hide what he'd really been up to this evening. But Elin knew he wasn't lying.

"Do you want to come over? But if you do, you'll have to leave before half-past seven in the morning."

"Course I do. I'll call a taxi."

Elin had butterflies in her stomach. Soon she'd feel his skin against hers. Even so, she tried to keep some sort of control and to think for a minute about why someone would go to such trouble to trick him like that about his mother. But she really couldn't come up with any likely explanation. She couldn't think of how she was going to tell Gunvor she was meeting Chibbe either.

The next time he texted she ran downstairs to open the main door but also carefully left her own door wedged open outwards against the corridor wall so he wouldn't see their surname above the letterbox. Not that she imagined he would actually give it a second's thought, but she'd rather not risk him discovering she lied about it. Maybe she'd just pretend it was her mother's maiden name or something. Twenty minutes later, she and Chibbe were lying in the narrow bed in what still had the air of a teenage girl's bedroom. They held each other tight and kissed and talked until animal instincts took over.

43

It was just after five when Manuel shook Gunvor awake. He didn't want to wake David, so he put his finger to his lips and mimed for her to get up and join him in the living room. Gunvor went to the toilet first and took the opportunity to rinse her face with cold water. Her sleep had been short and fitful, but she felt more or less ready to work. Waiting on the coffee table was a steaming fresh latte and a warm baguette dressed with ham and cheese.

"Oh, lovely, thanks."

"You're welcome. It's the least I could do."

"How's it going?" Gunvor sat down on the sofa and took a long sip of her latte before tackling the baguette.

"The body's been sent to Södersjukhuset."

"Why? The body is supposed to be sent to the forensics."

"Yes, I know. But sometimes forensics have problems with the transport. So, the ambulance that was in place brought the body to the emergency where it can be stored in the cold room until forensics can pick it up." Manuel seemed tired and a little fraught. His normally well-presented black hair was sticking up in all directions, and he had bags under his eyes.

"I can call the emergency. I am not sure they know anything about her but we have to give it a try."

"I thought you knew all about the routines in the hospitals."

"I haven't worked much with violent crimes and don't know how they go about dealing with the bodies. The ones I had been involved in were still alive when they came into theatre for emergency surgery. When someone had died, they called the coroner, not a surgeon." Gunvor did her best to remember what she might have heard about this when she was still practicing, but not much sprang to mind. So she was either not very observant, or she just didn't store any information that wasn't relevant to her job. She was the type of person who knew a hell of a lot about things that interest her but next to nothing about anything beyond her immediate concern. At least that's how it was when she was a doctor. As a private detective, she quickly realized that you never know what might be important, so she had learned to be much more observant and tried to remember even the most irrelevant details. But that was of no help in this case.

"It's not even certain they've identified her yet. Whoever did this might have burned everything to help cover his tracks."

"True, but we have to try. I'll call emergency. It's not, strictly speaking, their job to deal with bodies, but the nurses there usually know what's going on. If Alice had ID on her she'll hopefully be in the database. She was half-naked when she died, but maybe the killer wanted her to be identified," Gunvor got up, still holding her latte. "Is it okay if I go out on your balcony?"

"Of course. But isn't it a bit cold this time of the morning?"

"Absolutely, but I need to wake up."

Gunvor thought for a moment then looked up the number to the surgical emergency unit at Södersjukhuset. She still felt uncomfortable about getting involved with hospitals, and she didn't like the idea of lying to people for whom she had the utmost of respect. So when someone finally answered, she felt a slight tremor in her voice. She reassured herself that this was actually good, as she was supposed to sound worried. The usual thing, of course, would be to call the police in this sort of extreme situation, but she hoped to maintain as much distance as possible from the forces of law and order.

"Surgical Emergency Unit, Sister Anna."

The voice at the other end sounded pleasant enough, although a little stressed.

"Hi, I'm not sure if I should be calling this number, but I'm worried about a friend. We were supposed to have had dinner together last night but she never turned up and she's not answered her phone all night. I know I shouldn't be ringing the hospital straight away, but she's not been feeling well lately. She's been quite down actually."

"Does she have a friend or partner that you can contact? That's usually the best place to start."

"She's single and I don't know any of her friends or family. We got to know each other at an AA group and we've been speaking a lot since then, just the two of us."

"I think you should call the police if you're worried."

"Can you just tell me if you've admitted a woman, born 1986, name of Alice Hamrin?"

The silence at the other end of the line was telling, even if it only lasted for seconds.

"Maybe if you come here, we can talk. Do you know how to get to this unit?"

"So she's there?" Gunvor noticed just how on edge she was when she heard her own voice.

"It would probably be best if you came here."

Gunvor disconnected, but she knew everything she needed to know. There was no need for her to go off to the hospital and get mixed up in conversations with the staff and the police. She'd spread enough lies about that poor dead woman already.

She met Manuel's eyes through the balcony window and nodded. Then she called Elin's number. The phone rang a few times before Elin answered, sounding quite drowsy, which was not surprising since it was about five-thirty in the morning.

"I thought we were going to be in touch about half-past seven? Has something happened?"

Gunvor thought she heard a man's voice in the background. "Who's there with you?"

"Wait."

Gunvor heard Elin whispering, obviously not to her. Then she heard quiet footsteps and a door being carefully closed, "Who's there with you?" she asked.

"No one special," whispers Elin.

"That's about the dumbest answer I've ever heard. You've got someone, oh, just someone, in your bedroom at five-thirty in the morning. I guess you're not awake enough to think of a half-decent lie. Who is it?"

"It's not like you think."

"Oh, how exactly do I think?"

"Can't we talk about this later?"

"So it's Chibbe?"

Elin's silence spoke volumes and chilled Gunvor to the bone. In the worst-case scenario, Elin had shared her bed with a murderer. She couldn't say that now because Elin would get scared and then she'd probably give herself away and get herself into an even worse situation.

"We need to meet. Something has happened and I can't tell you over the phone. I'm in Årsta right now, but we can meet at my place in an hour."

Gunvor hung up to emphasize there was no room to negotiate the time of this meeting. She went in to tell Manuel about Elin and Chibbe.

"I'll take David back to my place. We'll run through all the details with Elin and then we can be in touch later."

"Okay, fine. I'll get a couple of hours' sleep and then go to the office."

Manuel called a taxi while Gunvor shook some life back into David. He had a tortured look, but he didn't complain. He was silent for the whole cab journey to Elsa Beskows Gata. At Gunvor's flat, she sent him through to her room and told him to go and lie down. She went into the kitchen to make another coffee and let out a groan when she saw the empty bottle of wine.

"Shit, I haven't exactly brought Elin a lot of happiness, have I?" she muttered. Her guilty conscience hit hard again. There was no avoiding the fact that she had exposed an innocent and inexperienced young girl to situations where she was way out of her depth. There was no point being strict and hard on her. It was time to dig out some patience and to explain things to her as clearly as possible.

44

D espite the situation, Gunvor determined to compose herself and make the most of this rare moment with a freshly-made latte on the balcony in the bright morning sunshine. She sat down with a fleece blanket around her shoulders.

The phone rang. "They've taken Mikael. I don't know what to do." Nadia sounded devastated.

Alarm bells went off in Gunvor's head. According to her plan, Nadja was supposed to be far away out of reach and Mikael under safe protection at the hospital.

"Who? The same people that beat him up?"

"No, the police."

Gunvor was lost. She couldn't understand why the police should have taken Franzén, but Nadja soon explained. "They are going to question him about killing a woman. Someone who apparently reported him for harassment just yesterday."

Gunvor would have loved to be able to say something wise and reassuring, but she was unable to utter a word. It was not only the phone that had gone quiet, but it was also as if her very thoughts had stopped as if her mind had become a vacuum. Not even the tiniest piece of the jigsaw was falling into place because this didn't add up at all. After a moment, she managed to compose herself sufficiently to continue the conversation.

"But isn't Mikael in the hospital?"

"He was discharged yesterday. As soon as I got home after meeting you in that café, he phoned and said he was on his way. So I packed and waited for him."

"Were you together later? If so, you are his alibi."

Nadja didn't respond, but Gunvor head her sob.

"You weren't?"

"As soon as he got home, I told him I'd spoken to you and that you'd said I should go away for a few days. I told him I thought it was a good idea too, but I'd waited because I wanted him to come with me. He agreed to sit in the car and drive to some hotel in another town. I'd already withdrawn enough cash to pay for it. Like you said, I just wanted us to be safe somewhere until we heard from you that everything was sorted out. And, I thought it would be a good idea for us to be somewhere neutral where we could talk through everything, without any interruptions from work or whatever. But then someone called him."

Nadja was suddenly silent. A few seconds later Gunvor heard more sobbing, heavier this time.

"Who was it?" Gunvor was aware that Nadja was finding it extremely difficult to talk, but she had to get information fast.

Gunvor heard Nadja take a deep breath and she was suddenly almost back to normal.

"I don't know. I am guessing, but I think maybe it is all connected to this whole shitty business because suddenly he didn't want to go away. He said something about an important meeting. He suggested I went away on my own, so I did, but I wasn't going any further than the Grand Hotel. I spent most of the evening sitting in the bar there. I wasn't getting drunk; I just didn't want to be alone. When the bar closed, I went up to my room. But I was too worried to sleep, so in the end I took a taxi home. When I got there, Mikael was sitting up drinking whisky.

He was drunk, and he was crying. He muttered something about being trapped. I thought it was just drunken nonsense, and I tried to calm him down and get him to sleep. But he continued to cry, and cry. And while all this was going on the police came to get him. Two of them stayed and asked me what I'd been doing. I told them the truth and that's when I found out what it was all about."

Gunvor was speechless. Either everything that happened was a collection of incredible coincidences or they were dealing with a real, calculating and resourceful psychopath—assuming Franzén wasn't the killer, that is. Maybe he had had more fantasies than rape that he had wanted to live out. Maybe just stepping into one of his fantasies had caused him to flip, maybe he couldn't find peace until he killed Alice, because it was clear that the killing had strong sexual undertones.

Gunvor waved to Elin, who was walking across the central courtyard area.

"What shall I do?" Nadja sounded desperate.

"Have you got a friend who can be with you? All you can do now is wait. I reckon that the people that sell these so-called rapes blackmail people and Mikael is almost certainly one of many. But it's up to him now how much he tells the police. They might let him go if they believe him and manage to find the people who are behind all this, but he might get charged even if he tells the full story because he paid for a sexual act, which is against the law.

Nadja was silent for several seconds.

"How can this all have happened?"

Gunvor had no good answer, so they ended the call after agreeing to get in touch the moment anything happened.

45

E lin was totally freaked out when Gunvor had called much earlier than expected. Still half-asleep, she picked up her phone as if on autopilot, yet terrified something bad had happened. The call woke Chibbe, so she went into the kitchen and closed the door. From Gunvor's curt tone and the timing of the call, she realized that there was a crisis, and having her cover blown by Gunvor's call would not exactly improve the situation. This was not how she had planned to start her morning. Chibbe was going to get breakfast and a bit of love before she hurried him away at quarter-past seven. She went back into the bedroom. Chibbe was sitting on the edge of the bed, looking confused.

"What's happening?"

"My mum's got sick and she's on her way home, so you'll have to go."

"Can't I stay and meet her?" Chibbe looked hopeful.

"She's sick. She doesn't know we've met and she's throwing up. I think we'd better wait for a better time, don't you?"

"Okay, sure." Chibbe looked dejected but started dressing.

"I'm sorry."

"It's okay, no worries. Maybe we can meet when you've finished studying today?"

"Aren't you working?"

"I don't know. I've not heard anything. They're probably out at the country house, but I'll go into the office after I've had a bit more sleep. Someone's been keeping me awake all night." Chibbe got up and pulled her to him, and she couldn't resist staying there a little bit longer.

When Chibbe finally left it occurred to her that he'd said something that rang a bell. Something about being at the country house. She must mention that to Gunvor.

She saw Gunvor on her balcony almost as soon as she entered the area. She waved but Gunvor appeared to be busy on the phone. The downstairs door was locked. Elin waited. After a few minutes, Gunvor came down and opened the door. Seeing Gunvor close up finally confirmed to Elin that something had gone badly wrong.

"What's happening?"

"Come in first."

Elin went in and closed the door.

"Alice was murdered last night. David watched it all on a laptop. The police have just arrested Mikael Franzén on suspicion of murder."

The floor beneath Elin's feet began to tremble. What the hell was going on? Everything was supposed to be sorted out now. Gunvor took her into the living room and wondered whatever had happened to her plan to break things gently to Elin. But what the hell, at least she'd been unambiguous.

They sat for at least an hour talking about what had happened. Elin came clean and told Gunvor all about her evening. She watched the space between Gunvor's eyebrows furrow in concern when she told her Chibbe got a call from the hospital. She didn't explain why she was so concerned, and Elin couldn't bring herself to ask. While Gunvor noted everything down on her laptop, Elin went through to the kitchen and made more coffee. At Gunvor's request, she made coffee for all three of them and put a few frozen croissants in the oven. Then she remembered and stopped in the living room doorway. "There was one other thing."

Gunvor looked up.

"Chibbe mentioned a country house a few times that might have something to do with the people he works for. I don't know if it means anything, but I thought I should tell you."

"In what context did he mention it?"

"Yesterday, when I asked if he was going to work, he said he probably would, but he hadn't heard anything yet. This morning, he said he still hadn't heard anything, but this time it was probably because they were at the country house. I remembered he'd said the same thing when I thought someone was watching us in the office. He mumbled something about how they were supposed to be at the country house."

"Good work, Elin. I know they owned some sort of big, country house a long time ago, but they don't appear to still have it. I'll ask Manuel to see if they are renting something."

Elin and Gunvor froze when the bedroom door opened. David's hair was a mess and he looked half asleep. "Did I smell coffee?"

Gunvor sent Elin and David off to the kitchen for breakfast. She was soon going to join them. But only after she had implemented her idea. She hoped for some information. It was probably too early to get an answer, but it was not too early to send a text message.

— *Hi. Did you see Alice or any of her friends in Sturehof yesterday? Something terrible has happened and I need to know if they were seen together with another man.*

She hardly managed to get up out of her chair to go into the others when her phone bleeped.

— No. Off sick.

Gunvor was confused. She'd seen Fredde yesterday, and he'd looked well enough. Weird. But maybe he was the sort who called in sick just because they didn't feel like working. Some people were like that. It wasn't something she'd ever considered. In fact, she couldn't remember ever taking a day off sick since she started working. Mind you, she was also aware of how she had never been particularly good at looking after herself. Throughout her years as a surgeon she used to say there were very few symptoms that couldn't be erased by a cocktail of Panodil and Ipren.

They sat for a while at the breakfast table. Elin asked David question after question. At first, Gunvor was afraid that David wouldn't cope, and she was ready to stop Elin's endless stream of questions, but she saw David gradually begin to relax, so she left them to it. This was probably exactly what he needed—to talk it through again and again and again.

Although Gunvor did her best to remain neutral, she knew her displeasure would be clear when Elin started telling David about Chibbe. Gunvor noticed how their energy, engagement, and drive was returning as they dissected all the events, so she started gathering up the dishes so she could get out of their way for a while.

"You should be able to find out who rents or owns the apartment or whatever it was where they filmed it. We should go there and find the exact address. I saw what it looked like. The camera was filming when they walked up to it as well." David seemed to have completely come out of his state of shock now and was ready to work again.

"It's probably sealed off now, what with the fire and everything," said Elin, looking thoughtful as she brushed the crumbs from the croissants together into a little mound on the table.

"Yes, but you should be able to get a decent look if you walk past down the street. It depends which door it is."

"Good idea, David. They gave a street name on the news, so it

won't be hard to find. But take your time and finish your breakfast first. I need a shower."

Gunvor walked towards the bathroom but stopped in the
doorway. "I need to ring Manuel as well. To tell him what
happened to Mikael Franzén and that Chibbe mentioned a
country house. And I need to Skype Aidan too."

46

As they drove toward the scene of Alice's murder and fire, they saw police cars blocking the entrance to the street, so they parked a block away and walked down Instrumentvägen. Further on, at the bend in the road, they saw more police cars. That end of the road didn't appear to be sealed off, but they couldn't see round the bend to the parking area where Alice had been found.

The wind was gentle and the sun was quite warm. If it weren't for all the tragic events, it would be a lovely September day. Oblivious to the awful happenings just around the corner, this part of the street maintained a sense of suburban tranquility. Gunvor was suddenly hit by thoughts of how deceptive life could sometimes appear, and how easily one's whole world could be shattered between one second and the next. Over recent years, based primarily on her own experiences, she had found it very difficult to believe that good things ever lasted. Positive emotions, good people, times in life when things seem to be going well, they could all disappear so easily; no matter how hard you tried to hold on to them. Like now. They walked down the same quiet street that just a few hours ago had witnessed someone else's final walk.

To what extent she would be missed was something Gunvor didn't yet know, but whatever dreams Alice had for her own future were now gone forever.

As they walked further, David staid at the bend in the road to keep watch. Elin and Gunvor also stopped and looked further down the left-hand side of the road at the area the police had sealed off. The easily recognizable police tape was holding the curious away from the last door of the red brick building a short distance further down the street. Just beyond that building they saw the parking area.

"This is it," David said.

"Are you sure?" Gunvor saw from his expression that he was, but she asked anyway.

"Positive. I recognize the block and the broad street with no pavements. She must have walked from here like we're doing now."

"The fire has probably not been that widespread. There is no sign of it from here. Where do you think the camera was installed, David? Above the door?"

"Definitely. But I could do with having a closer look."

David and Gunvor walked towards the sealed off area while Elin waited, checking her iPhone for news updates. When she finally started moving she was still looking at her phone, so her walk was slow and the others continue to walk ahead.

"Our paths cross again. What joy! Good morning, beautiful miss."

Elin came to an abrupt halt as she saw a man standing in front of her. He was wearing a formal suit and a hat which he politely raised in greeting to her. She realized he was the same man that bought her champagne in Riche.

"Oh, hi. Thanks for the champagne the other night." She couldn't think of anything else to say. It was just so weird that he had suddenly turned up here of all places. And now.

"The pleasure was mine, dear. All mine. And many thanks for your kiss."

Elin blushed as she remembered how much his attention had meant to her that night. So much had happened since then. But she didn't have to tell him any of that.

"Chestnut and I eagerly await your visit."

She remembered his fantasy and smiled. Although Chibbe took up most of her thoughts, it didn't hurt to flirt a little with this inoffensive man who seemed so incredibly taken by her. "I'd better start combing my hair out then. So it can hang long down my back."

"Oh, darling girl, it is already perfect. Totally, completely perfect."

Elin smiled at the man, strengthened by his undisguised admiration for her. Then she pointed towards Gunvor and David. "Sorry, I've got to go."

"My heart longs for our next meeting. Until then..." He bowed to her and strode purposefully on.

Gunvor and David were already level with the cordoned-off crime scene and scanned the wall for traces of a camera. A few curious bystanders were hanging around along the length of the sealed off area, trying to get a glimpse in through the open windows to the right of the door. They could smell the smoke now. Two police officers had been allocated the task of ensuring no one got beyond the cordon. They chatted to each other and eyed the crowd, while other plainclothes and uniformed officers moved around both inside and outside the building.

The parking area behind the building bustled with activity too. Tall, tightly-set bushes lined the outer walls and the footpath that led to the spot where Alice's body had been found. When Gunvor noticed this, she quickly understood the murderer's chosen route. There certainly wouldn't be many people walking about here after midnight, and the bushes hid the walkway from the nearby apartments. But why the killer took time to drag her body out was still a mystery. Maybe he wanted to be sure she would be found quickly. Or maybe he just didn't like the thought of her being burnt up and seeing his work destroyed. The staff at the hospital knew Alice's name, so there must have been something that identified her. The killer clearly wanted her identity known.

The killer disappeared before the camera stopped filming. But perhaps he went no further than out of the camera's line of vision, then waited. Did he see when the camera stopped? Or did he stop the camera? Or did he just go to get something to protect himself from all the blood when he dragged her out? Did Lacke stop the filming in a panic? Imagine if Lacke saw more than they had.

"Did you see that guy?" asked Elin.

The others looked at her, puzzled.

"The one who walked past you, in the suit and hat."

"We didn't notice anyone."

"Shit, how weird. It was that guy that tried to chat me up in Riche the first night. He was the reason I didn't want to go back there the next night. You remember, don't you, David?"

David smiled and nodded in answer. "Yeah, it's a small world sometimes."

Elin felt bolstered by the encounter but still thought it was a really strange coincidence. Gunvor had barely been listening as she tried to build a picture of how the body was taken from the building and into the parking area.

David was glad, as this confirmed that Elin was telling the truth about why she wanted to swap the bar for reconnaissance that other night. That she was not pitying him for being forgotten so quickly by that girl. But at the same time his pleasure made him feel a bit stupid. He realized how important it was to him that Elin saw him as serious and professional, not just someone who would get distracted by the first attractive girl that smiled at him.

They stayed where they were for a while, watching the activity at the scene of the murder and the fire, each caught up in their own thoughts. Gunvor wanted to know why the killer dragged

Alice out. Elin's mind wandered between the encounter of a few minutes ago and Chibbe. David was more practical, and it was he who broke the silence. "It's about time we found out who owns this flat or whatever it is."

"Good man. You're getting better at this." Although he tried to mask it, Gunvor couldn't resist smiling at the look of pride that was so plain to see in David's face.

"On the news, it says the property was vacant," Elin added. "I read that while I was walking behind you, but I forgot it when I bumped into that guy. Apparently, there are rumors the place was squatted."

"Squatted?"

David looked puzzled, and Elin wondered if he didn't know the word or if he was just wondering who was squatting it. She assumed the latter and replied. "Druggies maybe?"

"Oh shit, well, we won't get very far following that alternative, will we?" David sighed in exasperation.

"True. Now I really haven't a clue what to do next," said Gunvor.

"It's all screwed up. We know loads but, in a way, we know nothing. If we don't do anything, Mikael might end up in jail even though he's innocent." David was so frustrated by how far they seemed to be from solving the case regardless of how hard they'd worked.

"Unless Mikael did kill Alice, in revenge or to escape from the people who are blackmailing him." Elin didn't believe that, but she wanted to try saying it to see how the others would react. It seemed to fit with the police's theory anyway.

"What the hell do we know?" Gunvor's frustration was threatening to overwhelm her. "Go home and spend some time with your mothers and try to remember that life can be good too. I'll be in touch after I've spoken to Manuel and hopefully found out how things are going for Mikael Franzén."

47

Elin ordered a glass of rosé, despite having toyed with the idea of staying sober. It was the same bartender as Saturday, but he showed no signs of recognizing her, which in itself was no surprise considering the number of people that came here on any normal day. He filled her glass, took her money, and offered her a small bowl of roasted almonds before leaning back against the wall and concentrating on his iPhone.

Elin took a seat at the same table near the terrace where she sat that first evening with Mikael Franzén. Most of the clientele were sitting outside, but there was a steady stream of people coming in to order at the bar.

She had not told Chibbe about her plans to come to the bar. She thought there was a good chance he'd be here already. He wasn't, so she could pretend she came here to surprise him. If she'd texted him from home and he'd told her that he couldn't meet her today, it would have looked a bit strange if she'd come here anyway. And that would not have been to her advantage as it was specifically Sturehof she wanted to come to. Not just to meet Chibbe, but also to look for Lacke. If he were here now, she would have been able to get a pretty good idea of his emotional state. She would try to see whether the murder had affected him in some way or whether it was just par for the course for him. She wanted to see whether this seemed to be a one-off drama or just another day at the office. But Lacke wasn't here either, so she waited. The night was still young so she put her Plan B into action and texted Chibbe.

— *Meet me at Sturehof as fast as you can.*

He answered straight away.

— *Cool! On my way. Leaving Karlaplan in 10 minutes.*

Elin checked the subway timetable to give herself a rough idea of how long it would take for Chibbe to get there. She readied a number on her mobile that she would call just before she expected him to arrive. Each minute she waited felt like an eternity. She managed to go to the loo, order another glass of rosé and make the call before a smiling Chibbe appeared. He kissed her and went to buy a beer. He greeted the bartender with a handshake and they exchanged a few words.

When Chibbe finally sat down at her table, Elin blurted out the words. Quietly, so no one else could hear. She'd been preparing for hours, uncomfortable of where the conversation might lead. But, at the same time, she saw no alternative. Soon there would be no turning back.

"I have something to confess."

Chibbe looked at her, not knowing whether to be excited or worried.

"Or rather, I have two things to confess." Elin tried to smile at Chibbe before continuing, but she quickly realized that neither he nor she were taken in by her forced smile. "You could say there's some good news, as I see it, anyway, and some maybe not quite so good news."

Chibbe looked even more insecure when she mentioned the not quite so good news.

"I haven't lied to you, but I've kept something from you."

"You've got a boyfriend?"

She could read Chibbe's face like a book. When Elin shook her head, he breathed a short sigh of relief.

"But you're maybe going to be pretty pissed off with me anyway. It's just that… Well, I'm doing some work as a private detective."

"Are you having me on?" Chibbe grinned and seemed to think she was joking. His smile faded as he saw that Elin was serious and was slowly shaking her head. But he didn't seem as angry or suspicious as she had expected. "Wow!" he exclaimed.

Elin was confused. Chibbe seemed more impressed than pissed.

"My assignment was to follow Mikael Franzén."

Chibbe's face didn't change. He sat there, full of anticipation like a child waiting to hear the end of an exciting story.

"The guy you two beat up."

Chibbe tensed for a few seconds, then finally composed himself.

"Ah, I didn't actually know what his name was, but Alice and Daniel said he'd become obsessed with Alice and was following her. That's why I was hanging out with her a bit more than usual for a while, to protect her from that madman. Why were you watching him? Is he involved in more shit?"

"Chibbe, I want to tell you the other thing before I go on."

"Okay, tell me. That'll be the good news, will it?"

"I'm in love with you."

"Oh, love." Chibbe leaned forward to kiss her. She kissed him back for a few seconds, then pulled away.

"I need to carry on."

Chibbe still looked happy. Elin knew that what she was about to say could ruin everything between them, but at least he was aware of how she felt. She was certain that she would remember the sparkle in his eyes at this precise moment forever. Whatever happened next, she would always have this memory to savor, a memory of someone looking at her with love. It was the first time she had experienced it, which made it even sadder that the moment would presumably very soon be over.

"I don't know how to say this in a good way, so I'm just going to say it." Elin took a deep breath to calm herself, then she began, "We were watching Mikael Franzén because he was behaving strangely at home. That's how we ended up seeing you beat him up. Or, to be totally honest, it was just me that saw that. I came across you when you were coming back from the park."

Chibbe remembered and nodded.

"When my colleague tried to speak to him in the hospital, he was terrified. It was obvious he felt threatened. But we didn't know why." Elin forced the words out. She felt like it was now or never, "But when a colleague of mine was offered sex with Alice, the pieces started falling into place."

She stopped for a moment. Chibbe said nothing. He just looked at her through serious eyes.

"Your friend Lacke offered my colleague the chance to be a bit heavy-handed—as in violent—with Alice. We suspect that Lacke is involved in both prostitution and extortion. My colleague didn't want to miss the chance to reveal these crimes, so he ended up paying ten thousand for sneaking a peek on a violent sex act. But when my colleague, at Lacke's suggestion, sat in a room at the Clarion to obtain photographic evidence of these crimes being committed, all hell broke loose."

"What the hell are you talking about? What do you mean, the Clarion?" Chibbe's surprised reaction sounds convincing.

"In what looked like a live transmission, you could see a man following Alice and then attacking her as she was going into an apartment. There was a mixture of sex and violence until suddenly he stabbed her. My colleague witnessed the whole thing without being able to do anything about it because he had no idea where she was at the time of the incident. He didn't know who she was with either, as the man was wearing a mask. Please, Chibbe, tell me everything you know."

"Stop!" Chibbe was totally confused. He tried to work out in his mind what was supposed to have happened but found that was an impossible task given what he had been told. He had lost track of it all a long time ago. "Is Alice hurt?" His eyes were wild as he looked at Elin.

"She's dead, Chibbe. Murdered."

"Dead?" Chibbe repeated in astonishment.

"Yes, I'm sorry, but it's true. Haven't you seen the news today? Woman murdered in Hägerstenshamnen."

"What? In the flat?"

"You have to tell me about the apartment. David saw her being killed there. A few hours later she was found in a nearby car park. There was a fire at the flat too. Please, Chibbe, tell me what you know before you ask any more questions. Whose flat is it and what was Alice doing there?" Regardless of how hard she tried, Elin couldn't hold back the tears.

Chibbe sat silently for a while, considering how much he should reveal to her. Because he was facing the person who over the last few days had given him a hope of a relationship far better than those he had previously experienced. He decided to come clean and tell her what he knew. His voice was exhausted and dejected as he began, "Yes, sure, he sells her. As some kind of escort, as it were. But I always thought the punters were kind of nice. They were old blokes that could never get anyone as beautiful as Alice. I wasn't born yesterday. I knew she slept with them, even though it's never mentioned. But in a way she makes them a bit happier and calmer, so I don't see anything too wrong in it."

"Apart from it being illegal?" Elin smiled at him to show she was not an enemy, she wanted him to understand the situation.

"Well, yes, there is that…" Chibbe seemed slightly ashamed.

"You said that he sold her. Who is he?"

"Her brother."

"So, you're saying that her brother is the one behind it all?"

Elin's thoughts drifted to the moment she thought she saw someone in the office before Chibbe disturbed them.

"Yeah, he always has been. He has a way about him. A way of getting people to do what he wants, even me. It's basically him that I work for. And sometimes I look after her, but I've got nothing to do with this. I always said no."

"So how is it that you work for them?" Elin wondered because so far she hadn't heard him say a single positive thing about his employers. Maybe that was often the case in the real world, but his boss certainly was strange. And now she knew he was a criminal.

"Sometimes it feels as if I've always worked for him. I've known him for a long time, since we were kids basically."

Chibbe stopped. He didn't know what to say, so Elin tried to help him along.

"Tell me about them. Tell me everything you can think of. Even if you're not involved yourself, you might know something important that could help, even if it doesn't seem important to you. We want to know what happened to Alice, of course, but also what happened to Franzén. To be honest, we're doubtful that it is quite as straightforward as him becoming obsessed with her. We know he was being blackmailed over a film from what I presume was the same apartment."

Chibbe appeared not to believe what he was hearing.

"So, you're saying that ..."

"I'm saying that someone filmed Mikael assaulting Alice so they could blackmail him. This someone could be Lacke, Alice herself or her brother, or all three of them. But now someone has gone and actually killed Alice, and finding whoever did that is our priority now. That's who we want to stop first."

Chibbe had gone deathly pale, but he began to tell her everything that came to mind.

"I knew Alice at school. We were in the same class. She was always different, really wild. Her brother Daniel was a lot quieter and a bit sad. Different too, but in another way." Chibbe laughed, almost to himself, before continuing. "Like someone who was grown-up even when he was a child. He never played. He didn't have any friends. He seemed to be obsessed with money, although he had loads. He took money from lads so they could touch his sister's breasts. But on the other hand, he would pay you well if you did the things he told you to."

"What things?"

"Like steal stuff. Protect him. Scare or beat up anyone who he thought was threatening him or his position. Or, maybe someone who didn't obey his rules. You know," Chibbe shrugged.

Elin thought about Daniel and shivered. "What's your role in this anyway? With them, I mean. What do you actually do?"

"My work is to make sure that he is safe. And, that people follow the rules when they do business with him. It has just kind of carried on, almost the same as when we were kids. Daniel has lots of different things going on, but as far as Alice is concerned, me and Lacke are always there when some guy is going to check her out. Basically to just let them know that she has backup in case they get any ideas. But that is as close as I get to that side of the business, and it's closer than I'd like, to be honest."

Chibbe reached carefully across the table for her hand. She let him take it and attempted an encouraging smile though tears were slowly filling her eyes. She needed to keep him talking.

"But then maybe you know who the killer is. It must be the last one who... er... bought her, as it were."

"It was the guy at Berns. I don't know much about him, nothing at all, actually. It is mainly Lacke that arranges these things. I turn up to show a bit of muscle."

"And Mikael Franzén?"

"After what you said, I don't know what to believe anymore. But according to Lacke, he was totally obsessed with Alice. He was stalking her and being a real pain, so we gave him a slap, just as a warning."

"Who do you think was blackmailing Mikael? If you had to choose one of them from what you know about them."

"Right now, I feel like I don't know anything for sure. Lacke is certainly keen on money. But so am I, I guess, though I wouldn't kill anyone. Alice and Daniel have always been mad. It's hard to know how someone so different from yourself thinks. They've both done some weird things over the years. So you do wonder just what it is that's wrong with them. They've already got loads of money and they're not afraid to chuck it about. You can't imagine they would think it was worth their while getting mixed up in something like this."

"What? Are they like super rich?" Elin was confused. Gunvor had said something about them not having that much money, but she probably hadn't listened properly to what Gunvor was saying, so now she was unsure.

"Oh, God, yeah. And they always have been—which is good for me, of course. Daniel is happy to give me 5000 kronor to hang out in the bar with Alice for an evening. Not to mention what we got for kicking the crap out of that guy. That was enough to pay my rent and keep me in beers for a good few months."

She was concentrating on trying to ask the right questions, in the right order, and on seeing things objectively, but the more they spoke, the more relaxed she felt. She was certain that Chibbe hadn't been involved in the murder, but what bothered her was that she still hadn't gotten any proof that he hadn't been there on the night it happened. It would have felt a lot better if he had been with her instead of at the hospital, but if he got so angry there, they should hopefully remember him.

She tried to work out what else she should ask him now that he had opened up. She ought to focus on the killer. But as Chibbe didn't seem to know anything about Alice's last client, she asked him a follow-up question that could maybe help shed some light on the murder. It could also give her a better understanding of Chibbe's background too, as he, Alice, and her brother had been friends for most of their lives. "Can you tell me more about what Daniel and Alice are really like? As people, you know."

"She had the looks and he had the brains," Chibbe paused to think for a moment then continued, "The brains and the greed. He only thinks about money. Money, money, money. I don't think he's ever had a girlfriend, or boyfriend, for that matter. Mind you, he's obviously not good-looking, or nice, or particularly normal."

Elin looked at Chibbe with tenderness. She knew he was telling the truth. She felt it in her heart and saw it in the sadness in his eyes.

"I need to ring and check." He was already pressing out the number.

"Who are you calling?"

"Daniel, then Lacke. I mean, I texted and called both of them yesterday but got nothing back. It's always like that with Daniel, especially if he's out in the country with bad reception and that. But Lacke usually gets straight back to me."

Chibbe let both calls ring until they went to voicemail. He looked concerned again. "I can't understand why they aren't answering." He took Elin's hand, drew her face close to his, and looked into her eyes. "I know I'm a loser and my folks didn't have any money and I'm not particularly clever either. But we all need to make money, especially when you live in Östermalm." He tried to laugh, but it didn't ring true. "I've done so many stupid, bad things over the years to get money from Daniel. He pays too well for me to walk away. I've put the frighteners on plenty of people. But it's always been people who got involved, who chose to play the game, so to speak. I've never knowingly hurt anyone who was innocent. That guy I beat up... I was convinced he'd hurt Alice. And you, you could be a cop or a mad politician or whatever ... but I'm not going to let you go. Not unless you let me go."

He leaned forward and kissed her. But Chibbe was still restless and full of questions, so when their lips parted, he stood up again.

"I'm just going to nip up to the office for a minute. Maybe they're sitting there, in shock or something. I'll be right back."

As the door closed behind Chibbe, Elin lifted her phone, which had been in her hand throughout the conversation, and said, "Did you hear everything?"

48

W hen Gunvor got home and closed the door after dropping Elin and David off, she finally allowed the mask to fall. Her whole frame started to heave and shake, and the tears came. It was such a relief, but not knowing what to do next fueled her desperation. However much she cried, the feelings of loneliness and failure didn't go away, because she hadn't managed to understand nor stop whatever it was that had been happening.

She suddenly felt an urgent longing to be with Kjell. Above all the other overwhelming emotions was the guilt she felt when she thought of him. She worried that he would tire of her and find himself another woman who was there for him where he was whenever he needed her. Someone who at least had time to speak to him every day. So when the heaving of her shoulders and chest subsided, she called him on Skype. She was amazed at her good fortune, he was home.

She needed to see his caring eyes and loving stare so she could finally calm down. Despite it being in breach of all codes of practice and ethics, she told him everything that had happened. It wasn't as if he could affect the case from so far away. The news obviously worried him, but at least Gunvor felt better. His deep voice was like a balm to her soul, and bit by bit as the conversation progressed, her spirit climbed up and out of the dark hole into which it had fallen.

"Can't you call the police and tell them what you know? And then get yourself on a plane over here so I can cheer you up properly?"

"You know I can't do that. I let the boy get too close to the horrors. I owe him a solution. I owe him some closure so he can walk away from this with his head high. He went along with it for the money for a start. But already, after just these few days, he seems bit by the private investigator thing. He wanted it on his CV and he wanted to be able to boast to his mates about it. Manuel will never write him a reference now. That would mean admitting that we've been involved in illegal activities. If we solve the case then everything changes. But right now, the fact is that he is witness to a murder that he can't risk telling the police about without risking going down himself."

"Okay, I understand. And, I know you well enough by now to know that this would be your answer." Kjell smiled at her with a warm look in his eyes.

"Do you want me to come over there?"

Gunvor wanted nothing more but, at the same time, she didn't want to pressure him into leaving his beloved Island just to sit in her bare apartment and watch her while she thought and spoke on the phone. They had so little to go on they'd have to put all their efforts into coming up with a good way of getting hold of Lacke or of getting the right info from Chibbe. Of course, it would be great to have Kjell around if she needed to spend time in bars carrying out surveillance, especially as Aidan wasn't in town. "You know I would appreciate it. But no pressure, my love."

"I'll come. I'll text you when I've bought my ticket. Love you."

"You are fantastic, Kjell. I love you too." He broke the connection and she was alone again. But knowing Kjell would soon have his strong arms around her made it easier.

She had a quick shower and got herself ready for the evening. They had decided that she, David, and Manuel would look for Lacke. If they managed to find him, the plan was that David would make contact and ask him what had happened. Elin had promised to stay away from Chibbe until they found Lacke. Gunvor's backup plan was to force the truth out of Chibbe, but she was keeping that to herself for the time being. If they could sort things out differently, it would be best that Elin didn't give herself away—especially as Chibbe knew where she lived.

The phone rang. It was Elin, speaking quietly and sounding stressed. "Hi, Gunvor. I know you are probably going to get mad, but you have to keep quiet or you'll give me away. In a few seconds, Chibbe is going to come through this door and I'm going to ask him what's going on. I just want you to listen. He's coming now."

Gunvor was caught off guard by Elin´s call, and her last words.

"No!" she screamed. But there was nobody listening. Elin had already put her phone down. A feeling of terror rocked Gunvor. Elin was alone with Chibbe, and she had no idea where. She grabbed a pen and writing ped. Ready to jot down anything she was able to make out over the phone. What she then heard turned almost all her presumptions upside down. Suddenly, she saw the whole picture. Not because Chibbe knew everything, because it didn't appear that he did, but because he was providing the missing pieces of the jigsaw. Gunvor was now beginning to feel more proud of Elin than worried about her. She was suddenly seeing what a strong and clever young woman she was.

As she listened on the phone, Gunvor sent off an email to Manuel, adding a red flag to the message so he would see it was important.

"Did you hear everything?" Elin said eventually, as she came back on the line.

"Yes, and I have to say that despite being uncomfortable about you deciding to go it alone in such a foolhardy manner, I'm really proud of you. Listening to your conversation answered a lot of questions. One being that Chibbe doesn't appear to be involved, another that I have now seen both Alice's brother and the killer with my own eyes."

"Thanks."

Gunvor could hear that Elin was pleased from the tone of her voice. She felt a twinge of guilt about the times she had been a bit harsh on her. When they first met, she had put her heart and soul into helping her fight back against David, but lately, if she was honest, she had disapproved of her excessive drinking and her relationship with Chibbe. But Elin was just an ordinary young girl who'd suddenly fallen in love. Gunvor knew how quickly she tended to become overly focused on details of cases and their results and realized that when that happened it was easy for her to forget the human and emotional side of things.

"You took a massive risk. Far too big. Don't ever do that again! But I have to admit that I am truly grateful. Still worried though. I want to be sure that you are safe. Stay where you are and wait for David and Manuel. Where are you, by the way?"

"Sturehof. You know I love this restaurant. What is it? Do they want to speak to Chibbe? Shall I tell him they're coming?"

"Yes, do that. He's seen the killer too and he's the only one who can put us in contact with Daniel and Lacke."

"We'll wait here till they come."

Gunvor saw Manuel had replied. He was ready to collect David and go straight into town, so Gunvor sent off a quick response telling him where Elin was.

"They're on their way. But it could take about a quarter of an hour before they get to you. Just stay where you are. Do not. Repeat, do not go anywhere with Chibbe. Even if we trust him, we have to play it as safe as possible. Let's not put ourselves at risk unnecessarily."

"Okay, wait."

Then immediately she said, "Right, give you a call later, bye."

It was obvious that Elin said that to Gunvor, but the call was still on so she'd either forgotten to end the call or deliberately left her phone on. Gunvor continued to listen to try and work out which of those alternatives it was. In just a few moments Elin was talking to someone. Gunvor could hear their voices as clearly as she had heard her and Chibbe. The conversation had only just begun but Gunvor tensed.

49

As she talked to Gunvor on the phone, Elin had a good view of the room from where she was sitting. She caught sight of him the second he entered. The man from Riche whom she bumped into again just a few hours ago. He seemed surprised at first, but then he raised his hat and greeted her in a very polite and formal way. He walked in her direction, so she pretended to end the call while moving the mobile to her left hand and holding it under the table, out of sight.

"Once again, fate is on my side. Such joy," he said as he bowed slightly.

Elin smiled at him, wondering what the hell he was doing here, but she didn't really have the patience for him this time. She was fully focused on the job at hand. It might have been flattering and fun when she first met him but now coming across him twice in one day she felt he was a bit much. She didn't have the patience to humor him and put up with his weird behavior now.

"May I pull up a chair and offer the divine young lady a drink?"

He didn't wait for her reply. He sat straight down. Seconds

later, the bartender appeared from behind the bar with two glasses of champagne.

"I'm sorry but I'm with someone tonight. He'll be back any minute."

"Then I shall sit here only until he comes. I'm sure he'll be thankful that I take care of you. There you go. To your health, young miss."

She wondered what Chibbe was going to think, but surely he'd realize that she could have her own friends. The man had already sat at her table and probably wouldn't go until Chibbe got back, so she gave in and raised her glass to his toast. The champagne tasted good. She thought she noticed an aftertaste that she didn't remember from the time before, but guessed that must be because the champagne had been a different brand. It was good though, and she relaxed even after the first mouthful.

"Dear, you remember Chestnut, who I told you about before? She's out grazing just now but is so looking forward to meeting you."

The next thing she knew, he had placed his hand on hers from across the table. It didn't seem entirely appropriate, what with Chibbe on his way back and all. But, at the same time, she didn't want to cause a fuss. And it seemed like that would be the only way to get him to loosen his grip. He wasn't hurting her. His hand felt warm and tender, even though she thought he was holding her's unusually tight.

"Chestnut is longing, though not as much as I am, my princess."

The situation was, to say the least, odd. She drank a little more champagne, mainly because she didn't know what else to do, sitting here with this man who talked in riddles and looked at her with his dark, thunderous eyes.

Things gradually felt better and better. She relaxed and embraced the moment. Chibbe would be back soon and then the guy would leave her alone. Until then, why couldn't he hold her hand? In fact, he did seem like a good and loving man. He was just really odd and probably a bit lonely.

She felt a little dizzy now but imagined it was because of everything that had gone on. It was hardly surprising that her body was feeling the physical impact of being tossed between hope and despair, and love and death.

"My dear, you drink so fast, but that is fine. It suits me just fine. After all, time is short. I believe my princess knows that. It must be a sign. You want to be with me, don't you?"

Elin didn't understand what he was getting at. *Why is time short? What sign?* she thought.

She was getting more and more tired. In a way that made it hard to think. And to move. It felt as if she was turning into stone. Quickly losing control of her body.

"What have you done? Why …?" she said, as she lost control of her speech.

"Please do not worry, I will take good care of you. Everything will be as we want it."

It felt like she was falling asleep. She could see, hear, and feel what was happening but now she couldn't form any words to speak.

"My darling love, you don't seem well. Are you fine? Maybe you are cold, my little love. Look, I have something here that will warm you."

He draped a shawl around her shoulders. She thought she recognized it as being the scarf she had lost in the office. She tried to work out how that could be, but it was really hard to think straight. Fear took more and more control of her.

"Fredrik, can you help me take my fiancée to my car?" he called out. "She's not feeling well."

Her mobile slid out of her hand and onto the floor.

Gunvor heard banging and crashing over the phone and voices fading out. Then a dragging, scraping sound followed by... Nothing.

"Shit!"

She grabbed the phone and called Manuel. He responded in a second.

"Manuel. It's an emergency!" She felt like crying but put herself together. "Where are you?"

"Just passing Hornstull."

Gunvor battled to stay calm. But it was far too late. From Hornstull it would take them at least ten minutes to get to Elin. Ten long minutes. Far too long for them to keep bad things from happening.

"Just hurry. I´ll get a taxi. There´s a bartender. Fredde. Make him talk. He helped the kidnapper, probably without knowing it. But he has some information. If nothing else, put the fear of God into him if you have to. Whatever it takes to make him tell who took her. Now, go!" she yelled, slamming the phone down before she ran out the door.

"Nooo, no, no, no, no! This can't be happening. Not to Elin! I can't cope with this shit anymore. We've got to call the police." David was devastated when Manuel told him what had happened.

"We will call the police. Let's just make sure we know what's happening first. They can't help us if we don't know what we need help with."

"But what can we do, man? We haven't done anything right so far!"

"Yes, we have, David. But it's like that in this job. One step forward, two steps back. But we get there in the end." Manuel did his best to calm David, while at the same time forcing himself to believe what he was saying.

"If we can just focus on finding out where Elin is, we can call the police then. And they can help her."

They drove silently for a while before Manuel aired his thoughts.

"Gunvor thinks the guy we are looking for is the same one that last bought Alice, for want of a better expression. Gunvor and Aidan have seen him. Aidan is not around at the moment but

Gunvor knows what he looks like, so we at least have a description of who we're looking for. She can check that with the bartender when she arrives. Chibbe has seen him too, but he doesn't appear to know his name, though he should be able to ask Alice's brother. If he's left Elin to go to the office, he maybe has that information already. So if all goes well, we'll just need to call the police and give them an address where they can find Elin and bring her home again."

"How come Gunvor knows the bartender?"

"I don't know. She just said he's her contact."

"Strange that she never mentioned it. Does he know about us?"

"I've no idea, but if she has followed my guidelines then no. That's the best way of checking whether one's informer is telling the truth."

"Or whether we're doing our jobs properly. It's maybe us she doesn't trust."

"Of course, she trusts you. She presumably made contact with the bartender earlier, as she hasn't been inside Sturehof since you've been involved, has she?"

As they raced down Birger Jarlsgatan to Stureplan, Manuel said, "I'll let you off here. Find Lacke. Or Chibbe. I'll be there shortly after you. Are you okay to do this, David?"

"Course I am. I'm not giving up 'till Elin comes home."

David stepped out of the car and ran the last hundred meters to Sturehof. It was very quiet inside, just a few customers in the bar area. There were more outside on the terrace, but none that he recognized. He didn't care that people were looking at him wondering what he was doing as he walked around searching, looking at the floor. He soon found Elin's phone. Gunvor was still on the other end, and he told her that he'd found it then disconnected the call.

David rushed up to the bar and asked, "Are you Fredde?"

The bartender was puzzled, but nodded.

"What happened to the girl that was here a few minutes ago? Who did she leave with?"

"There are lots of girls here, which one do you mean?"

David couldn't tell whether Fredde was being evasive or genuinely unaware.

"The girl who was here with Chibbe." David was losing his patience

"She got sick, I think."

"You think?"

"She was drunk."

"Who did she leave with?"

"Some guy."

"Some guy?" David knew he was going a bit further than planned but couldn't stop now, "Some guy who knows your name. How could he know that?"

Fredde looked like he didn't understand what David was talking about, so he held up Elin's phone, "Surveillance."

Fredde was nonplussed, but eventually the penny dropped, "Ah, you work with Miss Marple?"

"Correct. So tell me who that guy was who took Elin. The guy you helped take her. Because I know she didn't go voluntarily."

Anger was rising in David. He couldn't for the life of him understand how the lad in front of him not only let a young girl who was clearly unwell be dragged away by a dodgy character but actually helped him carry her out. She must have been half unconscious, and she was certainly defenseless. Wasn't it part of a bartender's job to suss out these situations?

Manuel must have got lucky finding a parking space, or parked illegally, as he was suddenly standing next to David. Hearing David's aggressive tone towards Fredde, he placed a hand on his arm.

"I'll take it from here."

Before anyone managed to say anything, Chibbe walked in,

went up to the table near the bar then turned to Fredde, "Have you seen my girl?"

Manuel reacted before Fredde. He held out his hand in greeting, "Hello, we're Elin's colleagues. It would be great if you can speak to David here." He shook Chibbe's hand and guided him to a quiet corner near the entrance.

"David? Can you take over?"

David was struggling to take his eyes off Fredde, but in the end he went over to Chibbe.

"Where is Elin?' Chibbe asked. David saw no fear in his eyes, only a steady stare with maybe a touch of threatening puzzlement.

"She's gone. Someone took her. I'm sorry." Suddenly David was hit by a feeling of despair.

"What do you mean? Who? She was here with me."

"Our boss was listening in on your conversation." David paused to see Chibbe's reaction, but he just looked at David with deadly concern in his eyes now.

"She was what?"

"I think Elin wanted to prove to Gunvor that you are innocent —of Alice's murder, that is. Gunvor had suspicions that you were involved but Elin was sure you weren't so she put her phone on so Gunvor could hear everything you said."

Chibbe nodded solemnly, but David caught the hint of a smile while Chibbe heard him say that Elin was sure he wasn't involved.

"After you went, our boss spoke to Elin on the phone. Elin pretended she was finishing a call as a man approached her."

"What man? I was only gone a few minutes."

"My boss can give you more details later, but what I'm saying is that she suddenly sounded like she was passing out or something like that. She dropped her phone on the floor and now she's gone."

Chibbe stared at David with a look of murder in his eyes. Then he suddenly went up to the bar. Manuel was standing there talking to Fredde and had no time to react before Chibbe interrupted their conversation, "What the fuck happened to Elin? Why didn't you do anything? You knew she was with me. How could you let someone take her like that? Come on!" he snarled as he grabbed Fredde's collar and raised his fist, ready to strike.

Manuel held out his hand in an attempt to calm Chibbe, who pushed it away. Fredde backed away, despite still having the bar between them.

"I can't watch everybody."

"Everybody? Just how many million people have been in here tonight?" Chibbe growled sarcastically.

Suddenly, Chibbe turned away from the bar and shouted: "Did anyone see the girl who was sitting here?"

It was empty in the bar area apart from four men in their forties who shook their heads before going out to sit on the terrace. Three girls were sitting at the table on the terrace closest to them. They turned around when Chibbe shouted, sat totally still and looked at him in silence.

At that point Gunvor came in. Manuel felt relief in the midst of all the anger. Despite her being quite new to this line of work, she had seen a lot and had a lot more experience of life and work than he had. Manuel nodded discreetly in Chibbe's direction and Gunvor went straight over to him.

"Hi, my name's Gunvor and I'm a private detective. Can we talk?"

52

Elin never went fully unconscious while they were in Sturehof or en route to wherever they were going, though it felt like she was going to. In the restaurant, she had tried to keep hold of her iPhone as the two men pulled her to her feet and helped her stagger outside, but the little push they gave her as they took hold of her arms was enough to make her drop it. It slid down her leg and then beyond the reach of her hands, which she no longer had control of anyway. The sound of it hitting the floor was drowned out by their footsteps. Despite her weighing only a little more than fifty kilos, all three of them almost lost their balance for a moment when Elin swayed and nearly fell. A completely relaxed body always felt heavier, and for a second Elin felt that it was almost impossible for the two men to maneuver her.

Elin was being taken, against her will, out onto the pavement. She could see that people were staring at her with puzzled expressions. But she had lost the ability to ask for help. And then she was pushed rather too firmly into the back seat of a car and made to lie across it. Once she was in the car, she flitted in and out of consciousness, lost in the confused world of her own thoughts. At some moments she was fully conscious of what was happening. At some moments it felt like a bad dream.

At her clear moments, she was well aware that Gunvor and the others now had no chance of finding her. Elin was filled by a sense of hopelessness that threatened to outweigh her fear. All she wanted right now was to be with Chibbe. She saw her life pass like a film before her eyes, and was saddened to realize that it was a mostly grey and uninteresting mass of nothingness. A life in the shade, up until the moment Gunvor gave her the opportunity to do something completely different, a chance to be important and to be loved. And right now, the thought of never again being able to be with Chibbe was frightening her more than the thought of dying.

She suddenly thought about how she wanted to complain about not having a seatbelt on. A second later she remembered she was actually being kidnapped before sliding back into thoughts of Chibbe and forgetting about the back seat for a while.

Her body was now anaesthetized but lying crushed up in the small space was more than uncomfortable. It reminded her again of where she was. She thought it would be better if she had a cushion, but it hit her how ridiculous she was to be thinking like that when she was in the process of being abducted. Of course, she didn't want a cushion, all she wanted was to be freed so she could go back to Chibbe.

She heard how the man spoke, quietly and kind of colorfully. It took a while before his words started penetrating her confused mind.

"Darling, my dear beautiful darling. You know how much I have longed for you to come out to the country, to come home to me and the horses. I am so happy that the time has finally come, but I am obliged to confess that I am rather disappointed in you. Surely you understand that you can't play with other boys, not now that you know that there is only you and me."

Elin didn't understand. *What boys?* She was still struggling to structure her thoughts when she suddenly drifted out of consciousness again. In a dreamy haze, she felt the car stop and the engine go silent. Someone pulled her out of the car. She was so tired she couldn't even open her eyes. But it made no difference, as she could sense herself being carried. It was quite hard to tell, but she was pretty sure she was being carried by two men and they were not very coordinated, they seemed to be pulling her in different directions. It didn't hurt. It was just annoying. She wanted to sleep. A quick nap. Maybe for just a few minutes. Then when she woke up, she could work out what had happened and explain to them that she wanted to go home. Home to Chibbe.

They finally set her down on a soft bed and started taking off her clothes. She realized that wasn't a good thing, but her main discomfort was how cold the air felt on her naked skin. She wanted to ask for a blanket but couldn't work her mouth. A sense of calm gradually returned. It was still cold, but now it didn't bother her as much because someone was stroking her hair. Again and again, slowly and gently.

"Rest now, my lovely. Rest while I work, and then I promise to give you all my attention."

53

D avid was standing on his own for a moment, a little apart from the group while Gunvor steered Chibbe away from Fredde. He realized it was best to leave Manuel to speak to Fredde alone, because he was finding it extremely difficult to contain his anger, which wouldn't help anyone.

As he took a few steps away from the bar he made eye contact with one of the girls at the outside table. She had long reddish hair and looked a bit like an elf or a fairy. Not that he had ever met one, but if he had, it would've looked exactly like her. He imagined they were wondering what was going on, and at the same time he saw this as an opportunity a real private detective would never let slip. So with an attempt at a smile, he approached the girls and asked if he could sit down for a minute and talk about what happened. The girls exchanged glances before nodding.

"This is how we work. We're private investigators."

David felt his mood rapidly improve when the girls sounded impressed.

"Elin, the one who's been abducted, is a member of our team. So you can appreciate we are extremely concerned."

The girls were instantly horrified.

"Oh, my God! That's terrible," the fairy redhead said. "I had no idea that was what was happening. Then again, we were in our own little world here chatting away, I suppose."

"I didn't see anything," one of the other girls said. "Apart from when Chibbe came in and sat down with that girl. Then I turned 'round and looked, but only 'cos Bella said he was here."

The redhead—Bella—nodded in confirmation.

"So you know Chibbe?"

"Kind of. We hang out here a lot and he's always here. He tries to get off with everyone and he's a bit of a pain sometimes. Not exactly the sharpest tool in the drawer, if you know what I mean."

The others supported Bella's opinion by nodding and laughing.

"He's tried to pull all of us at one time or another," said Bella, raising her eyebrows suggestively, "you know the type."

"Yeah, I know, but did any of you notice when he left that Elin was joined by someone else?"

The other girls looked at Bella, who was the only one of them sitting in a position that had a clear view of Elin's table.

"I saw Chibbe go, and then straightaway another guy came up and sat where Chibbe had been sitting."

"What did he look like? What sort of age was he?"

"Kind of like a businessman, not the sort you'd look at twice. I don't think he was that old, but there was something about what he was wearing that made him look older than he is. More than that, it was the way he carried himself. It's hard to say, you'd think at first he was about 40, but I reckon he could have been a lot younger."

David knew exactly what she meant. But there was still one thing he was wondering about, "But, didn't you think it was odd that Elin suddenly went off with another guy when she'd just been sitting with Chibbe?"

Bella smiled at David before answering, "When you've been

hanging around these bars for a while you stop getting surprised by the things people get up to. You see all sorts sometimes. It's not exactly unusual for a girl, or a guy, to head off with more than one person the same night. There are girls who come here with one lad, shag him in the toilets and then go home with someone else. As for your friend, she seemed in a bit of a mess when she was leaving and I thought, well maybe she's upset about something and the other guy was helping her. I thought, Chibbe's been up to his usual tricks and he's dumped her, and she's got herself drunk. So it seemed good that someone was helping her. But now, of course, it's really scary to think some madman was, like, kidnapping her." Bella was really upset now, "I'm really sorry, I can't tell you anything more. I was so in my own bubble here chatting and having a laugh with my friends." Bella nodded towards the other girls, "Is there any way I can help?" Bella's eyes seemed full of both worry and hope.

"I dunno. Not that I can think of just now, anyway."

Bella reached for her bag and dug about for something. When she found it, she took hold of David's arm and pushed his sleeve up a little then wrote on the outside of his forearm, just above his hand.

"Call if you need help. Or just to tell me how it's going, I really hope you find her soon."

She let her hand rest on his after she had finished writing and put the pen away. David allowed himself to enjoy her touch for a few seconds before his worries drove him onwards, "Okay, thanks for your help."

He took her hand as he passed and squeezed it gently before going back to the others.

54

Gunvor quickly realized Chibbe wasn't going to tell her anything she didn't already know. Not because he didn't want to share what he knew, quite the contrary, but the fact was she'd already heard everything he had said to Elin earlier. He told her that his main source of income was being the heavy when Alice's brother dealt smuggled booze to bars, but that wasn't something that was of any interest to her right now. But the fact that he told Elin these things reassured Gunvor that he could be trusted. Maybe not total trust at this point, but at least he was willing to cooperate and might possibly help find Elin.

Gunvor felt she'd reached the end of the road with Chibbe, and summoned Manuel and David. Time was moving fast and they had to act before the trail dried up. "Have you got anything new we can use?"

"Fredde didn't seem to react when the man knew his name," Manuel said. "He reckons about three-quarters of the customers know his name without him knowing theirs. He knows he's no celebrity but understands how people you don't necessarily remember can sometimes remember you."

Manuel went on to say that Fredde thought there was something familiar about the man but he couldn't put his finger on it and the things he did think of were far too general to be of use in their current crisis. Regarding the actual abduction, Fredde admitted to helping the man take Elin out. Elin had drunk champagne with him and champagne can go to your head quickly. Fredde thought she was already a bit tipsy, and the champagne had taken her over the edge.

"As a bartender he's seen that happen often enough, it is nothing strange." Manuel seemed convinced by Fredde's story. Chibbe was more skeptical.

"It is still well out of order that he lets some punter he doesn't even know just carry her off."

It was entirely understandable that Chibbe was more than disappointed in Fredde, but Gunvor considered Fredde to be guilty of nothing more than a cynical and blasé attitude. Something that was hardly surprising considering what he saw every day in his line of work. Elin would certainly not be the first to go home with someone other than the man she'd come out with. And even though Gunvor was certain that wasn't the sort of thing Elin would do, Fredde didn't know her in the same way. But there was a feeling of guilt that kept chewing away at her, thinking that if she'd told Fredde that Elin worked for her, he would have protected her. "Yes, of course it is," she told Chibbe, "but now we have to focus on finding out who took her. "Did he remember what kind of car? Color? License number?" Gunvor looked at Manuel.

"Not much. A dark-colored car," he explained that he was stressed by leaving the bar and had been just concentrating on returning as quickly as possible."

"I saw you spoke to some of the other customers, David. Did they tell you anything useful?"

"The girls saw Elin leave with the man, but not much more than that. To them, the situation didn't seem threatening and they were busy with their own stuff, so they didn't take much notice."

David looked dejected. "I can't see how we're going to solve this. We don't even know whether it was some totally random guy who gave her Rohypnol just to get a shag, or whether there's a psycho serial killer on the loose."

"That's true. It feels like an almost impossible coincidence for the same person that murdered Alice to have taken Elin. But the world can be strange, and coincidences do happen. And in this case, that is the only thing we have to go on. We have to find out who Alice's brother sold her to on Sunday."

Manuel, David, and Gunvor all looked at Chibbe, who said, "He wasn't in the office and hasn't answered his phone for a few days now, which is not at all like him. I've been wondering if he's pissed off with me. That's how he normally reacts if I've upset him. The silent treatment. But I really don't know what it could be about this time."

"What were you doing for so long in the office anyway, if he wasn't there?"

"I was looking to see if there was anything that might help me find him. He goes out to their country house quite regularly, especially if something's happened. If some punter's been heavy-handed with Alice, they'd go there 'till she's okay again. I've never been there and I don't know the address."

"It's strange because I haven't managed to find any property in his name in any of the land registries—apart from the one they inherited when their parents died. And that one's not been registered in their names for years." Manuel wondered what he might have missed.

"He sorted that by giving the house away to some secret trust. Some kind of tax dodge or other."

"Ah, well that explains that then. Did you find any clues?"

"Yes, right down in the bottom of one of the drawers was an old invitation card. He must have had some sort of gathering. Not that he is at all sociable. It looked more like a business thing."

Chibbe pulled a folded piece of card from the pocket of his hoodie. He unfolded it and held it out for the others to read.

It was an invitation to a luncheon for small businesses in the catering industry, with the tasting of some new wines. The reason was irrelevant, what was important was the address. David got up, "What are we waiting for?"

"True, let's go. Are you coming?"

Manuel had turned to Chibbe who nodded eagerly, "Course I am."

*

They are on their way.
But the knight is home.
He is waiting for them.
One step ahead.
Protecting his princess.

55

E lin had either been asleep or unconscious. She couldn't be sure which. Whatever the details, she knew she'd been out of it. It's hard to remember and hard to move. And hard to open her eyes.

"So, my beauty awakens. What joy that you want to be with me again. I was beginning to wonder whether you were so tired or were merely teasing me. Let me wait for my sweet pea."

Elin heard his voice and felt a wave of panic. She couldn't remember technicalities but she knew she was in danger. It was impossible to open her eyes, however hard she tried. His laugh cut into her like a knife.

"My little lamb, can't you even look with your own eyes? Must I help you with everything?"

Then suddenly she saw. Right into one of his eyes. It was up close, and her vision was blurred. Everything was blurred at first. But his grip was tight. He was using his fingers to hold her eye open. He stayed close, staring into her eye until she focused properly and saw his face. They stared at each other for what seemed an eternity. This eternity was interrupted when she felt his other hand sliding across her stomach. His warm hand reached her breast and she remembered that she was naked. She shivered as she noticed his breathing become heavier.

"Now you are mine, only mine. From now on, you can only play with me and I promise I will only play with you. I've already done away with my last playmate."

His hand squeezed her breast. "But you have been disobedient. You've caused all sorts of problems. Now I have to tidy up after you. You understand I cannot allow him to be scampering around between your legs."

Elin's mind felt like treacle. The man took his fingers from around her eye so she closed it again. Suddenly it came back to her, how he had come into Sturehof when Chibbe had gone to the office, how he offered her champagne. After that she only recalled fragments. She was in a car. He was rambling non-stop and touching her. He held her hand and stroked her hair. He rubbed her arm gently. She remembered waking up to being caressed, but then panicking when she realized it wasn't Chibbe. It felt like it happened a few times, but that could just as easily have been her dreams.

She managed to open her eye again, this time by herself. His face was still close. She tried to move, but she failed. Her hands were stretched out above and behind her head. She didn't know if it was because she couldn't move them or because they were tied there.

"Good morning, my little sleepy love. I do believe madam appreciates a little intimate massage. You've woken up and you want more?"

He squeezed her breast harder. "You must have patience, my princess. Soon you will make me your king and I will make you my queen. Soon, soon. Oh, so soon we shall be alone. But we can surely snatch a stolen kiss right now, while no one is looking."

He leaned over her and put his tongue in Elin's mouth. All she could do was lie there and let it happen. It seemed to go on forever and all the while her breast was hurting as he squeezed it harder.

"Oh, how you excite me, my darling. I know you are longing for our first time. Just like me. I can barely hold myself back, but you understand, don't you, that I need to clear up a few things first? So we can have peace and be alone, just you and me."

56

The mood in the car was tense. Gunvor was in the front seat next to Manuel, trying to assess the likelihood that the man that held Elin was the same one who killed Alice. She thought it unlikely, as she could see nothing that connected the two incidents. But it was harder still trying to work out who else it might be, and it was even more frightening to think that Elin had not been kidnapped by Alice's killer, but by someone they know absolutely nothing about. Someone they might never find. At least they had a chance of finding Alice's murderer via her brother if he was at the country house. Hopefully, he'd be so shaken by what had happened to Alice that he would talk, even if doing so revealed his own dirty affairs.

Chibbe had been sitting staring vacantly into space as the plains surrounding Uppsala began to broaden out. He turned to David and said, "She is so lovely. The nicest girl I've ever met. She's got to be okay. If anything happens to her, I won't be able to go on."

Suddenly Chibbe looked small and lost. He fiddled with a thread from his hoodie, winding it tight around his finger. "Has she talked about me? Has she said anything, anything at all?" A wave of uncertainty passed through him. Reality had caught up with him, reminding him of the unreal situation that had developed. How did he find himself sitting in a car full of strangers looking for a detective called Elin with whom he was rapidly falling in love?

"She doesn't say much. We're both quite shy really." David surprised himself with his openness, though it felt good to try and bond with Chibbe. "We've become good friends, though. As good as you can be when you haven't known someone very long. But in our job, it's crucial that you trust each other. And I trust Elin, even though I don't know everything about her. And yes, I know she likes you. She really wanted you not to be involved. That's why she tried to persuade you to go 'round to her place last night, even though we all told her to keep her distance. She knew something bad was going on. Do you know I saw everything? The murder?"

David's voice trembled suddenly. Chibbe looked wide-eyed at him and patted him on the arm, realizing that things were tough for him too. Gunvor and Manuel were silent in the front, listening to the conversation in the back.

"It was a weird evening," Chibbe said. "I wanted to go 'round to Elin's, but I had no idea that shit was going on. I don't understand what the hell they were up to. Filming his sister? How sick is that? Daniel will do anything for money. He's got absolutely no scruples."

"Have you?" Gunvor couldn't resist butting into the conversation. She was concerned that the question might seem too blunt and judgmental, but at the same time she wanted Chibbe to understand that her sympathies lay with Elin. Elin would always be her priority— as long as she remained alive.

Chibbe gave a long sigh before replying, "No, you're right. I've done a lot of bad things over the years, but I was never involved in anything that went on at that apartment. I swear. And yesterday I was at the hospital."

"You could almost think someone was trying to frame you and

make sure you don't have an alibi. Someone asking after their mum is forgotten pretty quickly. Sometimes you being big and aggressive can come in useful." Gunvor offered Chibbe a wry smile in the rearview mirror.

"The question is, who would want to stitch me up? And why?"

Chibbe's words offered food for thought and the group fell silent. The car turned onto a narrow dirt road. They peered into the late summer evening, scanning the prickly overgrown bushes that were illuminated by the car's headlights.

*

I have bided my time.
Spared myself for the right one.
Waited for her to come.
Now she is here.
I no longer have need of any other.
From now on it is only you and me, my princess.

57

T ime passed in the strangest of ways. Elin had no idea how long she had been lying on her back staring at the crystal chandelier. It could have been a few minutes or a few hours, because there was nothing to measure time against. It was silent and still there in the room with nothing to focus on, apart from the well-polished pieces of glass that made up the chandelier. Then suddenly she heard agitated voices.

"What the hell is wrong with you? Your sister's been killed. The police could turn up any minute. What made you come up with the idea of kidnapping Chibbe's girlfriend, of all people, in the middle of all this? How's that going to help anything? You're fucking mad!"

The door swung open and banged against the wall. The voices came nearer. It was hard for Elin to direct her gaze but she managed to see that it was Lacke coming in with the man who kidnapped her at his heels. "What the fuck?" Lacke shouted in shock when he saw her. "She's naked! What have you done?" he screamed.

The man hurriedly laid a blanket over her. Lacke's eyes met

Elin's as he moved towards her. "I'm so sorry about this," he said. "You shouldn't be here."

The other man quickly stood between them and raised a warning finger to Lacke.

"Lennart!" The man's voice was harsh. "Which one of us gives the other lots of money to carry out these piss-easy little jobs?"

"This isn't a job. This is a kidnapping."

"As opposed to all your other honest and diligent work?" Despite her confused state, she detected the distaste in his voice. "My dear Lennart, you are up to your neck in this mess, so you can stop playing the hero. End of discussion. Now if you'd be so kind as to do as I say, go and park your car behind the stable. We'll soon be having visitors."

Lacke looked at her with sadness in his eyes before disappearing from her line of vision. Instead of following him out, the other man approached Elin and removed the blanket covering her.

"He doesn't understand that you will do anything for me. He doesn't realize that you and I are together. But don't worry, very soon he won't be able to bother us. Him or anyone else." Then he leaned over her and began to suck on one of her nipples.

Elin could hear him moaning, then he raised his head and looked at her again, "You and me, my princess. You and me."

He laid the blanket back over her, switched off the lights, and closed the door behind him as he left.

58

It took a while for them to wind their way up to Daniel's house, although it looked so close on the Sat Nav. The dirt road was narrow and bumpy and the September evening had gotten much darker. There were no street lights and no houses nearby to give off any light. They couldn't make out any roads leading off the one they were on either, so it was almost certainly some sort of private road.

The Sat Nav lost its signal after a while, which made them unsure whether they'd taken the right road. The one they were on appeared to keep on going, and they hadn't come to any places wide enough to turn around in, so they kept going. Suddenly they saw lights coming from the windows of a building a bit further on. Even from this distance they could see that it was a large building. Gunvor looked at her watch, which told her they had now been driving along this same dirt road for almost 15 minutes. She glanced at the speedometer, which said they were going at 40 kilometers per hour, so by her reckoning this must be the house.

Gunvor thought she saw a movement in one of the windows on the ground floor as they drove onto the driveway and into the well-maintained grounds of the house, which was a large, yellow stone building on two floors. *A house with attitude*, thought Gunvor. The imposing main building appeared to share its air of class with the smaller buildings that surrounded it, which Gunvor assumed were stables. She was not an expert, but she imagined that the stables were in the same style as the main house. Not that architecture mattered right now, but she just wanted to feel some sort of control over pretty much anything. The need to ground herself was so strong in her now that not knowing the history of the buildings was almost a physical ache. Gunvor felt a sudden wave of regret over ever having gotten involved in the private detective business. She wanted to be safe on the island with Kjell. Manuel parked the car as far away as possible from the main building.

There was another car parked on the other side of the graveled space in front of the house, just in front of the stone path leading up to the elegant steps that climbed to the front door. And not just any old car either, it was an S-type Jaguar. In this light it was hard to say what color it was, but Gunvor guessed dark grey. She'd never been interested in cars, apart from the eternally elegant Jaguar. During her marriage she'd owned a few, including an S-type, but after the divorce she left that world behind. Seeing Daniel's expensive car now it occurred to her that it was not exactly the ideal car for driving the last bit of the journey out here. That car would be far happier on a motorway, unhindered by restrictions.

They didn't have time to discuss what they were going to do next in any great detail. Even Manuel, who was an old hand in the game, had never been in a situation quite like this. Gunvor felt smaller and more afraid when she heard the uncertainty in Manuel's voice, even though he was trying his best to take control of the situation.

"Okay, the road ends here so this must be the house," Manuel turned his head and looked towards the back seat. "And now it's time for you, Chibbe. Do you want someone to go in with you?"

"No, I reckon it's best if I go in alone. Daniel is weird. The chances are he's already annoyed because someone's on his land. You know what I mean? Even me, and I've known Daniel most of my life. If you want something from him, it has to be on his terms."

"Okay, you know best. Good luck."

Gunvor rolled down the window to let in some fresh air. They heard the gentle crunch of the small stones under Chibbe's black sneakers as he made his way across the drive.

"Let's hope he bloody knows something," David said. The others responded to him with murmurs.

～

CHIBBE STOOD motionless for a moment then stepped in. They couldn't tell if someone let him in or if he had opened the door himself. He came back out a few minutes later looking clearly dejected.

"Shit," David said. Gunvor tried to maintain her spirits but shared exactly the same feeling David had just expressed. Chibbe went into the car and looked like he was extremely pissed.

Chibbe took a deep breath and said, "Daniel has been trying to get hold of the bastard who was with Alice that night, but he seems to have just vanished. And it seems the person he said he was doesn't actually exist. He used false ID and paid for everything in cash. Well, I saw that much myself."

"So did I. We were watching you that night. Did he say anything about the flat?"

"No. I asked him why he hadn't told me they had cameras there and all he said was he hadn't wanted to get me involved in that side of things. He said he knew I wouldn't like it. Having the

cameras was definitely something new. But I don't get it. You
want to make money, but you have some limits, don't you?"

"But he must know something about that guy. Where did he
meet him, for example?" Gunvor had turned around and was now
looking at Chibbe.

"I don't know, to be honest. I always assumed that he put
adverts up somewhere or ran dodgy websites or something. Now
and again he's asked me to put the word about, when I'm talking
to people in the bars and that. But I've always said no."

"Is he doing anything now to find this man, or has he
given up?"

"I don't know. He looked really down. That's why he came
here, he said. To be on his own, to grieve in peace."

"I'm not going to accept that. We must be able to get something more out of him. I'm going in." Gunvor released her
seatbelt.

"That won't work. He'll never admit he's involved in prostitution or extorsion, let alone murder."

"I'll think of something."

Gunvor got out of the car and Manuel followed suit, "I'm
coming with you."

Nobody protested. Definitely not Gunvor, who was more than
happy to not have to go in alone.

When the door opened, Gunvor immediately recognized the
man she saw at Berns. As Chibbe said, Daniel indeed looked
depressed. He didn't ask who they were. Instead he asked them to
follow him into the drawing room. Gunvor guessed Chibbe must
have told him about them.

"Please, sit down," he said in all politeness.

Gunvor and Manuel sat down, each in a green velvet Rococo
chair. Daniel walked up to a Drinks cabinet in the form of a globe
positioned centrally in the large room. He took his time to pour
two measures of whisky. Manuel and Gunvor said nothing, they

just waited for Daniel to be ready. Daniel handed each of them a finely cut heavy-bottomed glass, then stood facing them and raised his own.

"We don't know each other but I hope you will share a solemn toast with me. To the memory of Alice."

He lifted his glass and drank. Manuel and Gunvor raised theirs but Gunvor only pretended to drink. She was on high alert to ingesting liquids after what she suspected had happened to Elin at the restaurant. Besides, she had a particular dislike for whisky and also wanted to ensure there was nothing in her system that might impair her thought processes. She saw Manuel take a long drink from his glass. She thought it was probably a good idea that at least one of them met Daniel's need to indulge in a proper toast, but noted that it would be her that'd have to drive them home.

Daniel lowered his glass and looked at them in a way that suggested they should explain why they were here. So Gunvor began, "A very close friend of ours has been taken away against her will. The man who took her may well be the same person you came into contact with. The man who committed those terrible crimes against Alice. I appreciate that circumstances could make it difficult for you to go to the police. We haven't been in touch with the police either. Yet. All we need is enough information to have him put away for what he has done to Elin. In that way you would have your retribution, if that is something you would like, without needing to be involved."

Even though they were in such an unbearable situation, not knowing where Elin was or how she was, Gunvor relaxed a little. Now, with the chance to talk to a witness, she was on more familiar territory. Gaining people's trust and making them want to speak to her had always been one of her main strengths. At last she could do something that might make a difference.

"I don't know what to say. I am feeling so utterly devastated. My heart and soul are crushed beyond repair," Daniel wiped his brow.

For a moment Gunvor thought he was trying to mask a smile, but she assumed it must have been a grimace as he was on the verge of tears. "Just tell us everything you know about that man and we can assess whether there is something we can use to help us find him," she said.

"All the information he gave was false. And it's impossible to trace him through his payment for Alice's services." Daniel took a deep breath before continuing, "I can't cope with this. I just want to be with my fiancée."

Gunvor froze. Suddenly she recognized the voice. She stared at the man who had now lowered his hand and was smiling at her. She turned to Manuel, who fell from his chair onto the floor.

"Oops," Daniel's voice sounded terrifyingly cheerful, "Lennart, please come and help."

Gunvor stood up and bolted for the door. She was stopped cold by Lacke who had come running in from the hall and grabbed her hard, nearly knocking her to the floor. Before she had time to resist Daniel was holding a pistol to her head.

"Now calm down, little lady," he said.

Lacke loosened his grip but kept a strong hand around her neck. Daniel had a broad smile across his face, "I must apologize for not coming up with a new method of subduing your good friend." He nodded towards Manuel, "A tad unimaginative, I know. But your visit was arranged a little hastily, so I was forced to use the same trick I used with little miss Elin. But I do promise to be more imaginative when it comes to your turn. And it will be very soon."

As he spoke, Daniel took Gunvor's mobile from her jacket pocket and asked Lacke to take care of their guest. He tied her hands behind her back and pushed her into an adjoining room at the rear of the house. Daniel followed close behind. Gunvor was almost paralyzed with fear, but was suddenly struck by a glimmer of relief as she saw Elin lying on the bed. Elin stared at her through glazed eyes. Gunvor now understood what Daniel was talking about. He must have drugged them both.

Lacke pushed Gunvor onto the bed next to Elin and tied her legs up as well. Then he dragged Manuel in and left him lying in the middle of the floor. The two men left the room, switched off the light, and closed the door as they left the room.

59

Watching Gunvor and Manuel walk across the driveway, David saw a curtain twitch in one of the unlit rooms to the left of the main door.

"Did you see that?"

"What?" Chibbe hadn't noticed anything.

"There's someone in that window, just left of the door."

"Do you think so? But there's only Daniel in there."

"Just watch for a second," David said.

They both sat silently looking at the dark window, but they didn't see anything.

"Shit, that's weird. I honestly saw something."

"Probably just the wind. God, it is creepy here, isn't it? Like something out of a horror film."

"Yeah. Imagine living out here on your own. Shit."

"I know. I'm a total city boy."

"I'm more of a suburban kid. I've never been out in Östermalm before. Not even to the city, really."

Chibbe looked surprised, "All my friends hang out at Sturehof. It's more because of that than just because it's Östermalm."

"Pity a few of your friends weren't there tonight then. And saw what happened to Elin."

"No. And I was so pissed off with Fredde. I really thought I could trust him."

David pounced, "You know Fredde?"

"I've known him for years. He's an old schoolmate."

"Oh, shit!" The realization spun around David's head. If Fredde was an old schoolmate of Chibbe's, then he went to school with Alice too. So he'd been lying the whole time. A jolt of adrenaline shot through David's body when he realized that Fredde might be in collusion with the killer—the killer who now had Elin. And they were sitting here in the middle of nowhere unable to do anything.

"I've got to speak to Gunvor. Now," David said as he turned towards the house.

"What's going on?" Chibbe couldn't work out David's sudden reaction.

But David was already on his way. Chibbe jumped out of the car and followed right behind him. On David's instructions, the pair moved as quietly as they could. David wanted to check out the situation in the house before he went barging in. They didn't want to risk interrupting Gunvor's talk with the grieving brother, which would hopefully give them some more information. But it was hard to walk in silence on gravel. Walking past the Jaguar, David used the car's bonnet for support.

"That's still warm," David whispered to Chibbe. "Did he say anything about how long he'd been here?" Chibbe shook his head in response.

As they reached the stone pathway leading up to the front door, David indicated a way in over the pristine lawn surrounding the house. He gestured to Chibbe, who was a good bit taller, to try and get a look through the window to check things out.

"See if they're in the middle of a conversation and if Daniel is talking. If he is, we'll wait a bit."

Chibbe carefully approached the window and stood on tiptoes. "What ...?"

"What is it?"

"There's only Daniel there. Where are the others?"

David got his phone to call Gunvor and find out.

"Shit. No signal."

Chibbe got his mobile out of his pocket.

"Me neither. That's what it's like out here. We have to call on the landline when Daniel's here. Ridiculous really. It's not exactly that far from civilization."

"Okay, that's how it is. Can you look in again? Look around and see if you can see anything strange or different. Or if there's any sign of Gunvor and Manuel."

Chibbe looked in again and then looked at David. "It's crazy. He's just sitting there, totally calm, staring at the wall. Shall I go in and check?"

"I don't know. Something's happened. Maybe we should get the car and drive a bit further away so we can get a signal and call Gunvor."

"No, fuck that. I'll go in and ask Daniel. If he tries anything, I'm at least twice his size."

"But there might be someone else in there."

"I don't think so. I reckon you were just seeing things."

Chibbe went up to the door and quietly checked to see if it was open. *Nice,* he thought as he pulled it open and walked in. David was close behind him, but stopped for a moment as Chibbe moved on through a door on the right. He had spotted a telephone on a dresser in the wide hall.

60

G unvor got used to the darkness quite quickly. Her eyes had
always been good in the dark. And that was at least one
ability that age had yet to weaken. She spoke to Elin as quietly,
calmly, and slowly as she could, all the while desperately hoping
that Elin was conscious enough to understand what was
happening.

"We're here now. Chibbe's with us. He and David are coming
to help us."

Gunvor was far from convinced herself, but she saw no alternative other than to hope they were coming, while at the same
time trying to free herself. She managed to get into a sitting position and then onto her knees beside Manuel. Her movements had
not exactly been pain-free, but the adrenaline helped her ignore
the aches and twinges she was feeling in what seemed like all of
her joints and muscles. She sat with her back against Manuel's
unconscious body and used her hands to feel backward towards
his leg. She found the knife inside a small leather sheath attached
to his ankle. For once she was pleased about his habit of not only
carrying concealed weapons but also telling her all about them.

Once she'd managed to roll his trouser leg up and take out the knife the rest was quite straightforward.

"Now I'll sneak out and go and get help. I'll be back soon. I'll leave the light off so they don't suspect anything."

Despite the darkness, she could see that Elin was looking at her, just staring and making no reaction. Her gaze seemed so apathetic that it was hard to work out if she was awake or not. To be safe, Gunvor felt her neck for a pulse. There was time for a shudder of fear to pass through her before she eventually found the faint yet steady heartbeat. For a moment she was frozen by a brutal image of Elin lying dead beside her. Before she went to the window to plan her way out, she rearranged the blanket covering Elin and kissed her maternally on the cheek.

"I'll be back soon. I promise."

61

Daniel sat smiling at Chibbe as he rushed into the room, "Christoffer. To what do I owe this honor?"

"What have you done with them?"

"The question is rather what you got them into in the first place. I can't recall giving you permission to bring your new friends here."

Chibbe was thrown by Daniel's frank admission that he had done something to Gunvor and Manuel.

"I certainly don't recall inviting you here either, my dear Christoffer." Daniel frowned at Chibbe, then his eyes moved to something behind him. "Ahhh, another guest. Well, I never! Look how popular I am today." Chibbe spun around and caught his breath when he saw Lacke holding David firmly by the neck with one hand and pointing a revolver to the side of his head with the other. He turned back to face Daniel and found that he was now holding a gun too and realized that all four of them had walked into a trap.

"What the hell ..." Chibbe's shocked eyes flashed from Lacke to Daniel and back.

"I'm sorry," Lacke looked at Chibbe a little desperately.

"Oh Lennart, pull yourself together, stupid boy, Daniel chided. We don't want you standing here feeling all remorseful. You never showed any regret before, when you led Christoffer along and made more money than him. On the contrary, I believe you have thoroughly adored being involved in bigger things than Christoffer has ever come close to. The only thing that's ever bothered you is that you weren't able to tell him about it. You've never been able to brag about it like the little child you are."

"I can't see why we have to do this, Chibbe's okay."

Chibbe was more than unhappy with the situation. But whichever way he looked at it, there was a gun pointed at David's head. And even if Lacke were to lower it, Daniel was still armed.

"This is insubordination beyond belief. I will not tolerate it."

"But they want the same as us, to find whoever killed Alice." Lacke was more than a little confused by the last few hours' events.

"You will stay out of matters that are beyond your comprehension."

Despite the way Daniel had always suggested Chibbe was not very smart, the pieces suddenly fell into place.

"It was you..."

62

The window opened easily, without creaking. It wasn't too high up either, so Gunvor sat on the window ledge and dropped down onto the lawn at the back of the house. She suppressed a cry of pain and leaned against the wall to rub the aches from her knees. This area was in total darkness. She moved silently along the rear wall, looking carefully around the corner before creeping along the side wall in the shadows until she came to the edge of the front face of the house. She saw their car and was surprised because it looked empty. She hesitated before walking out onto the gravel, then removed her shoes and headed for the car. The stones were hard and sharp underfoot, but the pain hadn't stopped her yet and it wouldn't now. She moved as quickly and silently as she could over the graveled turning circle. She now saw for certain that the car was empty. She couldn't imagine where everyone could have gone, so she headed back to the house to look for an explanation. Then she saw that there were more people in the room.

63

Chibbe was staring at Daniel and David sensed he was on the verge of snapping. With a wild look in his eyes Chibbe walked towards Daniel, who retreated a step and cocked the pistol as he pointed it at Chibbe.

"Not another step. Stay where you are!"

Chibbe ignored the warning and took a further step towards Daniel, "Why? Won't it be easier to hit me if I come closer? 'Cos it looks like you're planning to shoot me."

"I'm serious. Stay where you are."

Chibbe stopped and stood still, glaring at Daniel, "Are you the one who's behind all this? Is it you that's got Elin?"

Daniel said nothing but David shuddered at the smile that suddenly wiped away the fearful look he had a moment ago. He looked like a real psycho.

"What have you done with her? Where is she?"

Then Chibbe noticed the door to the inner room and set off towards it. Things happened very quickly. There was a shot and Chibbe fell. Lacke jumped back in shock and his grip on David's neck loosened slightly. David seized his chance. He twisted a little then swung his elbow into Lacke's throat. Lacke choked desperately for breath, and David pushed him away and ran for his life. The hall door was closed, but he managed to get through it and the outer door beyond it as he heard another shot ring out.

64

Gunvor had no problem seeing what was happening inside the house even though she was still some distance from the window. She realized Daniel and Chibbe were in there. Then to her dismay she saw that David and Lacke were there too and that Lacke was holding a gun to David's head. Suddenly Chibbe turned and rushed away. She heard a pistol shot and Chibbe went down. At first, Gunvor froze but came to the instant she saw David come running out.

"David!" She called.

David covered part of the driveway before he stopped. He looked at Gunvor with an air of total incomprehension. Gunvor's relief at seeing him in one piece lasted only seconds as Lacke appeared, racing towards them with his gun pointed at David. He was startled at the sight of Gunvor. He ran between Gunvor and David, turning and pointing the gun at each of them in turn.

"You stupid bastards!" Lacke shouted. "Why did you come here? Why couldn't you just let things be?"

"Don't you see what you've got into?" Gunvor said. "I know you aren't a murderer, but you know that Daniel is, don't you? It must have been him that killed Alice and now he's planning to do the same to us and Elin. You don't think he'll spare you, do you?"

Gunvor walked slowly towards Lacke, all the while trying to find a suitably trusting and confident tone of voice.

"Stay where you are," Lacke's voice was shaking slightly. She tried to convince herself that he wouldn't shoot. Well aware that this was probably their only chance, she carried on walking slowly but steadily towards him.

"We will tell the police that you weren't involved in the murder. That it was Daniel who killed Alice and Chibbe and that you didn't know anything about it."

"No way am I going back inside again. I don't give a rat's ass about you, I'm gonna take my money and go. I mean it. Stop!"

But Gunvor wasn't stopping. Lacke was stressed and didn't know who he should point the gun at. Gunvor was getting very close but it seemed like he still saw David as his biggest threat. An underestimation most people would make.

"Stop! I'm gonna shoot you, bitch! You, too, punk!" he said as he then pointed the gun at David.

David yelled "No!" and took a step backward.

When Gunvor saw Lacke was momentarily distracted with David, she hurled herself forward and pushed Lacke. Hard. With all her might. Lacke fell backward and fired a shot, but missed Gunvor by a hair. In an instant, he regained his balance and made a lunge for Gunvor, but she was ready. He took her underarm to throw her to the ground, but she quickly sidestepped his move and redirected his strength to achieve a yonkyo move. Ever since she had learned the yonkyo it had been her favorite aikido move. It had taken her hundreds of hours of practice in the dojo to learn how to effectively invert the hold, but once she'd gotten it, it never mattered how strong her opponents were, she always took them down. Then, in an instant, she would lock their arm against her leg. So, in a stunning blur of instinctive reaction, Gunvor flew into violent action.

It happened so quickly that David hardly had time to react. He saw Gunvor throw herself forward and started to move himself. Hearing the shot, he instinctively stopped. In what seemed like a split-second later, Lacke was on the ground and Gunvor was holding him there, apparently with no effort whatsoever.

"Wow!"

David couldn't believe his eyes when Gunvor threw Lacke to the ground in one remarkable, fluid motion as Lacke was twice her size and half her age. But he remained alert enough to rush forward and recover the gun when Lacke dropped it.

"Can you hold him? I know how to use a gun so it's best if I go inside," Gunvor gasped.

After what he had just seen, David was ready to believe anything Gunvor said, so he took over the hold on Lacke and handed her the gun. It didn't actually require any strength at all to hold Lacke immobile in the aikido hold Gunvor had him in. He was lying face down on the gravel with his arm stretched out and twisted behind his back, locked against David's leg. Gunvor showed him how to press Lacke's hand painfully if he started playing up. Even how to break his wrist if it became necessary. David nodded his understanding and whispered to her to be careful. Gunvor began moving towards the house and Lacke wasted no time at all before starting to bargain with David.

"Please let me go. I can help you stop this madness. This time he's gone way too far. Give me a chance."

"Just a few minutes ago we asked you to help and you said no. You had your chance and didn't take it."

"Come on, I swear," Lacke was desperate and tried to worm out of the hold, but David instantly tightened the hold as Gunvor had instructed and Lacke got nowhere.

"Too late," David was managing to extract some pleasure from the situation despite being worried about events in the house. The thought of letting Lacke run so he could go and help Gunvor was tempting, but he knew Gunvor wouldn't be happy, so he maintained his steel grip on his helpless victim.

65

Battered and bruised, Gunvor reentered the house. She knew Daniel was fully armed and assumed that he knew she was on her way in and was waiting for her. But what choice did she have? If she didn't go in now it might be too late for Elin and Manuel.

There was an eerie silence in the house, apart from a crackling noise in the hall. It was the telephone, lying off the hook, as if someone left it in the middle of a call. Gunvor thought it odd, but it wasn't anything she had time to sort out for now. She peered into the living room where she and Manuel were offered whisky. She slowly and quietly slipped up to the door and made a quick peek into the room to check whether Daniel was lying in wait in some corner of the room. He wasn't. The room was clear, so she went in.

A pistol was lying on a small table standing against one wall, near the door to the inner room. Gunvor hoped this meant Daniel was unarmed, but she certainly wasn't going to take that for granted. The guy was acting like an unhinged lunatic, so it was unlikely he would have left anything to chance—unless he had full confidence in Lacke being able to manage the rest of the situation.

Chibbe was lying motionless on the floor in a pool of blood. It was hard to be sure just how seriously wounded he was. His hoodie was dark, and it was impossible to see where he'd been hit.

To her relief, Gunvor saw that his eyes were open, and they met hers. He pointed his finger towards the inner room. She nodded. Thank God Chibbe was alive, at least, although he looked to be in urgent need of help. She sent up a silent prayer and motioned him to lie still on the floor and play dead, as he could be seen from the inner room.

She was still barefoot, so she could move more or less silently around the room. She took one step at a time. Adrenaline filled her every tissue. Her heart was pounding like a drum inside her chest. It seemed to her that people outside the house could hear it. She struggled to keep her breathing quiet, which was not easy as she was still trying to catch her breath from the fight outside. Besides all this, she was terrified she was about to walk into a trap. Every nerve on her tingled with anticipation as she walked with ghostlike steps towards the next room. After what seemed an eternity, she made it to the room where Elin and Manuel were being held.

She tried to compose herself before she appeared in the doorway. Her pistol was raised, ready to fire, while she focused on keeping her breathing calm and steady. She went in.

Daniel was sitting on the bed with Elin's head on his lap. In his hand was a huge hunting knife. He held it with both hands on the hilt with the point of its blade resting on Elin's chest, above her heart. Daniel didn't look up when Gunvor stepped over the threshold, he just carried on staring at Elin. Elin looked to be a little more alert than earlier, and Gunvor could see her trying to turn her head. But Daniel turned it back again so all she could see was his face.

"My sweet love, we don't have time for others. We must devote ourselves to each other now. When you are better, we shall ride together. You shall ride Chestnut in your long, white dress. Just like we said that first time we met. Do you remember? A beautiful memory. Our first shared memory."

"It's over now, Daniel," Gunvor commanded. "Drop the knife, or I'll shoot to kill."

He still didn't look at her, "It is over when I say it is over. As always, it is I who will dictate the rules. And I will never let her go. She is my princess and I am going to make her my queen."

"Isn't that enough now?"

Holding her pistol in a two-handed grip, Gunvor was braced, aimed, and ready to fire. But she wasn't sure if she could shoot to kill the bastard. Of course, if he twitched a muscle with either knife hand, she would absolutely do it. But her hands were shaking so much she was afraid she would probably miss anyway. She imagined that Daniel also realized that she wouldn't shoot, whatever happened. They were in a deadlock.

66

L acke stopped trying to bargain with David when they heard a shot ring out inside the house. David's immediate instinct was to run in, but he didn't. Gunvor had trusted him and he was determined not to let her down. And, he wasn't going to screw this up if his life depended on it. If she had the upper hand inside then he'd doing the right thing in keeping Lacke down. If she didn't, they were doomed anyway. And in that case, they'd done everything they could and he would hold his position as long as he could. And if they got lucky, help would soon be there.

"Daniel, Daniel! Hey!" Lacke shouted out as well as his circumstances allowed, causing David to press his arm down even harder, almost to the breaking point.

"Shut it," Daniel breathed.

When Lacke stopped shouting, David became aware of just how silent it was. Then he heard a car in the distance, getting gradually louder. It must be coming along the dirt road to the house. Soon David saw the car's headlights and seconds later it drove at speed into the grounds. It braked hard a short distance away from them, spraying them with gravel. A man stepped out.

David saw straightaway who it was "Just what the hell are you doing here?" he exclaimed.

David struggled to stay calm, even though he suddenly understood the big picture. He felt an incandescent rage begin to boil up inside himself.

"Never you mind, just let Lacke go."

Fredde was looking menacing as he approached, but before he had gone a few steps they heard police sirens. David still didn't know what had happened inside the house, but the sound of the police cars was a huge relief. Fredde turned on his heels and ran towards the rear of the house. David didn't know where he was going, but assumed he knew the place and thought his best escape route was that way.

"Fredde!" pleaded Lacke in desperation.

"Great friends you've got," For less than a split-second David actually felt a shred of sympathy for Lacke.

The household grounds were soon full of police cars and policemen.

As a trooper ran up to David with his gun raised, he yelled, "It was me that called." As he did so, he released Lacke and put his hands up in the air, hoping they wouldn't see him as a threat.

67

Gunvor heard Chibbe moving behind her. She guessed he felt a bit stronger or safer now and was trying to get himself into a more comfortable position. She quickly shut out all thoughts of Chibbe and focused entirely on Daniel, "Can't you understand that it's over? Let her go, she's done you no harm."

"She is mine."

"No, she's mine."

Suddenly Chibbe staggered into the room. In his hand was the pistol Daniel had shot him with. Before anyone had time to react, Chibbe shot Daniel in the head. Daniel's head snapped backward and blood sprayed the wall behind him. Then he slumped down over Elin's shivering body. Gunvor lurched forward and managed to deflect the knife away from Elin's chest as Daniel dropped forward. Blood from his shattered head ran straight into Elin's face. Gunvor heard Chibbe collapse as she struggled to get Elin off Daniel's lap. Once she had succeeded with this, she maneuvered Elin into a sitting position and sat next to her with her arms around her. Elin was groaning and was now able to turn her head and take in the devastation around her. She started to sob when she saw Chibbe lying motionless on the floor. Gunvor pulled her closer into her and they both remained that way, unable to do anything else.

They sat there for a good while before they heard the sirens. The sound got nearer and nearer and eventually Gunvor saw the policewoman burst into the room. It was over, yet it wasn't. She receded into herself, reeling from a particularly strong anxiety attack. Elin was checked for injuries and carried out by the ambulance crew, but Gunvor was incapable of going with her.

After a few minutes a police officer sat down next to her and helped her to stop hyperventilating. When she finally started to cry, it was a release. She cried and cried on the comforting shoulder of the officer.

When she had calmed down a little, she found out that Elin, Chibbe, and Manuel were being taken to Akademiska hospital. None of them were in life-threatening condition. Lacke was in custody and was being transported straight to Kronoberg. Gunvor felt grateful and relieved, although her body was still heaving from the anxiety attack.

The female police officer walked outside with her. David was there, standing talking to another police officer. He looked small and tired, yet Gunvor saw the man he was well on his way to becoming. A courageous man who knew the difference between right and wrong and who would do the right thing whatever it took, even if that meant pursuing a crazed killer. It occurred to her David was a man she hadn't known even a short week ago.

The officer patted David on the shoulder and, as Gunvor got nearer, she heard what the policeman was saying to him. "What you did was admirable. Thanks to you leaving the line open we were able to hear the gunshot and locate you. You have most certainly saved lives today."

David beamed at Gunvor when she interrupted their conversation.

"You called the police?" Suddenly Gunvor made the connection. She had noticed the telephone was off the hook and could hear interference crackling from the receiver. She hadn't given it any more thought while she was trying to creep up on Daniel.

"David, we are so lucky to have you with us!" Gunvor meant what she said and David knew she did when he saw the tears in her eyes.

"I'm just happy I was able to do something. And anyway, you didn't do so bad yourself, sorting Lacke out like you did. That was awesome!"

David and Gunvor embraced each other before they were each taken away to the precinct station in a police car for questioning.

68

The next evening they were together again, sitting on Gunvor's balcony. They had all been served snacks and drinks. The evening was warm and windless. But their greatest pleasure this evening was the relief that the case was closed.

"The police asked so many questions. Exhausting but interesting." David was excited.

"That could be you some day, if you play your cards right." Gunvor smiled at him. "And you, Elin? How did you experience the hearing?"

"The police took it really easy on me. They did the questioning at the hospital, and I was still dizzy even though I had gotten some IV drip. But their questions helped me to structure the little I remember."

"The drip did a remarkable job of helping me to recover." Manuel let himself into the conversation. "And, I can't tell you how sweet they were to me at the hospital.

"Sweet or good-looking?" David was teasing. "Did you find yourself a nurse?"

They all laughed.

"Not really. But true. They were both sweet and good looking."

"And the questioning?" Gunvor was curious.

"Fine. I know those policemen from before."

"Great. So we are all fine then." Gunvor smiled happily. "And I've talked to Aidan and gave him all the details. He greets everyone, by the way. And Chibbe?" Gunvor turned to Elin.

"Doctors said he was really lucky. The bullet passed through his shoulder. He had some surgery during the night. The police were hearing him under doctor´s surveillance. But he has to talk to them again. Off course. He is a main witness as well." Elin paused. "These last couple of days. They feel so unreal."

Elin's words made them all quiet for a while. Elin drifted into her thoughts. Her mother had gone crazy when she told her what had happened. She was going to ground her indefinitely until Elin explained that she was over eighteen and had been for a while, and tonight she was going over to Gunvor's whether her mother wanted her to or not. Her mother was actually quite appreciative of the chance Gunvor had given Elin, though she did think she hadn't handled some of it quite as responsibly as perhaps she should have.

"Mum, I've lived with violence my whole life and we've stopped some violent men now. I'm not hurt. I'm safe and sound. It appears I have a new, well-paying profession in my future. Don't you think that's worth celebrating?"

Elin's mother didn't like it, but she couldn't argue with her daughter either. She loved seeing Elin's persona blossom from that of a shy, bullied girl to a strong, confident woman right in front of her eyes. Her passion and spirit could not be denied. So, after shedding a few tears, she went out and bought a cake which she suggested Elin take to Gunvor.

Manuel still had a headache but couldn't help smiling as he wondered how he was going to write up the case for their website. It was the biggest and most dangerous job he'd ever worked on.

David was thoroughly enjoying telling the story of how they

went and rescued their friends over and over again. Seeing how Elin's eyes sparkled when he told it, he even mentioned Chibbe's courageous contribution.

They reflected for a while on Daniel's ruthless and calculating nature.

"I wonder what it's like inside his head. Was it all some sort of crazy, sick game to him? They must have had a really destructive relationship. Alice seemed to have had a whole lifetime of being used and abused by Daniel. Now that she's gone it's going to be difficult to find out whether she got anything from it herself." Gunvor was more than happy that they'd solved the case, but couldn't stop feeling frustrated by the fact that they would never know the whole truth.

"Hard to know, but there seemed to have been a strong bond between them. I mean they were both over thirty and still lived together," Manuel made his contribution around a mouthful of cake.

Gunvor nodded in agreement then turned to Elin, "Well, you certainly made a strong impression on him, strong enough for him to do away with Alice. It's horrific to think of how he so cold-bloodedly planned for Alice to report Mikael so the police would suspect him. Because that's what I'm convinced happened. I couldn't sleep for thinking about what might have happened if we hadn't found you. He was pathologically obsessed."

"Yeah, but even though I was petrified it didn't seem that he wanted to hurt me. It was you who were in the most danger, you and Chibbe. It must have driven him mad seeing me and Chibbe in the office. Because it was Daniel who was there, I realized that as soon as I saw he had my scarf."

"And it must have been him that tricked Chibbe into going to the hospital. Presumably so Elin would think he was involved and leave him. But we'll never know for sure." Gunvor realized she would be wondering about this for a long time to come. There were far too many questions that would more than likely never be answered. They would be forever buried with Daniel and Alice.

"I expect they'll reopen the investigation into the murders of Daniel and Alice's parents now. There are too many similarities to Alice's murder. What a madman! Lucky it wasn't him you fell for!"

Manuel turned towards Elin when he said this. Elin shivered. For her, things weren't quite so straightforward; fate had probably influenced events more than her own choices. After all, there had been something about Daniel that attracted her. If Chibbe hadn't made a move on her, she would have carried on thinking he was an arsehole and Daniel's old-world, gentlemanly charm might well have won her over.

The doorbell rang, and joy and longing seem to bubble over inside Gunvor. She opened the door and threw herself into Kjell's arms. Their lips met and they kissed, then they stood for a while just holding each other in a strong embrace. He whispered in her ear, "I'm here now. And I want to take you home with me so I can sleep at nights again. You can take a month or two off from all this crime and death."

Gunvor merely nodded her head and laid it back against his shoulder.

Before they went inside to the others, the doorbell rang again. It was Ciwan and Tara. Gunvor invited them in, primarily to celebrate the successful outcome of the case, but also to meet Kjell. The newly-arrived guests put some food on their plates in the kitchen and then joined the party in the living room.

The group from the balcony now came inside and added details and embellishments to Gunvor's summary of their recent dramas.

"So your contact was actually one of the bad guys?"

Gunvor nodded and reminded herself never again to give her trust to someone so casually as she did with Fredde. It came out in questioning that Fredde had been working for Daniel for many years. His job in the bar was set up mainly so he could solicit customers for Alice, which meant he took home quite a good share of profits.

"My choice of contact couldn't have been worse. It meant that Daniel knew about me right from the start."

Gunvor suddenly remembered the man who had been staring at her when she sat on the balcony that evening. And the man on the jetty near Mikael and Nadja's place who had appeared from nowhere. Whether it was Daniel or not, she would never know. She tried to shake off the uncomfortable feeling the thought gave her and allow the successful closure of the case to make her feel content for once.

"Okay, now we are all here, I'd like to say a few words." The room fell silent while Gunvor raised her voice just slightly, "We have been on a pretty crazy journey, personally and professionally," She looked at David and Elin who nodded in unison. "I am incredibly grateful that I've been able to make this journey with you. A toast to the Fruängen Bureau."

Manuel put his glass to his lips but suddenly stopped.

"Gunvor. What's in my glass?"

They looked at each other with a twinkle in their eye.

"Oh, just whisky. But by the way...sleep tight."

Everyone let out a laugh. Then Manuel raised his glass in salute to Gunvor and said, "Here's to Gunvor Ström, our savior and heroine. Your clever mind and well-trained body have saved our lives. If it hadn't been for you..." Manuel slowly shook his head before he continued. "If it hadn't been for you, we would not be here today. I am so grateful to have the honor to work with you." After waiting a moment for the emotional praise for Gunvor to subside, he turned in Kjell's direction, "And let's drink to the kindest and most patient of men," he said.

Kjell smiled and reached for Gunvor. Gunvor squeezed his hand, drank the toast then disappeared into her own thoughts for a moment. She thought about how it all started when Nadja commissioned them for an assignment. That poor woman had been to hell and back, she thought. Hopefully, things would be better for her now. Whether it was Fredde or Lacke that had threatened Nadja was still unknown. However, Mikael had been released earlier that day. He probably still had some things to explain. Both to the police and to his wife.

It would be an understatement to say they were all exhausted, but their need to get together to meet was stronger than their desperation to rest. Now they had eaten, drunk and talked through everything several times, it all felt better. They had been able to solve and finish the case together. Moreover, they had made the difficult transition from being a group of talented individuals working on a case to a beautifully bonded team.

They all embraced before leaving, each to their own homes. Very soon, Gunvor was making the most of every second as she climbed between the bedsheets and held onto her beloved Kjell.

69

E lin's emotions swirled around her head as she walked home. Yesterday evening had been horrendous on so many levels. Thankfully, she didn't remember all of it, and what she did remember was framed in a weird dreamlike haze.

Chibbe was back in her thoughts again. Her strongest memory from the previous night was seeing him lying on the floor, motionless and covered in blood. She was sure he was dead and wanted to scream out in despair, but not a sound passed her lips. The joy she felt upon hearing he was alive and that he'd make a full recovery was indescribable.

Earlier in the day, when she was discharged, she had managed to sneak into Chibbe's ward and give him a quick kiss before he was taken for questioning. At that moment, a tear had flowed down his cheek. But he had quickly wiped it with the hospital gown's sleeve.

He didn't want to worry Elin. But he was worried about the hearing. He had killed someone, even if it had been to save her. He was well aware that he was far from being a model citizen. He'd been on the wrong side of the law too many times in his life. But when he was with Elin, he regretted everything bad he had previously done. Everything he'd done that could put him away and separate them. He regretted it all, except shooting Daniel, because he did that for Elin.

Elin felt like she was a completely different person from the girl she'd been a week ago. Now she knew she was strong. She knew she was loved. And she knew she would do anything at all for her guardian angel Chibbe.

70

D avid hugged Elin again when it was time for them to go in separate directions. He felt real warmth for her now; she felt like a younger sister. He'd felt such anguish when she disappeared last night. The strength of his feelings took him totally by surprise. And when he held her now, it was with the utmost sincerity. He promised himself he would never let anything happen to Elin again. Not on his watch, at any rate. From now on, he wouldn't give a shit what people thought. Elin was one of his mates. They could say what they wanted. If he had to, he could drop them forever too, because now he's got a life. A life of his own. Besides, he was a member of the Fruängen Bureau.

He walked up the sloping path next to the school football pitch where he and Gunvor had met what seemed like a hundred years ago and rolled up his sleeve to see the carelessly written numbers on his arm for the umpteenth time. But this time, he wasn't just going to look. He tapped the number into his mobile. When he heard the tired but gentle voice, he got a warm feeling in his chest, "Hey Bella, it's David, the detective from yesterday."

EPILOGUE

The case is closed. Kjell will be successful in convincing Gunvor to return to the Canary Islands with him. Elin is looking forward to spending quality time with Chibbe, and David has good chances for a relationship with Bella. Everything is nice and quiet. But not for long.

Is it always a good idea to look for a lost person? Gunvor Ström is not entirely sure as she believes there are those who don´t want to be found. Despite this, she takes on the task of looking for Per Cedergren with the suspicion that he is on an adventure with a mistress and will soon return voluntarily.

Gunvor´s good friend Aidan also makes his debut as an investigator when he helps a new acquaintance look for her missing friend.

When Gunvor and Aidan enlist the help of their young friends Elin and David, they begin to see similarities between the two parallel cases. But how do they relate? And what do the disappearances have in common with the murders that at first glance seen to be hate crimes?

Soon they are in the eye of the storm, not knowing where the danger is lurking.

In the autumn of 2020, the first sequel to Looking for Alice in the Gunvor Ström series will be released.

ACKNOWLEDGMENTS

I would like to express my special thanks of gratitude to my hybrid-publisher Publish Authority. Because they share their great knowledge and are my wise guides through the winding paths in the land of marketing.

ABOUT THE AUTHOR

Swedish author Luna Miller (pseudonym) specializes in Nordic Noir and is the writer of the international best-seller *Three Days in September*, and is one of the authors of the international anthology *Love Unboxed 2*. In mid-life, after experiencing life and adventures throughout Europe, India, China, Pakistan, Iran, Thailand, and a host of other countries, with her studies, children, and work, Luna found quality time to write her debut novel *Den som ger sig in i leken*—the original Swedish precursor of *Looking for Alice*.

Her next book in the Gunvor Ström series is to be released in the autumn of 2020.

For more, please visit www.LunaMiller.com.

f y

A NOTE OF THANKS

Thank you for reading

If you enjoyed *Looking for Alice*, we invite you to review it online and encourage your friends and family to read it as well.

Publish Authority

Lightning Source UK Ltd.
Milton Keynes UK
UKHW021905080221
378428UK00011B/2549